WHISKEY ON THE ROCKS

REBEL VIPERS MC BOOK 1

JESSA AARONS

WHISKEY ON THE ROCKS

This book is a work of fiction. The names, characters, places, and incidents are all products of the author's imagination and are not to be construed as real. Any similarities are entirely coincidental.

Whiskey on the Rocks Copyright ©2023 by Jessa Aarons. All rights are reserved. No part of this book may be used or reproduced in any manner without written permission from the author, except in the case of brief quotations used in articles or reviews. For information, contact Jessa Aarons.

Cover Designer: Charli Childs, Cosmic Letterz Design

Editor: Rebecca Vazquez, Dark Syde Books

TABLE OF CONTENTS

WARNING	VII
DEDICATION	IX
PLAYLIST	XI
PROLOGUE	1
CHAPTER ONE	5
CHAPTER TWO	11
CHAPTER THREE	19
CHAPTER FOUR	25
CHAPTER FIVE	33
CHAPTER SIX	41
CHAPTER SEVEN	47
CHAPTER EIGHT	53
CHAPTER NINE	55
CHAPTER TEN	65

CHAPTER ELEVEN	69
CHAPTER TWELVE	75
CHAPTER THIRTEEN	85
CHAPTER FOURTEEN	97
CHAPTER FIFTEEN	105
CHAPTER SIXTEEN	115
CHAPTER SEVENTEEN	123
CHAPTER EIGHTEEN	131
CHAPTER NINETEEN	139
CHAPTER TWENTY	149
CHAPTER TWENTY-ONE	163
CHAPTER TWENTY-TWO	175
CHAPTER TWENTY-THREE	183
CHAPTER TWENTY-FOUR	197
CHAPTER TWENTY-FIVE	207
CHAPTER TWENTY-SIX	217
CHAPTER TWENTY-SEVEN	227
CHAPTER TWENTY-EIGHT	237
CHAPTER TWENTY-NINE	247

CHAPTER THIRTY	251
CHAPTER THIRTY-ONE	263
CHAPTER THIRTY-TWO	271
CHAPTER THIRTY-THREE	279
CHAPTER THIRTY-FOUR	289
CHAPTER THIRTY-FIVE	301
CHAPTER THIRTY-SIX	307
CHAPTER THIRTY-SEVEN	315
CHAPTER THIRTY-EIGHT	325
CHAPTER THIRTY-NINE	333
EPILOGUE	341
ACKNOWLEDGMENTS	346
ABOUT THE AUTHOR	348
OTHER WORKS	351

WARNING

This content is intended for mature audiences only. It may contain material that could be viewed as offensive to some readers, including graphic language, dangerous and sexual situations, murder, abuse, and extreme violence.

This story is for everyone who ever thought they couldn't do it. For everyone who's pushed through the doubt and gone out to get what they wanted. For everyone who has dug themselves out of the hole, brushed off their own dirt, and got themselves everything they deserved.
You are all amazing and brave and fierce. Stay strong and shine on, you crazy diamonds!

PLAYLIST

CLICK HERE TO LISTEN ON SPOTIFY
Whatever It Is – Zac Brown Band
Cherry Pie – Warrant
1, 2 Many – Luke Combs
Got What I Got – Jason Aldean
All My Favorite People – Maren Morris, Brothers Osborne
My Truck – BRELAND
Whiskey Drinking Song – Jackson Taylor & The Sinners
Queens Don't – RaeLynn
Redhead – Caylee Hammack, Reba McEntire
Ride – Chase Rice, Macy Maloy
Wine, Beer, Whiskey – Little Big Town
Whiskey in My Water – Tyler Farr
Little Red Wagon – Miranda Lambert
Jack Daniels – Eric Church

PROLOGUE

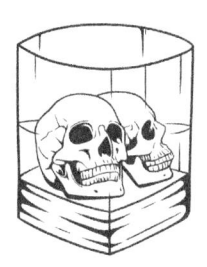

WHISKEY

"Enough!" My Pops slams his gavel and everyone in Church goes silent, giving him their attention. "Next order of business. I've discussed this with the officers, and it's time to bring it to a club vote."

What's he talking about? I quickly notice his attention is all on me. I'm sitting at the far end of the table, all the way across the room, but his laser focus has me pinned to my seat.

"I motion for Mountain to pass his President patch to Whiskey!" I hear coming from my uncle, Brick, seated at my right, and I'm stunned.

"I second," another officer, Bear, pipes up.

I can't believe what I'm hearing. President? They want me to be the club's next President? But why? I can feel my body respond to the words before my brain is fully engaged. I was lounging back in my chair, but I sit up straighter, my chest puffing out like a proud peacock.

"Why now?" Probably a stupid thing to ask, but like I said, my brain hasn't jumped on the bandwagon yet.

That gets my Pops' response. "Because I can't ride. Therapist says maybe one day, but not any time soon. That means I can't be a proper leader. Now's your time to step up. You've been preparing for this your whole life."

These last few months have been rough on him, but I never saw this coming. I thought he'd be President until the day I had to lay him six feet under. But if this is what he wants, I need to put on my big boy britches and take his word for it. He may be my Pops, but he's also this club's leader, and if he says he's ready to pass his patch down, I need to accept that.

"I won't lie and say I'm not hesitant, but I'll do you and this club proud." Shit, but what about Steel? "Wait . . . what about Steel? He's the VP."

He leans forward, hands folded on the table, eyes still locked on me. "There's just over a year left in his sentence. He called yesterday and I filled him in. He's good with whatever we decide. So, we vote. Everyone in favor, say 'aye'."

Okay, I guess that answers that.

Bear stands from his chair, starting the votes. "Aye."

Brick pops up from his left. "Aye."

Every single one of my Brothers stands up and says 'aye'. It looks kind of like the wave you see people do at sporting events. One person stands up, then the person next to them, and so on, until everyone's up on their feet. Everyone but me, that is. My ass is glued to my chair. I can't technically vote for myself, but I'm still frozen in my seat.

Pops stands up from his chair and slides his cut off his shoulders. He sets it down on the table and he holds his right hand out. I watch as Butch unclips his pocketknife from his belt and hands it over. Pops flips the blade open, and with near surgical precision, cuts the rectangle 'President' patch off the front of his cut.

That patch has been on his cut for just over thirty years. Longer than I've been alive.

When all the threads are cut, he hands the knife back and looks at me again. "Come here, son."

That gets my ass moving. I stand up and make my way around the left side of the table, to stand in front of my Pops and the whole club. He holds his right hand out and I reach to grab it, shaking his hand.

I didn't notice he had the patch in his hand, but as we shake, I feel the material sandwiched between our palms. He pulls me in for a hug and squeezes me tight. Hugging has always been a normal occurrence in my family, but this one feels different. A passing of the torch, if you will.

He slaps my back one time, then pulls back to look me dead in the eyes. "Aye." It's the last vote I needed, and he gave it loud and proud.

"That makes it official," Bear hollers. I see him reach forward, grab the gavel, then slam it on the table. "From this day forward, until the end of his time, Whiskey is President of the Rebel Vipers MC."

Holy fucking shit. I'm President of the Rebel Vipers MC.

Before I can speak, I'm attacked. "Hell yea!" I know who it is immediately. Hammer, my best friend and fellow second-generation member, hugs me from behind and lifts me clear off my feet. He almost knocks both of us to the ground, but I wrestle myself free and turn around to hug him back.

I stand by the Church room doors and as everyone walks out, I'm bombarded with advice, handshakes, and hugs, all congratulating me on my new title.

The last one in line is Hammer. He throws an arm around me and pulls me out into the main room. "Time to party and get you laid," he laughs.

I've got my arm around his shoulder, so I pull his head down and give him a noogie. "Fuck yea!"

First order of business as President—get shit-faced and laid, but not necessarily in that order. Time to get this party started.

CHAPTER ONE

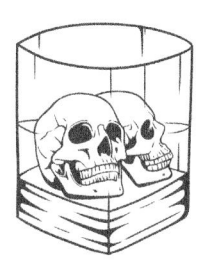

WHISKEY

There is no better feeling in this world than the roar and rumble of my Harley. Riding her is just as easy as breathing. I live for when I can cruise around the back-country roads, with nowhere I really need to be and the only things that matter are me, my bike, the wind, and the road underneath the tires. It's the best feeling in the world for a guy like me. But I have to admit, where I am right now is a really close second.

It's way too damn early in the morning to be awake, but I'm sitting on the back patio of the clubhouse all by myself. I'm halfway through my second cup of coffee and wishing things were always this simple and carefree. Unfortunately, I only got maybe three hours of sleep last night thanks to my brain working overtime, worrying about nothing. The mind likes to tell jokes sometimes, and I'll be the first to admit that I don't find them very funny.

Summer is on its way out and mornings now have that crisp bite of cool air. The end of September is a funny time of year in Wisconsin. You could wake up with frost on the ground, be sweating your balls off by noon, and be back to wearing a hat and gloves after dark. Mother Nature in the Midwest is seriously bipolar. One week, it's sunny and eighty-five degrees, then the next it's fifty and raining for five days straight.

One good thing about being up before everyone else is there are no loud and obnoxious sounds coming from everywhere. There aren't many times or places in this clubhouse that there isn't some sort of noise. I love my Brothers to death, but they sometimes don't know how or when to shut the hell up. All I hear are birds chirping, the wind blowing through the trees, and the occasional squirrel rustle from the woods surrounding the compound.

Creak. I may have spoken too soon.

I hear him before I see him. Jethro 'Mountain' Hill may have been a stealth motherfucker before his accident, but nowadays that damn wheelchair is like his cowbell. Not that any of us would be foolish or stupid enough to say that to his face. My Pops may only have one leg now, but he's still a one hundred percent badass. He wears a prosthesis the majority of the time, but he really doesn't like it. I can't blame him. I think not being able to ride his motorcycle makes him madder than actually missing a leg. It's a punishment no real biker would ever wish on anyone.

He rolls across the concrete patio and stops next to me. I try to ignore him, but I know he's too stubborn to leave me alone. He spins to face the open yard and lights up a cigar. I hate those damn things. It's like almost dying once wasn't enough for him, he has to keep trying until it happens on his terms. Apparently, almost dying in a motorcycle accident makes you pick up awful habits. The only thing that will bring Mountain down is a damn earthquake. Good thing we don't get those a lot here in Wisconsin.

"What are you doing up so early, son?" he finally asks.

"I could ask you the same thing, Pops," I say.

"Stupid meds make me have to pee all the damn time," he grumbles as he takes another puff.

"How does Blue deal with you? That woman is a fucking saint. Or maybe she's crazy for dealing with your stubborn ass for the last twenty years." She really is a saint, but don't let that fool you—when Blue gets worked up, she's like an earthquake in human form. Maybe we do get them here more often than I thought. They were made for each other.

"She's still asleep. That woman can sleep through a damn tornado. And don't talk about her like that. Remember, she's almost half your blood too."

As hillbilly crazy as it sounds, he's totally right. My father's wife, and Old Lady, is actually my aunt by blood.

A few years after my piece of shit mother went off and got herself killed, her younger sister showed up at the clubhouse looking for her. Pops fell head over heels for Lana and quickly made her his. He gave her the name Blue because of her eyes. It's a trait she and I share, and the similarity started our friendship. My Pops has brown eyes, so having blue eyes like her is kind of cool. He says her eyes are as blue as the sky is clear, so I guess mine are too, whatever that means.

I wasn't so sure of her in the beginning, but what else do you expect from a ten-year-old boy? I eventually realized that I couldn't have picked a better woman for my Pops if I tried.

"Now, quit lollygagging and answer my question, asshole." I guess morning grouchiness is inherited.

"Couldn't sleep," I mumble into my mug.

"What's that? Why not?"

"Not really sure, Pops." I rub my knuckles against my chest. "Was tossing and turning all night thanks to this unease and heavy feeling just sitting right here." I'm not honest and open like this with anyone else. Unless it's directly a club matter, it's none of anyone else's damn business. Club Presidents don't do weak.

"I hate to say it, son, but you're probably feeling restless. You've never been the type who sits still for very long. Hell, you had a broken arm at three years old because you wouldn't stop climbing that damn tree once you were tall enough to reach the lower branches." I chuckle as I take a sip of my now half-cold coffee. "And you know I'm not one to ask for any trouble, but things have been awfully quiet around here lately." He whispers that last part, like if he says it quiet enough, the gods won't hear him and cause problems. Unfortunately, that's not how life works for us.

"I hear ya, Pops, and I hate to say that I agree. We've been lucky so far to be in an area where we don't have much competition or problems. But I feel like our good luck time is running low." This isn't the conversation I thought I'd be having so early in the damn morning. "Why don't we pick this up later? I've gotta go open the yard and then we have Church this afternoon. Afterward, we can have a meeting with the officers to talk things out. That sound good to you?" I ask as I push myself up and out of the chair.

"Works for me, son" is his only reply before he rolls himself back inside. Good morning to you too, motherfucker.

I head back inside the clubhouse through the double back door and stop in the kitchen to switch my coffee mug out for a travel mug, then I make my way back upstairs to my room to get changed for work. As I head down the hall, I hear some rustling and showers running, so I know a few Brothers are starting to wake up. I change into a t-shirt, dark gray hoodie with 'Tellison Recycling and Salvage' printed on the chest, and clean jeans, then slide on my black boots. I make a quick pit stop in the bathroom to take a leak, brush my teeth, and tie back my hair. Before

I open my bedroom door to head out, I grab my cut from its hook and slide it on. I've been wearing this thing for the last twelve years and wouldn't go anywhere without it. But every day I look down and see that President patch, I thank my lucky stars that my Pops is still here and was the one who gave it to me.

I open the door and almost get knocked in the face by a giant fist. "Hey, Hammer. What's up, man?" He looks like he's had a long night too. "Everything okay? You look a little rough."

Hammer lowers his fist and shoves his hands in his front pockets. "I'm alright. Just got some things on my mind."

"Yea, sure. Why were you about to knock on my door?" I grab my coffee off the dresser, flip the lock on my door as I walk out, and pull it closed behind me. I rattle the knob a few times to double check and we take off down the hall. Walking and talking is the name of the game around here sometimes.

"Just checking to see if we still had Church this afternoon?" he asks.

"Of course we do. Why are you asking? It's the same day and time every week. Are you sure you're feeling alright, man?" What's going on today? Must be something in the water if we're both having an off morning.

"Yea. I just need to get my head straight. I probably need more coffee. I'll be fine by Church." Once we get down to the main room and out the front doors, he jumps on his Harley and takes off. Lucky bastard.

CHAPTER TWO

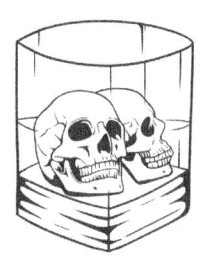

WHISKEY

I walk back through the front door of the clubhouse and notice my Brothers are all lounging around, just shooting the shit in the main room. They look way too comfortable for a Friday afternoon. Time to get their asses in gear. "CHURCH!" I bellow and everyone goes silent. I chuckle and make my way across the room, dropping my phone in the box by the door.

Number one rule in Church: No electronics. The only time we allow a cell phone or computer in the room is if Cypher is showing us some techy shit most of us don't understand, or someone needs a private room for a conversation. No ifs, ands, or buts about it.

Everyone follows me in, then Hammer shuts the double doors. I'm in this room several times a week, but it still blows my mind every time I walk in. The room is huge. Whether looking in from outside the warehouse-turned-clubhouse or from inside the main room, you can't tell how much room is really in here.

The table in the center of the room is enormous. When the original five guys bought this property with the intention of starting this club, I don't think they anticipated what they'd find. For some reason, there was a double lane bowling alley in a back room of this old meat processing plant. During the renovations, they carefully removed the wood lanes and used one of them to make our meeting table. They cut the lane in half and put the long pieces back together sideways. The table is seven feet wide and about thirty feet long. We have it set up to comfortably seat twenty-four people, but we've crammed almost sixty around it in the past.

As the President, I sit furthest into the room at the head of the table and next to me is an empty chair for my VP, Steel. He's currently doing a two-year stint in lockup for me. Thank goodness he'll be home next spring. Meanwhile, his chair remains empty.

"Alright, fuckers, let's get down to business." I slam the gavel and get this meeting started. "Before we get into the usual stuff, I need to say we're having an officer's meeting once we wrap up. Any problems with that?" I get headshakes and no's from the room, so we move on.

"Okay, let's get a quick rundown on all the businesses so we're all in the loop. Wrench, you start."

"Business at Rebel Repairs is up just a bit. People are bringing in their motorcycles for end of season oil changes. And calls to schedule for winterizing and storage are trickling in. I'm sure by the end of October we'll be set for storage to be full for winter," Wrench explains.

While Steel is technically the head honcho over at the bike repair shop, Wrench has stepped in big time while he's been away. He's a kickass mechanic and one hell of an Enforcer.

"Good to hear. Winter storage is filling faster each year. Ring, what's up at the brewery?"

"We released the fall seasonal beer three weeks ago and it's flying out the door. I can barely keep up production for all the orders we have. I'll probably keep it on the line until mid-October before we switch to the winter brew. Otherwise, everything else is running smooth. We just had our state inspection on Monday and all was good. They went through both Moraine Craft Brewery and The Lodge, so the liquor, bar, and food service licenses are up to date. We still need to find a front-end manager for The Lodge, but I don't even know where to start looking."

Ring is another one of our Enforcers. He's also Steel's best friend. To distract himself from missing his friend, he has thrown all his time and energy into running the brewery, bar, and restaurant. We really need to find him some help.

"If anyone knows of someone with a food service background, let Ring know. Cypher, can you also look on some job websites to see if there are any local people looking for jobs? I'd like to try and get someone from the area who knows about the club tie-in." Cypher nods, and I can already see his fingers twitching for his keyboard. "Next up is BIT. Buzz, whatchya got?"

"Dammit, Whiskey, you know I hate when you call the shop that. It's Bloodlines Ink Therapy," Buzz says through gritted teeth as he runs both hands over his bald head.

I can't help but bust his chops sometimes. If he wasn't so good at what he does, and the son of one of the founding Brothers, Skynyrd, I'd wonder what he's doing in this club. The man has no tattoos, for Christ's sake!

Through everyone's fist-hidden coughs and chuckles, Buzz continues, "All the artists are booked for three-plus months and piercings are about two weeks out. Adding walk-in times has helped keep customers happy, so no major complaints there. If any of you need ink, let me know. I've got a few days blocked out in mine and Dad's books. Other than that, business as usual."

"Alright, I guess that just leaves me. Both the recycling center and auto salvage are running at the same as last year. People are clearing out their garages, so we have lots of scrap metal coming in. That's all being set aside in the bigger bins to use for runs down to Chicago, and everything else is sorted and compacted. Any other business questions? Otherwise, we're moving on to club stuff." Sometimes I feel like I'm running a corporation instead of a motorcycle club. This shit is crazy. I'm glad we've built the network that we have, but sometimes I wonder if the old timers ever imagined how big we'd grow. The more money we make on the illegal side, the more we had to start earning legally to have a way to wash it clean. "Brick, are you good on your notes?"

"You betcha. This Secretary gig is a piece of cake." Brick clicks his pen, shuts his notebook, and kicks his feet up on the table. He's not only my Brother, but also my uncle. He's Mountain's younger brother and has been the club Secretary from day one. I've seen the notes that he takes, but I can't tell if he's writing in code or just doodling pictures. If he dies on us, I sure hope someone can figure out his system. Otherwise, all our past records are only going be good for fucking wallpaper.

"Next order of business is the run from yesterday. Trooper, you headed up that run. Anything out of the ordinary we need to know about? Any problems on either end?" I hate when I don't go on runs, but sometimes shit at home takes precedence.

"No, sir, everything went smooth. We got to the air strip about two hours early and did our searches. Everything was clean as usual. Plane landed with no problems and once it rolled into the hangar, we started unloading. It was refueling as we worked, so it was back in the air in forty-two minutes. Monty says he'll call soon to schedule the next drop off. Once he was gone, we waited about a half-hour and rolled out. We only had one stop for fuel along the way and got to the drop-off right on time. Scotty seemed in good spirits when we got to the docks and his guys did all the heavy lifting. Bins got emptied, reloaded in the truck, and we were headed back north by dusk."

You can definitely tell that Trooper used to be a Fed. His memory is sharp as a tack and he doesn't leave any detail out. Thank whatever deity you believe in that he got sick and tired of the so-called legal life and decided to join the dark side. Had we not met because of a bust gone wrong, and had he not shown how unhappy he was to be part of it, I would've shot him on sight when he showed up a few months later. He had quit the FBI and wanted to join the club. You might think I'm crazy for letting an ex-fed into the club, but there are just some things you don't need to worry about.

"I got a text this morning from Scotty and he said all was clear after you left. Kraken, did the money clear on time?" He's the club Treasurer and a whiz with money. Numbers are not my thing, and he can figure all that shit out in his head.

"All's good. I'll be doing deposits and have everyone's cash ready by morning. I also sent money in to Steel's commissary account. With as little as he spends, this should last him through the end of the year," Kraken explains.

"I guess we'll just wait for another call from Monty, and until then, business as usual. Any questions?" I ask.

"Who's supposed to stay for the officer meeting?" Hammer asks. Something's up with him and I'm starting to not like it. He's the club's Sergeant-at-Arms, so I don't know why he's asking.

"Everyone who wears a damn officer patch attends an officer meeting. You got a problem with that? You have somewhere more important to be?" I snarl.

"No, Prez. I'm good," he replies as he slumps down in his chair.

"Good. Anyone else got a problem? Too fucking bad if you do." *BANG!* I slam the gavel down. "Everyone who doesn't need to be here, get the hell out." As if my stress wasn't enough, Hammer has to go and ruin a perfectly good meeting.

The door shuts and I glance around the table. I look at my Pops and he nods his head. It takes me a second to calm my breathing, but I manage to rein it in. All that's left in the room is me, Pops, Hammer, Kraken, Brick, Saddle, and Bear, our club Wise Man.

"As officers of this club, it's our responsibility to make sure everyone is safe and try to be ahead of any trouble. We've been super lucky lately and haven't had any major issues or problems. That includes on our runs and with outside clubs. Unfortunately, when things are quiet for too long, that's when shit starts coming down hard," I say as I look at my fellow Brothers.

"Did something happen that we need to know about?" Saddle asks. Saddle is our Road Captain. He's in charge of setting up our run routes as well as planning the logistics of any long rides the club takes. Our cross-country trip to Sturgis is his biggest undertaking. We just got back from there last month and he's already in planning mode for next year.

"Nothing specific. Mountain and I had a chat this morning about how quiet things have been and we just need to be vigilant about any trouble. I don't want us to be up a creek without a paddle if something does pop up. Just keep an extra eye peeled for anything new when you're out and double check whatever you're in charge of. Basically, keep our bases covered. Now I feel like I'm rambling," I say with a chuckle.

"There's nothing wrong with being prepared or aware of your surroundings," Bear pipes up. He doesn't always talk a lot, but when he does, we listen. He's our club Wise Man for a reason. He was a chaplain in the Navy, is my Pop's best friend, and he's also Wrench's dad. Our club is a mix of real blood and close lifelong friendships.

"And that's why I wanted to pull you all aside. Just be aware of shit and report back to me if you see any problems." I stand up and start to walk out. "Get out. You're all dismissed. Do I need to hold your fucking hands?"

CHAPTER THREE

KIANA

This is definitely not a trip I ever thought I would have to make. I never wanted to be tracking down my little sister at the Rebel Vipers clubhouse. To say that I was very unhappy when Tempy decided to join the group as a club girl is totally an understatement. I almost lost my damn mind. I couldn't understand how she could allow anyone to treat her the way they treat women. She basically has sex with all of those men in exchange for a place to live. No one makes a commitment and she'll probably never be anything more to them than an easy lay. I don't see the appeal.

    She yelled and fought back and said that I should trust her judgment. She was twenty-one when she moved out of our family house, and now, two years later, I'm finally going to see where she lives. If she's even there, that is. I haven't heard from her in two weeks and I'm really worried. She's never ignored my texts or phone calls for more than a day, but lately, all I get is her voicemail.

The drive out to the clubhouse is actually quite nice. I've always known where it is, but I've never had a reason to go there. In the beginning, Tempy had tried to invite me to family get-togethers at the club, but I always refused. Then eventually, she just stopped asking.

If we wanted to see each other, she would drive into town and we'd meet at the house or a restaurant. Of course, she always had a chaperone tagging along watching us from a distance. She would ignore the biker, but I still didn't like it. She said it was for our protection—I said it was for control. We learned how to agree to disagree.

The further out of town I drive, the windier the roads become and the taller the trees seem to be. It's like being in a fairytale book forest. Autumn is in full swing and the leaves are in their prime color-changing phase. The trees line both sides of the road and create a canopy of colors. The yellows are super bright, the oranges almost brilliantly bold, and the reds have a subtle hint of maroon. The few that managed to stay green have a hint of brown as they turn crispy and float to the ground. The breeze that comes through the trees make them sway and spin, almost like it's raining a rainbow. I really need to get out more and explore. This area is so damn beautiful.

I'm almost in a trance when I come around a curve and realize I'm here already. I slow way down to avoid driving past. On the left side of the road, there's a huge white sign on top of a six-bay garage that reads 'Rebel Repairs' in bold green and black letters. Immediately to the right of the building is a tall metal chain-link fence topped with barbed wire. What in the hell are they trying to keep out, or maybe in? This place is ridiculously huge.

Up ahead, I see a break in the fence with a big sliding gate and a guy standing outside a small shack watching me. He raises one arm and waves me forward. I turn left into the driveway and stop just in front of the gate. He walks back inside the guard shack and I'm totally unsure of what to do. I quickly look all around me and in my rearview mirror. That's when I notice the building across the road behind me. The sign hanging on the fence says 'Tellison Recycling and Salvage'. I wonder if the club owns that too.

I look back ahead and notice the large parking lot full of motorcycles and the ginormous building behind them. It looks like it used to be some kind of factory at one time, but they've definitely maintained it very well and done some upgrades. There's a covered porch running the length of the main level and tall, skinny windows lining the second story. But the one thing I notice that's kind of eerie is there are no people outside. The guy still hasn't come back out of the guard shack and no one is walking around inside the fence. I need to find my sister and figure out what the hell is going on here, so I open my truck door and jump down. Just as my shoes hit the concrete, the guy walks back through the opening next to the gate.

As he gets closer, I notice that he seems a little on the younger side. He's wearing blue jeans, black boots, a white t-shirt, and a black leather vest. It's plain except for a patch on the left side that says 'PROSPECT'. I'm not one hundred percent sure, but I'm guessing he's not a full club member.

"Can I help you, ma'am? Are you lost?" he asks.

"No, I'm right where I need to be. I'm looking for my sister, Temperance. Do you know if she's here? I need to talk to her," I say as I tuck my thumbs in my back pants pockets.

"Don't know anyone here by that name. What does she do here?" I wish I could see his eyes, but his damn sunglasses block out any sign of emotion.

"She . . . uh . . . she's . . . uhm . . . she's a club girl." I mumble through the words.

"If she's a club girl, what's her club name?"

"Her name here is Wings, I think. Is she here?" I ask again.

"Nope. Haven't seen her here in a while."

"Look, I haven't heard from her in two weeks and she's not answering my calls. Can you either find her or someone who's in charge?"

"I'm sorry, ma'am, but the Brothers are in Church and I can't interrupt them. If you wanna speak to the Prez, you'll need to wait until they come out." That definitely got his hackles up. He's a rule follower for sure.

"Well, do you know how long it'll be? Wait, did you say they're in church? I didn't know bikers went to church." I'm so confused. I thought these were badass guys who didn't care about anything but bikes, booze, and boobs.

"Not church like with a pastor. Church is what we call our club meetings. I'm a Prospect, so I stay out here and watch over shit until I'm told otherwise. I'm sorry, but I can't help you. If you'll just wait in your truck, I'll let someone know you're here when I can. Once Church is over, most of the guys will come out and you'll know." He turns around and goes back into his little shack.

How frustrating. I climb back into my truck, but just as I get settled, the front doors of the clubhouse burst open and about a dozen guys come pouring out. It's like a cloud of black leather and denim. Talk about intimidating. A few men point and look my way, but I stay seated and lock my doors. The Prospect walks my way, so I roll down the window.

"I just called inside and Whiskey said he'll be right out." Then he walks away again.

I don't know who this Whiskey is that he's talking about, but I hope he has some answers, because I'm not leaving until I know something. I look up and almost lose my breath. The hottest guy I've ever seen is walking down the parking lot and is headed for the shack. He exchanges a few words with the Prospect but keeps his eyes on my truck. He's got sunglasses on too, so I can't see his eyes. But, wow, the rest of him is fine as hell.

He's got to be just over six feet tall and is as broad as the side of a barn. His hair is blonde, like the color of wheat, and it falls just short of his shoulders. It's wavy and the top half is tied back in a ponytail. He also has a short, scruffy beard the same color as his hair. He walks through the gate opening and is heading my way. I open the truck door again, jump down, slam it shut, and spin around to find him standing right in front of me.

"Damn, girl. What's a tiny thing like you doing in a giant truck like this? You lost?" He smiles with a smirk. That won't last long if I get my hands on him. He may be hot as hell, but that won't stop me from kneeing him in the balls. Cocky asshole. No, I can't be thinking like that. I need to think of Tempy.

"I'm guessing you're Whiskey. And for the second time today, no, I'm not lost. And yes, this is my truck, so don't worry about it. The reason I'm here is because I'm looking for my sister, and I need you to tell me where she is right fucking now."

CHAPTER FOUR

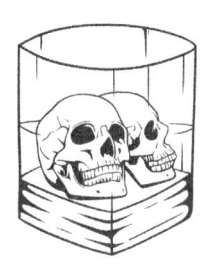

WHISKEY

It's been a week since I told the other officers to keep an eye out for trouble. Since nothing crazy has happened, Church this week was short, sweet, and to the point. Everyone gave their business reports and we were out of there in less than an hour. It's Friday afternoon again and everyone is ready for the weekend to begin. I close the Church room doors and grab my phone out of the box. I have a missed call from Jacob, the Prospect who is outside on guard shack duty. Just as I'm about to call him back, his name pops up and it starts to ring.

"What's so important that you call me during Church?" I bark into the phone.

"Sorry, Whiskey, but there's a chick out here who says she's Wings' sister and is looking for her. I told her she isn't here, but she won't leave until she talks to someone in charge."

"Alright, I'll be right out." I hang up the phone and shove it in the inside pocket of my cut. I walk down the hall to grab my sunglasses from my office, then head back through the main room, out the front doors, and down the parking lot to talk to Jacob.

"Did she say what her name is?" I ask.

"Nope. First, she asked for Temperance, so I had no clue who she was talking about. Then she said her club name was Wings. Told her I hadn't seen her in a while and she had to wait for Church to be over to talk to you."

"Alright. Head back inside and switch with someone else. I'll see what she needs," I reply.

I walk through the gate opening and head toward her truck. The thing is a beast and looks a lot like my cage. We both have excellent taste, driving a brand new Chevy Silverado 2500 Crew Cab. Hers is bright fire engine red, while mine is an all-black High Country. As I get closer, the driver's side door swings open and two tiny pinkish Converse drop into view. When the door slams shut, I see a wave of bright red hair.

I'm struck dumb and can't seem to stop the words coming out of my mouth. "Damn, girl. What's a tiny thing like you doing in a giant truck like this? You lost?" I try to cover my dumb mouth with a smirk, but I'm now lost in her pretty sparkling blue eyes.

"I'm guessing you're Whiskey. And for the second time today, no, I'm not lost. And yes, this is my truck, so don't worry about it. The reason I'm here is because I'm looking for my sister and I need you to tell me where she is right fucking now." Damn, she's got a feisty side. I like it.

"Whoa there, little lady. Yes, I'm Whiskey, the club President. What's your name?" I ask as I cross my arms and puff out my chest. Can't drop the tough biker President façade too much before I know who she is and what's going on.

"My name is Kiana, and just like I told your minion over there hiding in his little hut, I'm here looking for my sister. Her name is Temperance. I call her Tempy, but you Neanderthals call her Wings. I don't know why you all need nicknames. Such a stupid thing. But anyways, where is she?" Damn, she talks fast. When she's done, she takes a big breath and crosses her arms to mirror me.

Now that she's standing still, I get a really good look at her. She looks like a tiny Irish doll. Standing up straight, the top of her head is still below my chin. I probably have a good foot of height on her. Her hair is super curly and it flows over her shoulders, down to the middle of her back. The color is almost hard to describe because calling it red wouldn't do it justice. It's like a wave of fire and a vibrant ruby sunset mixed together. I'd probably get burned if I touched it—or she'd probably punch me. What I wouldn't give to spend a night burying my hands in that fiery mane and have her riding me like a fucking bull.

What the fuck?

I can't be having these thoughts right now. I shift my weight and take a step back, trying to will my dick to go down and not be too noticeable. Hopefully, she doesn't look below my belt.

"It's nice to finally meet you, Kiana. Wings has told us a little bit about you but said you didn't want to visit. I'm sorry you had to drive out, but she hasn't been here lately. We assumed she either went home to you or somewhere else." This is for sure not the answer she's looking for.

"What kind of place is this? You just let your whores run around and get lost and not worry about them? Tempy always defended you idiots and said you cared about women. I'm finding that really hard to believe right now." The red spreads from her hairline down to her cheeks. The ocean blue eyes I saw before are now nothing but black obsidian pits. She looks even hotter when she's pissed off. I just wish it wasn't at me. I don't tolerate backtalk very well and she's about to learn that the hard way.

"First of all, Wings is not a fucking whore. Why would you say that about your own sister? She's a club girl, by her own choice might I add, for the Rebel Vipers MC." I'm not going to let her think she can go and say whatever the hell she wants. "You will not come here and tell me how to run my club. The way things are done here have worked perfectly fine, and I won't change them because of you and your bitchy ass attitude. This is MY compound, MY clubhouse, MY club, and MY family!"

My voice gets louder the more I talk, and I fist my hands hard at my sides and walk forward until I have her backed against the bed of her truck. "If you want something from me and my Brothers, it would be in your best interest to ask me nicely. We don't take too kindly to outsiders who don't like us." I'm sure I look like a raving lunatic right about now, but she's pushing all the wrong buttons. If her eyes could pop out of her head, they probably would.

"What the hell's goin' on out here? We can hear you hollering from across the lot." Hammer rounds the hood of the truck and Kiana whips her head to the right to see who it is. As soon as she sees him, her body relaxes and sags against the truck.

What the hell?

"Oh wonderful. It's the babysitting biker," she snaps.

"What?" I ask as I back up and crack my sore knuckles. "Who's babysitting who?"

She points a finger at Hammer and snidely says, "Him. Every time Tempy comes into town to see me, this idiot follows her and watches us. Kinda creepy, if you ask me. We're grown ass adults, so why does she need a tail when she visits me?"

Hammer is starting to look uncomfortable and that's not good. He got his road name for a reason, and nobody who's been on the receiving end of his swing has lived to tell the story.

He finally lets her have a bite of his anger. "We take care of our girls just fine. And if you don't like it, you can get back in your big, bad firetruck and get the fuck off our compound."

"If you took such good care of your girls, why can nobody tell me where the hell my sister is? She's supposed to be here and safe, but she hasn't answered my calls or texts in over two weeks. Tell me where she is, if you care so much about her!" And the fire is back.

Hammer drops his attitude real quick and takes a step back. "What do you mean you haven't heard from her? She left here one day, saying she was going to your house, and never came back. I thought she was with you." Now he looks panicked. "Whiskey, where is she?"

"Brother, I don't know, but we'll definitely find out." I grab his shoulder and give it a tight squeeze. We make eye contact and I silently let him know we'll be having a deeper conversation about his feelings for Wings later. He nods his head and walks through the gate, back into the clubhouse. Once he's out of sight, I turn and look at Kiana. She's deflated, all her energy and gusto gone. I wish I could hold her and let her know everything will be alright.

What the hell is wrong with me? One minute, I want to reach out and strangle this bitch. Then the next, I see a sad look in her eyes and want to wrap her in my arms and not let go. I'm losing my damn mind.

"Look, I know you came here hoping to find your sister, but as you can see, she's not here. If you give me your phone number, I'll call you when I figure anything out," I say, trying to use a nicer tone of voice.

"I'm sorry, but that's not good enough for me. If you won't go out and find her, I will. She's my little sister and my responsibility. We're all that each other have. Our parents are gone, so it's just her and me. I'll find her on my own and you'll never see either of us again." She stomps her foot, pulls her truck door open, and jumps up and in like a goddamn gymnast. I wish she'd swing around me like that.

Shit. I really can't be thinking about her like that right now. She hates my guts. The truck roars to life and as soon as she throws it in gear, she's in reverse, spinning around, and gone in a cloud of dust.

Fuck my life—I want her bad. Maybe I just need to get laid. What am I going to do? Guess it's time to get to work and find our girl. No more boring and mundane days around here.

"Trooper!" I yell as I walk back up to the clubhouse.

He comes out the side garage door. "Yea, boss?"

"Follow her and keep an eye out for any trouble, but stay out of sight. I don't want her knowing she has a tail. Maybe take your truck." I don't need her having another reason to be mad at me.

CHAPTER FIVE

KIANA

"What an insufferable, idiotic man. Could he have been any more of a pain in my ass? How can he say he cares about his family, but have no idea that Tempy is missing? What's going on around here?"

I'm starting to wonder about my sanity. If I keep talking to myself out loud, someone is going to have me put in a padded room.

As I make my way back to town, I try and turn my angry off and switch into work mode. As much as I need to find my sister, I also need to concentrate on making a living. The house is paid off, thanks to my grandparents' lifetime of hard work, but my bakery mortgage and truck payments are not free. On top of that, I might have a small obsession with shoes. It all adds up quick.

I turn right at one of the two stoplights in our town and drive down Maple Street. It's Tellison's version of Main Street, USA. This is the road that leads from one end of town to the other and everything branches off from here. I pass the town hall and wave to our resident nosy neighbor, Mrs. Harris, and her dog, Sampson. If my brain wasn't fried, I'd wonder what kind of mischief she's up to today.

I pull into the parking lot next to my bakery and back up to the loading dock. This building and storefront used to be a butcher shop, so the sunken dock makes the perfect parking spot for my big truck. I may have to jump in and out of my baby, but I wouldn't trade him for anything. A few months back, I went to the dealership a few towns over, just to see what they had, and as soon as I walked down the row of trucks and saw him, I knew he had to be mine. A few hours later, I drove my Dragon home. Yes, I named my truck Dragon. If men can name their vehicles, so can I.

I get a little bit of butterflies every time I see my bakery. Owning a business has been a dream of mine ever since I was a little girl, when I would set up a play store and make my family members buy things from me. So, when I turned eighteen, and my grandma sat Tempy and I down to tell us about the money my parents had left us, I immediately knew what I would do with my half.

I opened The Cake Butcher the day before my nineteenth birthday. It took me months to pick a name, but as soon as I found the empty butcher shop building, the name popped in my head and stuck.

I walk around the building and enter through the front door. I sometimes like to walk in and see things from the customer's perspective. Plus, I like to surprise my employees and throw them for a loop.

"Good afternoon and welcome to the Butcher. I'll be with you in one moment," I hear from behind the swinging door that leads to the back room. I stand there and wait to see which lady I get to scare today.

"No hurry. It's not like I'm a paying customer or anything," I yell back.

Crash!

"Oh shit." I rush around the counter and into the kitchen, where I find Lynn sitting on the tile floor next to a box of smashed eggs. She looks up at me and we both start laughing uncontrollably. Pretty soon, I'm hanging onto the edge of the stainless steel table top to prevent myself from falling over and into the pool of egg yolks on the floor. Just as our laughter slows down a bit, I may or may not have snorted a few times, which causes another round of giggles to start.

"What the heck is going on in here?" We're laughing so hard, we didn't even hear Angie come in.

"Where did you come from?" I ask her.

"I was downstairs doing an order. What happened up here? Why are there eggs all over the floor?" Her mouth looks like it would be on the floor if it could be.

"I came in the front door to surprise you ladies and scared Lynn here. I guess she had butter-fingers and dropped the whole box. We probably should get these scooped up so we don't turn into fumbling figure skaters." The last thing I need is one of us falling and breaking something.

"I'll grab a dustpan to scoop them up, then dump them down the garbage disposal," Lynn says as she tries to stop her giggles. "What are you even doing here today? Weren't you going to try and find your sister?"

"Yea, I tried, but she wasn't at the clubhouse. They haven't seen her in a few weeks either. She left there saying she was coming to the house to see me and never returned." Just thinking about Whiskey's face is making me angry and flushed at the same time—and my girls don't miss a thing.

"Is that all that happened while you were there?" Angie elbows me in the side as she walks around the work table to grab some clean towels. "The color of your face tells me you found something nice to look at while you were there. They sure do make them stupidly handsome out there in the woods. I don't know what their mommas feed them at that clubhouse, but I wouldn't mind a taste of some of them. Every time I see those bikers ride through town, I can't help but stop and look. Yum."

"I didn't see anything other than a dumbass, rude biker who claimed to be their President, and he wasn't very nice. He tried to flirt with me until I somehow offended him. Then he started yelling about 'his club' and 'his family', blah blah blah. Then he asked for my number and said he'd call me when he figures it out," I say as I pace back and forth from the shelves to the stainless table and gather ingredients for a last-minute cake order for tomorrow.

"The club President? Isn't that Whiskey, the super tall blonde who looks kinda like Thor?" Angie asks. "I remember him from school. He sure grew up into a fine looking young man." She used to be a teacher and retired a few years ago. When she hated being home all the time, she started working here to "occupy her afternoons," as she calls it. I think she just needed to get out of the house and away from her husband for a few hours. Howard was my father's best friend, and my favorite guy ever, but he likes to get on his wife's last nerves, though we all also know she loves every bit of it.

"Angie, you shouldn't be saying things like that. What would Howard say if he heard you right now?" I sass back at her.

"He'd say that if I wanted to be with Thor, he'd just trade me in for Captain Marvel," she shouts over her shoulder as she pushes through the swinging door into the front room.

"I want to be her when I grow up," Lynn says with a sigh.

"Me too. Anyway, other than the now broken eggs, do you have everything set for the Wilson cupcake order? I got a call this morning from someone begging for a last-minute wedding cake. Apparently, they went to pick up the cake they ordered three months ago from the big box store and no one could find their order. So that's why I'm here when I shouldn't be. It'll just be a simple two-tier with piping and colored flowers."

"Honey, you're starting to ramble again. I've got the cupcakes baked and cooling. All I have to do is mix the frosting, frost them, and box everything up."

"Thanks, hun. I just can't help feeling bad that I'm just going through my days and can't find Tempy. What if something happened to her? Or maybe she's hurt and no one is there to help her." I sink down onto a stool next to the worktable.

"I know you miss her. And I know you don't want to hear this, but the club is probably your best bet in finding her. They don't flaunt it a lot, but they have some connections that you don't. You might just have to wait for their phone call. How about you worry about that cake and I'll go up front and help Angie close everything up. Sound good?" Lynn hugs me, then pulls back.

"Yea, that's fine. Oh shit, I never gave him my cell number. How is he gonna call me if something comes up? I really don't want to go back out there." Crap! I was so pissed at Whiskey, I left before we traded numbers.

"I'm sure he has his ways to find your number. Remember, they don't follow the light side of the law," she reminds me.

"Yea, you're probably right. Go on and help Angie. I need to get this cake started or it won't have time to cool, and I'll be here all night." Time to get back to work and put my worries on the back burner for a few hours. I'll try and call Tempy again when I get home.

CHAPTER SIX

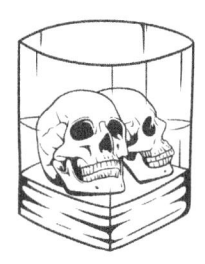

WHISKEY

I don't know how I managed to get a full night's sleep, but I thankfully did. Between Wings missing, her drop-dead gorgeous sister, and my worries about Hammer, I don't think I can handle any more on my plate. And to think that a week ago I was complaining that life was too quiet. Me and my big mouth.

I head out the front door and jump in my truck. I'm only going across the street to the recycling yard, but I've got the bed of the truck full of recycling from the clubhouse to dispose of. We definitely go through our share of glass liquor bottles and beer cans. I hit the button on the dash and the front gate rolls open, then I turn left out onto the road and just as quickly turn right into the driveway of the recycling center. I stop at the gate and honk the horn for Diego to come out the side door to swing the gate open. I drive through and pull around the main building to park in my assigned spot. It's not really my spot per se, but being the club President really does have its perks sometimes, and one of those is getting to park wherever the hell I want.

I pop the tailgate and start grabbing the garbage bags. When I turn around to drop them, I see Hammer walking across the road. He's walking my way, so I drop the bags and hop up to sit on the tailgate. He and I have some things to talk about regarding yesterday's red-headed visitor.

"Hey, Whiskey," he says. I guess I'm going to have to lead this conversation.

"What's going on with you and Wings? Is there something I need to know about?" I ask.

"Not really. We had a bit of a disagreement the night before she left. I tried calling her for a few days, but it always went straight to her voicemail. I figured she was still mad at me and needed time away. Like I said yesterday, I thought she went to her sister's, so I didn't know there was anything to worry about," he states. I can tell he's telling the truth. We've known each other long enough that I know his tells. Hammer is a trustworthy guy and I'm glad to have him at my side.

"Did you ask any of the other guys if they've seen her? Or at least her car?" I ask. "If it's not at the sister's house, it has to be somewhere."

"I asked a few guys, but no one has seen her. A few of the girls tried to call her but got her voicemail too. I'm lost. Where else would she go?"

"According to what Kiana said yesterday, they have no family. The parents are dead, so I have no idea. Let me call Cypher to see if he can trace her cell." I pull out my phone, wake up the screen, and hit the green button.

"What's up, Prez?" he rasps. I guess I woke him up.

"Need a favor. Can you put a trace on Wings' phone and see where it last tracked to? I think it's off because it's going to voicemail."

"Yea, one sec. Just gotta wake up the computers. Is something wrong? Is she still gone?" he asks, and I hear clicking in the background.

"She never made it to her sister's when she left a few weeks ago. The sister showed up here yesterday looking for her, and it was the first we knew she was missing." I have a feeling I'll be having this same conversation a few more times. I need to call emergency Church.

"Nothing is showing up, so I'd say it's either turned off or the battery is dead. The last signal I got was two weeks ago at the compound coordinates, so she might've turned it off when she left. I'll keep the trace open and set an alert just in case it turns back on and let you know. Anything else?" Cypher asks as he keeps typing.

"Can you send all the Brothers a text and let them know we have emergency Church tonight at seven? And call the ones who don't text. I know it's Saturday, but we're gonna have to let everyone in on the news." Hopefully, someone knows something.

"Will do. Later," Cypher responds, then hangs up.

I tuck my phone back into my cut, and drop back down to the ground. I reach down to pick up the bags, and start walking to the bins. "Cypher's doing his thing and we'll have Church tonight to update everyone else. Until then, we got work to do. Grab some of those bags."

"Fine. Do you need any help around here today? I need something to keep my mind occupied." Hammer hops up into the truck bed and pushes all the bags to the back, then jumps to the ground.

"Are you sure nothing is going on with you and Wings? Do you want to claim her? Don't think that any of us haven't noticed she's only been sleeping with you for a while now. No one else has tried to touch her in months," I ask him as I try to not laugh.

"Nope. And I'm not planning on claiming anyone, ever. You know how I feel about Old Ladies. My mother was the worst and I don't ever want one of those. In fact, I think I'm gonna stay away from the club girls for a while. It seems like bitches are nothing but trouble," he says as he slings bag after bag into the bin. I stay out of the way to avoid a face full of glass bottles—Hammer's swing is no joke.

"Don't forget that our mothers were not that different, so I know what you mean about the crazies." Both of our mothers ran away with men who were not their Old Man.

His mother was killed by her new boyfriend in a drunken fight, and mine met her maker when she crashed herself and her new lover into a tree. "If you're done with the ladies, that just means more for me," I say with a chuckle.

"So, you don't have any interest in Kiana then? I've seen her a bunch when I was following Wings. She likes to lay out on her back deck and looks pretty hot in a swimsuit. Maybe I should go for her, since she's not in the club," he says as he shoves me and tries to knock me over. He laughs as I stumble and tries to run away, but unlucky for him, I'm too quick and I grab the back of his cut to drag him backward and onto his ass.

"Don't talk about her like that, fucker. That woman is mine, or at least she will be if I have any say in it. She'll just need to learn how to watch her smart mouth, because she definitely knows how to talk back. I can't have my Old Lady disrespecting me like that in front of the Brothers."

What am I saying? Old Lady? What am I getting myself into wanting this woman?

"You know how rambunctious Wings is. If Kiana is anything like her, you're gonna have your hands full, man. Better you than me," Hammer retorts.

"Alright, asshole. I've got paperwork to do. Go find Diego and tell him you want to clean out the compactor. I'm sure he'd like a break from cleaning out that nasty thing." I hit the tailgate button and watch as it closes itself.

"Hell no. I ain't cleaning that fucking thing. Damn lazy bastard, you can't even close your own tailgate? What kind of man are you? I think you need to turn in your man card," he laughs.

I flip him off as I walk toward the building and prepare to lock myself in my office. I need to bury myself in weight slips and try to ignore the hard-on I've had since Hammer mentioned Kiana in a swimsuit. I'd love to see that, and then help her take it off. So much for trying to make my dick settle down.

CHAPTER SEVEN

KIANA

I stayed at the bakery way too late working on this wedding cake. I think I redid the buttercream flowers three times before I was happy with the way they turned out. I got everything put in the walk-in refrigerator and set out the boxes for delivery. I was so dead on my feet, I was afraid I'd fall asleep, face first, into the cake.

It's just after noon and I'm now leaving the barn where the reception is being held. I dropped off the cake, set it up on the table, and am now driving my tired ass right back home. I should be doing paperwork today, but I cannot imagine having to sit at my desk and think straight enough to do any work. I'd probably just make a bigger mess for my future self. Exhaustion and spreadsheets don't mix very well.

I pull into my open garage, shut off the truck, and let my head flop back onto the headrest. If my neighbors wouldn't think I was crazy, I'd probably allow myself to fall asleep and nap right here. Instead, I grab my purse off the passenger seat, push the door open with my foot, and slide out of the truck until my feet hit the ground, then I force myself to shut the door and go inside. I hit the garage door button and listen to it close as I open the house door and enter the mudroom. I left the windows open when I left this morning, so my house is nice and cool.

Fall is my favorite season and I love everything about it—wearing hoodies and Ugg boots, football season, dressing up for Halloween, and pumpkin everything. I would be happy if it was fall all year round. I absolutely hate sweating in the summer, and don't even get me started about the stupid white shit that falls from the sky in winter. I despise scraping windows and shoveling and salting. Give me temperatures in the range of fifty to seventy-five and I'd be a happy woman. I guess I shouldn't complain too much though, at least we don't have hurricanes and earthquakes here.

I drop my purse onto the kitchen table and drag myself down the hall to my master bedroom. A hot bubble bath sounds just about perfect right now, so I grab my tablet off the nightstand and walk into the adjoining bathroom. I reach down to plug the tub, turn the tap almost all the way up to get the water hot, and toss in a brown sugar bath bomb.

While the soaking tub fills, I strip down and throw my clothes into the hamper, putting my phone and tablet on the toilet seat. After dropping a towel onto the bath mat, I step into the water. Holy crap, this is just what I needed. I slide down under the bubbles and lay my head back in the little grove on the edge. Moments like this make me happy that my grandpa splurged on a bathroom renovation for my grandma. She used to love soaking in the tub on Sunday mornings.

Just as I'm about to grab my tablet to dive back into *Breakaway* by Heather M. Orgeron, and the adventures of Alexis and Colton, my phone dings with a text alert. I pick it up, thinking I probably should've called one of the girls to tell them I was coming straight home. I swipe to unlock the screen and see a text from a number I don't recognize.

> **Unknown:** Good afternoon beautiful.
> **Me:** Who is this?
> **Unknown:** I asked for your number yesterday but you wouldn't give it to me.
> **Unknown:** So I had to use my resources and find it myself.
> **Me:** Hi Whiskey. What can I do for you?
> **Me:** That's kinda creepy, btw!!

Why does he have to interrupt my quiet alone time? Cocky man. I change his name in my contacts and wait for his reply.

> **Whiskey:** I just wanted to check in with you and see if you've heard from Wings?
> **Me:** No word. I tried calling her last night but got the voicemail, again.
> **Me:** Anything on your end?
> **Whiskey:** Nothing. Had Church last night to fill in the Brothers, so everyone is on the lookout. We'll find her. I promise.
> **Me:** Don't make promises that you can't keep. I don't like liars.

Dammit, I didn't want to be upset today. Why does this man make my emotions so crazy? I'm angry one minute, and the next, my body is tingling under the water. I'm covered in goosebumps and starting to squirm.

> **Whiskey:** I'd never lie to you Kiana. I only want you to smile . . . and I think you secretly like me.
> **Me:** Oh really? What makes you say that?
> **Whiskey:** Cuz you answered my text and haven't yelled at me yet.
> **Whiskey:** I think you may like me more

than you want to admit.
Me: I have no idea what you're talking about. Can you leave me to take my bath in peace?
Whiskey: You're taking a bath? Like you're naked and talking to me?

Shit. I should really learn to think before I type. This is what I mean when I say that he messes with my emotions—I would normally never tell a near stranger that I was naked.

Me: Ignore me and my tired ramblings. I'm really wearing a long sleeve granny nightgown. No more naked talk for you.
Whiskey: Not happening, hot stuff. Now that I have the image of you all bubbly and in the tub, I won't think of anything else all night.
Whiskey: I think you should help me with my hard on. I always seem to have one when I talk to you.

Splash. Fuck! I just dropped my phone into the water while trying to sit up too quickly. I reach down to feel around and try to find my phone, hoping the waterproof case and phone really work like they advertise. Otherwise,

I'm in big trouble. My whole life is on that phone. My fingers graze it down by the drain and I scoop it up and out of the water, grabbing my towel and drying it off quick. I press the home button and it lights back up to show two missed messages.

> **Whiskey:** Want to tell me about touching yourself and we can help each other out?
> **Whiskey:** Are you there?
> **Me:** Holy shit Whiskey! Warn a girl before you start talking about your man problems. I just dropped my phone in the water. Thank God for waterproof technology.
> **Whiskey:** Hahaha! I'm glad to know that I affect you that much. Is your phone okay?
> **Me:** Seems fine but I need to take it apart to soak it in rice. Just in case.
> **Me:** No more naughty talk from you. Good night Whiskey.
> **Whiskey:** Good night Kiana. ;)

He sent a winky face? What guy does that? I think I'm out of my depths with this one. I'm just not sure if I want to keep fighting him.

CHAPTER EIGHT

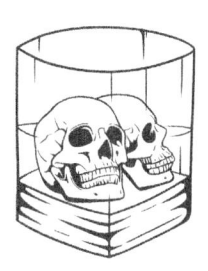

WHISKEY

Naked and in the bathtub? I'm in even bigger trouble now than I was when I started texting her. I debated waiting until tomorrow to text her, but I couldn't stop myself once Cypher forwarded me her contact information.

> **Me:** Update?
> **Trooper:** Her lights just shut off. Probably went to bed.
> **Me:** Sounds good. You can head back.
> **Trooper:** 10-4.

Yes, I still had Trooper following Kiana. But until we know more about her missing sister, I'm not taking any chances.

Now that's taken care of, it's time to take care of myself.

I strip as I walk into the bathroom, leaving my clothes where they fall, and crank on the shower. I get in, close the curtain, lean my head down, and wrap my hand around my already hard cock. I brace my left hand on the tiled wall and use the falling water to help my right hand slide up and down my dick. What I wouldn't give for Kiana to be bent over in front of me so I could be thrusting in and out of her tight, wet pussy. I try to draw it out, but with as hard as I've been all day, it doesn't take but a few strokes before I'm coming so hard I see stars behind my eyelids. I blast rope after rope up the wall. Holy fuck.

I spray my junk off the wall, then take my time washing my hair and body. I shut off the water, drag a towel over my hair, give my body a quick rub down, and wrap it around my waist. I climb out of the tub and go to the sink to brush my teeth and tame my crazy hair. I leave it loose and walk back into my room. I drape the towel over my desk chair, flip off the light, and crawl my naked ass into bed. Maybe tomorrow will bring some good news.

CHAPTER NINE

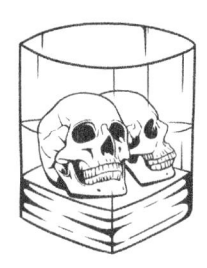

WHISKEY

It's Sunday night, so not much is happening around the clubhouse. Several of us are hanging out in the main room, relaxing on the couches, nursing some beers, and watching the Packers game. The refs make a shitty call, so the guys start shouting and yelling at the television. When the noise quiets down, I realize my phone is ringing. I grab it off the coffee table and see Gunner's name on the screen. He's supposed to be on his way to The Lodge to escort a few of the club girls back after their shifts at the bar and restaurant.

"Hey, Gunner. What's up?" I ask.

"Whiskey, man, we've got a bit of a problem." I hear him huffing into the phone, sounding completely out of breath.

I hold my phone in one hand and grab the TV remote with the other. I hit the power button and the guys about lose their shit.

"Shut the fuck up, assholes. We've got a problem." I toss down the remote and put my phone on speaker. "What's happening, Gunner? I've got you on speaker so the guys can hear too."

"Stiletto was attacked. When I got to The Lodge, I pulled around back and noticed the lot was dark. I saw some shadows moving by the dumpsters, so I rushed over to see what was happening and found some asshole standing over Stiletto, about to kick her. I hit him on the head with my gun and knocked him out. I need some of y'all to ride out and pick his ass up."

"We're on our way. Don't let him get away," I yell as we all rush out the front doors.

"I've got him tied up with some bungee cords. He ain't goin' nowhere," Gunner sneers. Now that he's got his energy back, his anger is kicking into effect.

"Alright, Brothers. This is the trouble we've been looking for. Trooper, Ring, Hammer, and I will lead. The rest of you split up. Half stay here to keep watch and everyone else ride back-up for the van. Doc, bring your bag to check on Stiletto. Mountain, you bring the van so we have a way to load up the fucker. Let's roll."

While we don't like going out looking for trouble, when it comes knocking at our door, we have no problem jumping to it. Whoever this idiot is that thought he could hurt one of our girls, he's going to learn not to fuck with the Rebel Vipers.

We roll out of the parking lot in a loud roar and ride straight to The Lodge. I look to my right and lock eyes with Hammer, and we exchange a nod and grab another handful of throttle. Whatever trouble is coming our way better be ready for us, because we won't stop until they're all dead.

We ride into the parking lot of the brewery and bar, half of the group staying close to the road to keep a look-out. Pops pulls the van around back and Trooper, Ring, Hammer, and I follow. As soon as the van stops, Doc jumps out the passenger side door and rushes over to the girls. Stiletto is sitting on top of a picnic table with a bag of ice held against the side of her head. Another club girl, Raquel, is sitting next to her with her arm wrapped around Stiletto's shoulders.

I use my left boot to lower my kickstand and let my bike settle in its leaning position. I lift my right leg and swing it back over the seat, then swivel around to stand up. I take a quick look around the lot and take notice of all the dead lights.

"Ring, can you figure out why all those lights are out?" I ask as I make my way over to where Gunner is standing.

"Will do," Ring replies.

"What have we got here?" I ask Gunner.

"Not really quite sure, Prez. He doesn't have anything in his pockets and I don't see a vehicle, but I didn't really walk around to look for one. He's got a few tattoos, but I wasn't gonna untie him to get a closer look. Figured it'd be better to wait for y'all to show up."

"Good thinking. I honestly could care less who or what he is. He tried to hurt one of ours, so he's getting a beatdown regardless. If he does happen to have answers to our other problem, that'll just be a bonus." I'm getting angrier with every word.

As I look down at the ground, I see garbage strewn around the pavement, and spot a high heeled shoe peeking out from under the dumpster. I squat down to grab it and notice a handgun about halfway under. I pick up the shoe but spin around and yell for Trooper.

"Trooper, grab your flashlight and come get a look at this. Gunner, did this guy have a gun when you hit him?" I ask.

"Not really sure if he did or not. I hit him a couple times with mine and he went down pretty quick," Gunner replies.

"Where's there a gun, Whiskey?" Trooper asks as he comes over with his Maglite. He carries that thing everywhere he goes. It's about twenty inches long and is its own built-in backup weapon. I've seen him whip that thing out faster than some Brothers can grab their guns. It's his go-to weapon of choice.

I stand back up and point at the dumpster. "It's about halfway under there, toward the right side. It might be this guy's gun, so I need you to bag it and see if Cypher can run it for prints."

"Cypher's out front, so I'll give it right to him," Trooper replies, then grunts as he lies down on his stomach and shines the light under the dumpster. He reaches back and pulls a big, clear plastic bag out of his back pocket. I'm not even going to ask what else he's carrying in his pockets. He uses the end of his flashlight to slide the gun closer, and once it's within reach, uses the bag to pick it up. "It's a Glock G19. Not a bad gun, but I personally prefer my Sig M17. I'll run out front and get it to Cypher. He can follow Mountain and Doc back to the clubhouse, with the girls."

I cross my arms and say, "Are you trying to do my job for me now, T? You want to start making plans for everyone?" I can't hold myself back anymore and bust out laughing.

"No way in hell, boss-man. I don't want to deal with all your bullshit. You can have it." Trooper chuckles as he walks to his bike, fires it up, and rides around the building to find Cypher.

Ring suddenly appears out of nowhere and is standing at my side. I grab my chest and take a deep breath. "Holy shit, dude. Give a little warning next time you wanna play ninja. I don't need to be having a heart attack right now."

"Gotta keep you on your toes, Prez," he says as he holds out his hand and shows me something. I look down and see a piece of round glass.

"What is that? Wait . . . is that a lightbulb? Did that come from the parking lot lights?" I ask.

"Yup. All the lights on this side of the lot are broken. Not sure if they were shot out or what, but there's glass under all the poles. I guess we just added another job to Cypher's to-do list. The security cameras should've picked up something. I'll text him and ask him to check them. He's gonna be so happy to get to use his fancy computers and gadgets," Ring continues.

"I guess it's a good thing everything is closed tomorrow. We don't need customers driving through the lot and getting flats from the glass. Can you call a couple of the Prospects and get them out here in the morning to clean it up?" I ask him. The club may own everything, but the brewery and bar are his babies.

"Already on it. I text Jacob and let him know to grab a buddy and be here bright and early," Ring states.

"Goddamn. If you guys keep doing shit before I get a chance to tell you, I won't be needed anymore. What am I gonna do with all my free time?" I joke and knock him in the shoulder with mine. "Oh yeah, I remember what I'm good for—beating down assholes like this fucker right here. How hard did you hit him, Gunner?" I ask as I kick the unconscious guy. "He's still out cold."

"I only hit him twice. He just must be a super weak pussy." Gunner takes a few steps forward and uses his foot to roll the guy over onto his back. His skin is filthy and he has blood running across his forehead. It looks like he hasn't taken a shower in a long time. "Ugh. Why are the bad guys always so gross? Do they not teach basic hygiene in asshole school?"

"Guess not. Let's get this trash loaded into the van so we can get out of here. I have a feeling it's gonna be a long night." I nod to Gunner and walk over to where Doc is talking to the girls. "How's everything going over here? What happened, honey?" I ask Stiletto as I climb onto the table on the other side of her.

"He came out of nowhere. I didn't even notice the lights were all out until it was too late. He grabbed my arm and pulled me backward. I lost a shoe and my leg twisted, so I fell down and hit my head on the dumpster." She paused to take a shuddered breath. "He was yelling something about needing me for his next shipment. I said I didn't know what he wanted, but he just kept rambling. Next thing I knew, he was falling down next to me and Gunner was standing there. He helped me up and called you."

I have to give her a lot of credit—for having been attacked, she sure has her wits about her. Our club girls are definitely some tough bitches.

"This yours?" I hold out the shoe I found. She nods and takes it. I lean forward, brace my elbows on my knees, and look over at Raquel. "Can you drive Stiletto and yourself back to the clubhouse? I'll have some of the guys follow you back."

"Yea, I can do that. Gotta run inside and get our stuff first," she says.

"I'll go inside with her and lock everything up. I'll follow them back, then meet you at the pit. I don't want to miss out on any of the fun," Ring says as he holds out his hand for Raquel. He helps steady her as she climbs down off the picnic table, then they walk toward the building.

I stand up to pull out my phone and dial my Pops.

"What's going on back there, son? All I can see from here is a bunch of walking in circles." Mountain is having a rough day of it.

"Can you back the van up here in front of the dumpster? But make sure to keep it straight. There's a lot of broken glass and we don't need to be getting a flat on the way back. We need to load up the trash and I don't want to carry it any further than I have to," I tell him.

"Oh hell. He smells? I hate when I have to be stuck in this damn van with a bunch of B.O." *Click*. He hangs up on me and I see the reverse lights kick on, then the van backs toward us until it's about six feet away.

I grab ahold of the door handle, pull the right door open, and unlatch the left door next. Once both doors are wide open, Gunner grabs the guy's feet and spins him around so he's facing the van.

"You can grab his arms. I don't wanna be near the smelly parts of him," Gunner grunts.

"Fine, but once this is all over, you're in charge of the Prospects cleaning out the van. I don't even want to know how much disinfectant you're gonna need to get rid of this stench," I say as we lift the guy into the van and roll him in. "He's all yours, Pops. Follow us back to the pit and we'll get him unloaded. Doc . . ." I look around until I find Doc as he comes out of the bar, followed by Ring and Raquel. "Doc, keep an eye on this fucker. Actually, why don't you put a bag over his head first? We don't need him waking up and seeing where he's going."

"No problem. It'll be my pleasure to knock him back out if he needs it," Doc says with a sparkle in his eye. Doc was a medic with the SEALS. These days, he enjoys inflicting pain on bad guys a lot more than he does bandaging us up when we need medical care.

"Alright, listen up, fuckers," I yell so everyone can hear me. "Let's get rolling. Ring and Cypher are gonna follow the girls back to the clubhouse. I need Trooper, Hammer, Gunner, and Kraken to follow me to the pit. Everyone else head back to the clubhouse. Once we get some info out of the trash, we'll let you know."

Everyone splits up and we walk to our bikes. Just as I get settled on mine, Hammer walks across the lot and leans back against his.

"Where the hell were you?" I ask him. "Don't think I didn't notice that you were missing."

"I was working on a hunch. I walked further down the road, about a quarter mile, and found an abandoned car tucked back in the trees. Looks like someone's been living in it for about a week. I didn't find anything but a backseat full of empty food wrappers and dirty clothes. My guess is it belongs to our guy. I sent a text to Wrecker. He'll tow

it to the yard and see if they can find something useful."
Hammer stands back up and straddles his bike.

"Sounds like a plan. Let's go meet our new friend."

CHAPTER TEN

KIANA

Sunday nights are always my lazy nights at home. The bakery isn't open on Mondays, so I don't have to worry about going to bed at a reasonable time, or getting a phone call about some last-minute change or an emergency order. We live in a small town of about three thousand seven hundred people, but you'd be amazed by the amount of people who think having a certain flavor of cupcakes is absolutely necessary.

I just changed into my pajamas and, after heating up a mug of water to make some hot chocolate, I toss a bag of popcorn into the microwave. While it's popping, I start to think about my parents and grandparents.

When I was sixteen and Tempy was twelve, our parents died from carbon monoxide poisoning. We were both at a friend's house for a sleepover. When no one came to pick us up the next morning, I knew something was wrong. They never forgot about us. Our friend's mom drove us home, and as soon as we opened the front door, I ran down the hall and into their room. I saw them lying in their bed, their skin was blue, and I immediately knew they were gone.

Since we didn't have any other relatives, we moved in with our grandparents. We used to see them several times a week, but moving into their house was a rough adjustment. Tempy cried every night for the first six months. After the first two nights of her sneaking into my bed, we decided to share a room. I tried to be strong for the both of us, but it was hard, so I cried in the shower and was brave in public.

Grandma Hannah and Grandpa Jack were all we had. They tried their hardest to make our lives somewhat normal, but they also hadn't had young kids in their house for quite some time. Then when I was twenty-five, Grandma passed away after a yearlong battle with breast cancer. After being together for fifty years, Grandpa couldn't live without his wife. Exactly one month after Grandma died, he passed away in his sleep. We would like to believe that he died from broken heart syndrome. We were sad that he was gone but happy that they were back together again, in heaven.

Tempy had just turned twenty-one, and three months later, she moved into the Rebel Vipers clubhouse. I don't really know what drew her to want to become a club girl, but every time I asked, she just said I wouldn't understand.

The microwave timer beeps, so I pull out the bag and dump the popcorn into a bowl. I grab my mug and the bowl, and head into the living room, setting everything down on the end table and curling up in the corner of the sectional with my favorite blanket. I turn on Netflix and try to find something funny to watch. I settle on an Adam Sandler movie and lounge back. Just as the movie starts picking up, I hear a noise from the side of the house. Pausing the movie, I listen for any more sounds but I don't hear anything else, so I try to ignore the uneasy feeling I suddenly have in my gut. I restart the movie and immediately hear the front step creak. I know that creak all too well. Any time I would try to sneak back in the house after curfew, that porch step would squeak and give me away. I knew when I woke up the next morning, I'd be hearing all about it.

I leave the TV playing, slowly stand up, and make my way to the front door. I look through the lacy curtain but don't see anything in the dark, so I flip on the porch light but there's nothing out of place. Leaving the light on, I decide it's time for bed.

I leave everything where it sits, turn off the TV, grab my phone, and head straight for my room, locking the door and checking both of the windows. Everything is like it should be, so I crawl under the covers. Deciding that right now isn't the time to be a stubborn woman, I send Whiskey a text message. Maybe I'm being paranoid and someone from the club tried to stop by.

Me: Hey. Just checking in. Any news?
Me: Did you send someone by my house?

I scroll through my personal and business social media pages to waste a few minutes, but nothing catches my attention for long. After ten minutes and no response from Whiskey, I call it a night, closing my eyes and shutting off my brain. I have a feeling it's going to be a night of little sleep and hearing strange noises. Thank goodness I don't have anywhere to be tomorrow.

CHAPTER ELEVEN

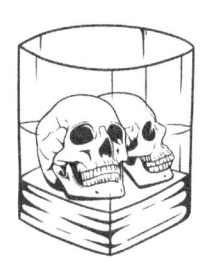

WHISKEY

When my Pops and his friends bought this piece of property, they didn't know what all was on it. They were mainly focused on the large amount of land, the privacy, and the rundown meat processing plant. They saw the potential these one hundred acres hold. The way Pops describes it is one day he and Bear went for a walk around the property line and were surprised when they came across this old barn. They had no idea if it was technically on their land but decided to explore it anyway. Later on, they were happy to learn it was in fact within their property lines.

The barn they found ended up being more than just a normal barn—it turned out to hold the incinerator the processing plant used to dispose of the dead animal carcasses.

Lucky for us, with a little elbow grease and some replaced and repaired parts, it works for our needs too. Disposing of an enemy's body, without leaving any evidence, is not always the easiest thing to do. So, when the guys discovered the incinerator and figured out what it was, they knew they had the perfect way to destroy any chance of future trouble.

But the incinerator wasn't the only surprise the barn held—it also has an I-beam hoist system, a ten-foot-deep concrete-walled hole, and a floor drain system.

Having a way to tie up and restrain the people we're interrogating is a major bonus. A system of steel I-beams run along the rafters of the barn, so we can hook a person to the chains and move them around within the open floor space. It also reaches over the hole, so we can lower a body down and leave them there if we need them to suffer for a bit longer. The floor drain is a great way to clean up any blood, or bodily fluids, that our brand of torture leaves behind.

Hammer and Gunner lead the way to what we like to call 'the pit', followed by Mountain and Doc in the van, and Trooper, Kraken, and I bringing up the rear. To get to the barn, we pass the clubhouse and turn left around the next corner. About a mile down the road is a gate that leads to a gravel path. I imagine at one time it was nice and smooth, but grass has grown up through the gravel and made it a more uneven surface over time. It's surrounded by pine and maple trees, so if you didn't see the approach over the ditch, you'd just drive right by. It's not the smoothest to ride on, so we go slowly to avoid the gravel kicking up and damaging our paint jobs. We may be badass bikers, but we take pride in keeping our rides looking good.

We all roll to a stop and shut our bikes off. As soon as Pops parks the van in front of the barn's sliding doors, the front doors fly open, and he and Doc almost come rolling out.

"Holy fucking shit!" Doc yells. Pops is bent over, leaning on his right leg, and it sounds like he's coughing up his lungs.

"What the hell is going on in there?" I ask as I walk to the van and pull on the handle. When the door swings open, I immediately regret doing so because it smells like a bomb full of manure exploded inside the van. "Did one of you rip ass or is this guy smellier now than he was before?"

"Son, I think this scumbag shit his pants. He started groaning and rolling around so much that Doc had to crawl back and knock him out again. But one thing I do know is I'm not getting back in that van to go home. I'll walk through the woods before I step my one foot back in that outhouse on wheels," Mountain says as he finally catches his breath.

I look around the group and see that everyone is trying real hard to not catch my eyes. "Question is now, guys, which of you fuckers gets to carry this guy inside and get him secured? Because I refuse to get that smell on my cut. That'll never come out."

"I call not it" Gunner says.

"You're all big fucking babies." This comes from Trooper. "I've dealt with worse drunks. Just don't complain when you see me in my skivvies 'cause I sure as shit ain't letting my clothes touch that nastiness." He pulls off his cut and hangs it from his handlebars. Next, he pulls off his Henley and then goes for his belt.

We hear a rumble and all quiet down as a lone headlight makes its way down the path. When we see it's Ring coming to join the fun, we relax. Yes, we may complain about it, but we're all fucked up enough to find this fun.

"Hey, I'm glad you didn't start the activities without me. T, why are you getting naked? I didn't know this was that kind of party." Ring chuckles as he fist-bumps Kraken.

"Aww, man, does your skin ever see the sun?" Kraken shields his eyes. "I'm gonna go blind from your pasty ass, vampire-lookin' skin." That lightens the mood and everyone starts laughing.

"Nah. I just don't enjoy burning like a fucking lobster. My skin's too gentle for that shit," Trooper says as he flips Kraken the bird. "Time to get this party started, boys. Someone get those doors open and flip on the lights. Once I get moving with this guy, I don't wanna stop until I get him inside."

Hammer walks up and unlocks the padlock that secures the doors, giving the left door a shove and then the right. He and Gunner head in first and split up to start flipping switches on the opposite walls, the fluorescent lights flickering as they warm up and quickly reach their full brightness. Gunner goes to the cabinet in the corner and grabs a folded-up clear plastic sheet. We try and keep as much blood off the concrete as we can—little drops are easy to scrub off, but a whole puddle leaves a big stain.

We all stand to the side as Trooper approaches the back of the van, opens the left door, and reaches in. "Fuck this," he says. "I ain't carrying this asshole." Instead, he grabs the guy by the ankles and drags him out, letting him fall to the ground. What a scene this is—a giant ass guy, wearing only black boxer briefs and boots, standing over a crumpled-up, dirty excuse for a man.

Trooper bends over, grabs the guy's ankles again, and starts to drag him backward into the barn. Once he reaches the middle of the room, he drops the guy and reaches up to grab one of the chains hanging from the beam above. Gunner drags a metal chair over from the corner and sets it down next to the body, then he and Trooper each lift the guy by an arm and set him down in the seat.

"That was my help for now. I don't wanna touch him anymore. I'm gonna be smelling shit for a week straight," Gunner says as he walks back to the door. He puts his hands on his hips and stands with his back to us.

"I'll get him secured with the chains and then I'm gonna need a shower. You losers can deal with this one. I'll drive the van back to the clubhouse, rinse off, and bring my truck back to get Doc and Mountain," Trooper says while he drags down more chain and wraps it around the guy's stomach, securing him to the chair. He grabs a length of rope from a hook on the wall and kneels down to tie the guy's legs to the front chair legs. He stands back up and turns to look at me. "That look good to you?"

"Nice work, man. Get out of here. Take your time. We'll probably be here for a while. Let the old fogies know you'll be back for them. Knowing those two, they'd really try and walk back through the trees," I tell Trooper.

CHAPTER TWELVE

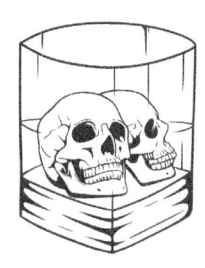

WHISKEY

I walk over to the tool bench that runs along the far wall. We like to keep our arsenal of weapons behind whoever we have in the barn. It's always fun to keep what's coming up next a surprise to our visitor. I grab a pair of black nitrile gloves and stretch them over my giant hands. It may make me sound like a whiny pussy, but I hate cleaning dried blood out of my fingernails. "Someone go and grab a bucket of water. We need to wake this fucker up. The surprise shower will hopefully help the stench some."

Hammer disappears into a small closet and comes out with a five-gallon bucket of water. He gets as close as he can to avoid the splash-back and tosses the water right into the guy's face. The guy starts to cough and squirm in the chair.

"Be careful there, buddy. Don't want you to tip yourself over. None of us wanna pick your smelly ass back up again. It was gross enough getting you here," Hammer warns as he holds out his hand for me to pass him a pair of gloves.

"Where the hell am I? And who the fuck are you?" he asks between coughs.

"Who am I? Are you just stupid or do you really not know whose territory you're in?" Hammer's taking the lead on this interrogation. As our Sergeant-at-Arms, this is what his job entails—he asks the questions that get us the answers we need. Hammer stands to his full height and begins walking circles around the chair. "My Brother over there," he points to Gunner, who's leaning against a steel support pole, "told me that he hit you a few times over the noggin, so I'll tell you a little story to help you remember what happened. You came to our business and tried to take one of our girls. You hurt her. We don't like when people touch things that belong to us. We just basically don't like sharing with strangers."

"She was outside all by herself. She was just out in the open for the pickin'," the guy says with a laugh.

Punch. Hammer throws a right hook and busts the guy's lip open.

"Is that all you got? I've gotten worse from my mommy." This guy definitely has an attitude problem.

"Don't worry about me and your mommy. After I take care of you, I'll go and pay her a visit. Hopefully, she's prettier than you are. Maybe she and I will become real good friends," Hammer taunts.

"My mom would kick your donkey ass. She don't take shit from nobody."

"Are you gonna tell me who you are or do I get to start getting creative? I know you have some ink hidden under that dirty shirt. How about I start cutting that off and see what I can find?" Hammer makes another circle around the chair and grabs a knife off the tool bench. "I think I'll start with your arms and see what you have hidden."

Hammer runs the knife blade up the left shirt sleeve and yanks up, splitting the material. That arm is empty, so he walks around and does it again to the right sleeve. Here's where we start getting some information.

"Who's Tiffany? Is she your girl or your mommy?" I ask.

"I ain't saying shit to you guys. You obviously have no idea what's going on around you. There's so much you know nothing about." It takes him a second to realize he said too much, too soon, then he closes his eyes and hangs his head.

"I think we need to get a closer look at that back piece. I have a feeling someone is part of our other problem as well," Hammer suggests. He looks at me and I nod.

I walk forward to grab a handful of the fucker's hair and yank it back. When his eyes meet mine, he sneers and says,

"I know I won't be getting out of here alive, so I'll let you in on a little secret. You won't find who you're looking for."

Hammer approaches from the front and slams a rubber mallet down on the guy's right hand. *Crunch*. That broke a few fingers for sure. "That's for talking back to our President. Show some respect, you pissant."

"Uhnnnn. Hurting me won't make me tell you what you wanna know," he grunts through his clenched teeth.

"Since this movie is really fucking boring, I'm gonna go outside. I can't stand the bad smell and bad acting," Ring says as he walks out into the dark.

"Time to get this shirt off you. Any last words to say before I start cutting you open?" Hammer asks.

"Fuck you" is all he says.

"No, thanks. I said I was saving that for your mommy."

He holds out the mallet to me, and I grab it and set it back in its spot on the tool bench.

Hammer places the tip of the knife right below the guy's chin and starts to slice down. From the sound coming out of his mouth, I'm going to assume the cotton isn't the only thing getting split apart right now. Once the knife gets low enough to meet the chains holding him to the chair, Hammer grabs the open flaps of his shirt and lifts the material up to rip it the rest of the way apart. Blood is dribbling out of the thin cut that runs between the guy's pecs. Thin, shallow cuts are sometimes worse than deeper ones. Just like getting a papercut, it hits all your nerve endings, so you feel it all.

Seeing the patch tattooed on the left side of his chest, Hammer busts out laughing. "Your name is Loony? Is that kinda like from the cartoon *Looney Tunes*?" The tattoo looks like the name patch we all have sewn to the front of our cuts. I'd bet a hundred bucks this guy belongs to another MC. Question is, which one?

Loony snaps back, "No, you fuck face. It's Loony, as in super crazy and gonna kill you assholes when I get out of here." Ooh, someone doesn't like us making fun of his name.

I can't hold myself back anymore. It's my turn to get some answers. "Apparently, this dumbass isn't very smart. I'm starting to think he fell off the stupid ladder and hit every rung on the way down."

"I'm a lot smarter than you idiots. There's stuff happening right under your noses, and you have no idea what," Loony smarts.

"Oh yeah? Like what? Like how you took one of our girls a few weeks back?" I ask him to see his reaction. Based on how white his face gets, I hit that nail on the head. "We know she's missing, but we didn't know who took her. But now that we've got you, it won't take us long to figure it out."

"Hammer, get the rest of this shirt off. I wanna see what he's got inked on his back. If it's what I think it is, we'll have our answers."

Hammer grabs hold of the material and yanks it up and back. The shirt rips again, but it's enough for us to see the words tattooed across the top of his shoulders.

CHAOS SQUAD MC.

As soon as he comprehends what he's seeing, Hammer loses him damn mind. "We know you're responsible for our missing girl. You can't deny it. Where is she? Where did you take my girl?" he yells.

"Your girl? She wasn't wearing a property patch. She's just a whore. Who cares?" Loony spits out and locks eyes with Hammer.

"She is NOT a whore! She belongs to this club and I wanna know where she is!" Hammer throws a one-two punch and Loony's head snaps back.

Loony rolls his head to the side and spits out some blood, then he looks around at all of us and starts laughing. "Sorry to bust your bubble, boys, but she was already bought and paid for, so you will never find her."

I walk around so that I'm standing in front of the chair. "Well, thank you for that information. Since you're not of any more use to us, I see no reason why we need to keep you around for any longer." I look back and forth to the other guys. "Do any of you have anything else to ask our friend before we kill him and burn his body?"

This is where he starts to panic. "Burn me? What the fuck? I didn't do nothin' to your girl. That was all Bullet. He's the one who makes all the calls. I was just supposed to grab the girl tonight and bring her back." This guy sure doesn't know when to shut his mouth. He spouts all the important stuff when he's put on the spot. Just a few simple threats gets me the information we need to start a search for the rest of the Chaos Squad MC.

"Bullet? Is that your leader?" I ask and Loony nods in response. "And to think I was just gonna stab you without telling you first. I sure am glad I waited until now."

I reach behind my back and grab the Ka-Bar knife tucked in the holster along my belt, then plunge it into the fucker's gut. I pull it back out and immediately start stabbing him over and over again. The last time I yank it out, I flip the knife in my grip and slice it sideways across his neck. I step back and to the side to avoid the spray that spurts out. With the stab wounds already in his stomach, it doesn't take but a few seconds for his head to drop and he's gone.

"Sorry I took the fun away from you, Hammer. I just couldn't listen to his voice anymore," I say as I walk over to the bench and grab a towel to wipe the blood off my knife.

"No problems here, Prez. Less for me to clean off myself," Hammer replies as he rips off his gloves and tosses them down on the plastic sheet.

"Gunner, go out and grab Ring. Kraken, the three of you are on clean-up duty. I want nothing left of him but ashes. Then you'll need to peroxide the hell out of this area once you move the sheet." I point to the circle of blood on the plastic sheet.

Heading for the storage closet, I rip off my gloves and throw them by the others, toss a clean towel over my shoulder, and grab a small bottle of peroxide off a shelf. I take it, and the bloody towel and knife, and head for the storage closet. "Hammer, wait for me. I want a word before we head back."

"I'll be outside," he replies.

I walk into the closet and flip on the light with my elbow. Inside is a wall mounted stainless-steel sink and a stack of empty buckets. Using the towel to hold the handle of my knife, I pour the peroxide over the blade and rinse everything off with super-hot water from the faucet. I leave the bottle and bloody towel in the sink and grab the clean towel from my shoulder to dry off my knife. Once it's shiny again, I tuck it back into my belt sheath.

I walk out of the closet to see Gunner and Kraken rolling Loony's body up in the plastic. "I'm out. There's trash in that sink, so don't forget to burn that too."

"Will do," Ring replies and heads in to grab it.

As I walk outside, the sky starts to show its first signs of a new day. It's pretty close to dawn and our day is just ending. Thank God it's Monday and the yard isn't open today. I need a damn nap.

I walk over to my bike and see Hammer sitting on his, looking down at his phone. That reminds me, I turned off my ringer earlier and need to turn it back up. Straddling my seat, I reach into my cut and grab my phone from the inner pocket. When I wake up the screen, there's two missed texts, so I swipe up to unlock and see the messages are from Kiana.

>**Kiana:** Hey. Just checking in. Any news?
>**Kiana:** Did you send someone by my house?

"What the fuck?" I wonder. What the hell is going on? Why would she ask that? I check the time stamps—10:57 p.m. and 10:59 p.m. That was just after I got the call from Gunner about Stiletto.

"What happened?" Hammer asks.

"Kiana sent me a text last night and asked if I sent someone by her house. You don't think someone from the other MC is watching her, do you?" I'm starting to panic a bit.

"Before our little chat, I would say I don't know, but now, I wouldn't put it past them. Who knows how long those fuckers have been watching us? If they're not wearing cuts or riding bikes past the clubhouse, we'd have no idea they were around." He's got a point. Until tonight, we didn't have a clue who we were looking for.

"I gotta go. I need to head to her house and see what's going on," I say as I fire up my Harley.

"Let me know if you need backup. I'm only a phone call away," Hammer yells over my rumbling engine.

"Thanks, man. We'll talk more tomorrow. Tell the guys we got Church at five p.m. and everyone better be there.

If this is what I think it is, I'll be bringing Kiana back with me. The girls will all be on lockdown." I pop the clutch, grab a handful of throttle, and I'm off. Right now, I could care less about the gravel driveway and my paint job—I've got a lady to see.

As I get closer to town, I slow my speed and start paying a lot more attention to the shadows. I want to see if there's anything that seems out of place. I turn onto Maple Street and coast past all the dark businesses. If I wasn't so worried about what I might find when I get to Kiana's house, I'd actually enjoy the quietness of our little town. I hang a right onto her street and see a few houses with lights on, but nobody is outside yet. Her house is straight ahead, at the end of a cul-de-sac, so I pull right into her driveway. I don't see her truck anywhere, so I'm really hoping it's parked inside behind the extra tall garage door.

I shut off my bike, hop off, and start to walk up the front porch steps. The first step squeaks under my boot, so I take the next few as gently as my weight will allow. I try to look in the front door's window, but there's some sort of curtain on the inside that doesn't let me see anything. I look to the left and see a bench made out of carved logs. Lucky for me, it looks heavy duty enough to hold my weight. I only plan to sit and wait for Kiana to start making noise inside, but before I know it, I feel myself start to doze off.

CHAPTER THIRTEEN

KIANA

I start to wake up and can't seem to remember how I got to bed last night, then I roll over and see my phone laying on the pillow next to my head. Instantly, it all comes rushing back. I lay still to see if I can hear any strange bumps or noises from outside. Now that it's daylight, I should take a walk around the house and check things out. With my luck, it was probably a tree branch that fell against the house and I was freaking out about nothing.

As I toss the blankets off and swing my feet to the floor, I look at my phone and don't see any response from Whiskey. He probably saw my messages and thought I was crazy.

After making a pit stop in the bathroom, I head into my walk-in closet to get dressed. I change into a long sleeved, black t-shirt and a pair of distressed jeans with rips in the front. With a plan to enjoy my coffee on the front porch, I pick out a pair of royal purple fuzzy socks to keep my feet warm.

I head down the hall and into the kitchen to make coffee and find something to eat. I don't have much in my fridge, so I settle for a couple pieces of cinnamon sugar toast. After everything is brewed and popped, I shove my phone in my back pocket and head for the front door.

I guess I'm not paying as much attention as I should be, because I miss the visitor who has taken residence on my porch bench. I can't see his face from where I'm standing in the doorway, but I'm not going to take any chances. Slowly taking a step back into the house, I set my cup and breakfast down on the foyer table and pick up the aluminum baseball bat that I keep next to the door. Resting the bat on my shoulder, I take a few steps forward so I can get a look at the stranger's face.

When I see who it is, I let out the breath I didn't even realize I was holding. I'm not exactly happy that Whiskey is sleeping on my porch, so I decide to have a little fun with him. Shuffling forward, I lean against the porch railing and let the bat fall forward off my shoulder. It makes a metallic *thunk* as the end hits the porch and Whiskey jackknifes up from the bench. What I did not expect was having a gun pointed at my face.

"Holy fucking hell, woman! You can't be doing that to a man with a loaded weapon," he yells at me and deflates back onto the bench. "I'm sorry about that, darlin', but you surprised me." This time, his voice is a lot softer and calm.

I don't respond to him because I think I'm frozen from shock. I let go of the bat handle and collapse to the porch floor, shaking. I don't even notice him getting on the floor with me, but the next thing I know, I'm picked up by two strong arms, placed in Whiskey's lap, and wrapped up against his warm chest. He starts rocking us back and forth, whispering into my hair. I can't understand what he's saying, but whatever it is, it's working and my heart rate is slowly coming back to normal.

I turn my head and look up at him. "What are you doing on my porch? I didn't call you in my sleep, did I? I've been known to talk in my sleep sometimes." Great, and now I'm sharing embarrassing secrets.

"No, you didn't call me. But I did get your texts at about dawn. I was worried that something was wrong, so I rode over to check on you. I couldn't hear any noise and I didn't want to wake you. What I didn't plan on doing was falling asleep out here," he says as he continues to rock us.

"I was having a rough night," I say.

"I got that from the texts. What did you mean when you asked if I sent someone to your house? Why did you think someone was here?"

That makes me snap out of my stupor. Why am I sitting in his lap? He's not my boyfriend. I climb out of his lap and get up on my own. "Nothing happened. I just thought I heard some noises outside, but when I looked, nothing was there. I was just overreacting and shouldn't have bothered you."

Whiskey unfolds his body from the ground and stands. When he's not standing in front of me, I forget how tall he really is. Being right next to him, I have to tilt my head back to get a look at his face.

"I hate to break it to you, but I'm not sure you were imaging things," he says as he grabs my hands and laces our fingers together. Damn it. Why do we fit together so well?

"What do you mean? Was there someone here when you got here?" I ask and start looking around the porch and out onto the street. I don't see anything out of place, but maybe he already chased them away.

"No. No one was here, but I do have something to tell you. Can we go inside and talk? This might be better if we go in and sit down." Before I can answer, Whiskey pulls me inside and shuts and locks the door. "Is this your coffee? Do you have any more? I need some caffeine."

He's asked enough questions, so now it's my turn. "No, you cannot have any coffee. I wanna know what the heck is going on. Why am I not imagining things? And what do you have to tell me? Is it about Tempy? Did you find her? Is she at the clubhouse? We have to go right now." I try to get around him, but he blocks my way into the kitchen.

"No, she isn't at the clubhouse. Let's sit down and I'll fill you in."

He grabs my hand and pulls me into the living room, leading me to the couch. I sit in the middle while he perches himself on the leg part of the L-shaped sectional. He leans forward, rests his elbows on his knees, and brings his head down to my eye level.

"I'm sorry to tell you, but I don't have the best news for you. We don't know where Wings is, but we did hear that she's alive. Someone took her. But I need you to know that I have a lead and we're doing everything to bring her home."

"What do you mean someone took her?" I ask as the tears start flowing. "Who took her?"

"I can't give you those details, but I can tell you they'll be sorry that they did." Whiskey is being very evasive and I don't like it one bit. This makes my tears dry up real fast and I can feel my face heat with anger. He tries to reach for my hands, but I slap his away.

I sit back, out of his reach. "That answer isn't good enough for me. I need to know what happened to my sister and you'll tell me right fucking now. She's my baby sister. What did you and your stupid club get her involved in? This is all your fault!" As soon as the words are out, I know I've made a big mistake.

In one fast, smooth move, Whiskey is on his knees in front of me and his face is an inch from mine. His hands are next to my shoulders and he's caging me in. "I know you're angry, but I will not let you speak to me that way. I'm the man here and you'll listen to what I say and not argue with me. Until I have more information, I can't tell you any more. This is club business, so you don't need to know every detail. Do not make me repeat myself. Do I make myself clear?" His eyes are bright blue, but you can only see a bit of silver because his pupils are dilated. And the woodsy and leather smell coming from his t-shirt and vest are intoxicating.

I don't know what comes over me, but having him be this hot and aggressive right in front of my face proves to be too much for me to hold myself back. I move my head forward that last inch and kiss the hell out of him, throwing my arms around his neck and pushing him backward. My forward momentum makes him fall back onto his heels and I use the opportunity to climb into his lap on my own this time.

Whiskey wraps his arms around my waist and uses his hands to pull us up onto the couch. Without ever breaking our lip lock, he lays me on my back and crawls on top of me. His tongue traces the seam of my lips and it's like an 'open sesame' message to my brain. My lips part and his tongue dives into my mouth. I could say that it's the best kiss I've ever had in my life, but that would require my brain to be functioning enough for me to remember anything other than what is happening right now. We continue to try and steal the breath from each other for a few more minutes before he slows down our kiss and leans his forehead down on mine.

"As much as I'd like to keep this going, we have to get moving." He sits back and pulls me up to sit next to him. "We need to get you packed and to the clubhouse. You can't stay here right now. It's not safe." He tries to stand, but I pull him back down.

"What do you mean you need me at the clubhouse? I don't wanna go there. I'm fine right here." I can hear the whine in my voice but can't seem to stop it.

"I can't let you stay here alone and I need to be at the clubhouse. Something else happened last night and we all need to stick close together. I shouldn't be telling you this because you're not in the club, but it'll be hard to hide once we're there. Another one of our club girls was attacked last night. She wasn't taken, but she was shaken up. We caught the guy who tried to take her, but we don't know how many more of the bad guys are out there. It would make my life a lot easier if you would just come with me."

The look on his face makes me think for a minute. Hearing that another girl was almost taken scares me more than I want to admit. Do I take what he says seriously and go with him? Is the clubhouse the best place for me? I'm not really sure.

"Why would the clubhouse be any safer for me? Tempy went missing from there. What's to say that someone can't get me there?" I ask.

"She wasn't taken from the compound. She left and something happened somewhere between there and here. The clubhouse and compound are extremely safe and secure. You saw the barbwire fence and locked gate when you were there last week. That goes all the way around our acreage. We also have motion sensors and security cameras pointed in every direction. If someone tries to get in, we'll see it." He scoots closer to me and pulls on one of my curls. It bounces back when he lets it go. "Plus, if you come back with me, we can do more of what we were doing before. Maybe we can do what we were talking about when you were in the tub the other day. What do you say?"

"How long would I need to stay? I have a business to run and can't not be able to get in my kitchen. I can stop the cupcakes, but I cannot cancel my cake orders. That's what makes me the money to pay my bills." I need to know all the details before I agree to anything.

"If you need to bake stuff, you can use the kitchen at the clubhouse. It's pretty huge and we'll get you any supplies that you need. Any deliveries you need to make, we can send one of the Brothers along with you. Until we know the full severity of what's going on around here, we have to be careful." The more he shares, the more I begin to take him seriously.

I nuzzle my face into his palm and put my hand on his thigh. I squeeze hard until he tries to pull away. "I'll agree to this under one condition. If you want me there with you, you won't be with any of the club girls. I know what they do for you there and I don't play those games. I will not share you. This may not be a forever thing, but it'll only be us while I'm there."

"Oh, sweet girl, you underestimate me. Once I have you in my bed, I don't know if I'll ever let you get back out. I just might have to keep you there forever." Whiskey's voice is as smooth as his name. "I won't be sharing you with anyone. Don't you worry about that."

He's way too happy that I've agreed to this. Time to knock him back down a notch. I get up from the couch and step a few feet away, then cross my arms and try to put on a straight face. "What if I want my own room? Can I stay in Tempy's room?"

"No, you can't. Her room is down a hallway with all the other club girls. I don't think you'd like to hear some of the things that come from those rooms. And I don't want one of the guys getting drunk and walking in on you. It would be best if you stay upstairs with me. My bedroom door locks and I'll get you the spare key. If they know you're there with me, no one will touch or bother you." It seems like there are some things I'm going to have to learn.

"Okay, fine. If I'm going with you, I need to go pack," I say and turn around to head back to my room. I make it a few steps before I'm stopped by arms wrapped around my waist. He pulls me back into his chest and I instantly feel his hardness against my ass.

"Don't bother packing anything to sleep in. I don't plan on you being wrapped in anything but my arms," Whiskey whispers in my ear. He lets me go and slaps me on the ass.

I can't help but laugh out loud as I walk away.

It doesn't take me very long to pack, but I end up loading a suitcase, two duffel bags, and a backpack with what I think I'll need. Not knowing how long I'll be there, I pack a little bit of everything.

As I back out of my driveway, I look at my house and get a strange feeling. It's like I'm saying goodbye. I don't know what that feeling means, but I hope it's a good thing.

Whiskey is leading me to the clubhouse and he looks so damn hot on his motorcycle. I guess I've never paid close attention to the way bikers ride, but seeing how effortless he makes it look, I wonder if he'll take me for a ride.

I glance in the rearview mirror and see a dark van a little ways behind me. It disappears when we go around the curves, but then it's there again when the road straightens. I wonder if Whiskey called for someone to follow us back.

As we round the last curve, I see the garage and clubhouse fence ahead. The gate starts to move and by the time we reach it, it's open just enough for us to pull into the lot. Whiskey rides toward the clubhouse and backs his bike up in the row of black and chrome. I slow to a stop because I don't know where to park.

I see Hammer walking toward my side of the truck, so I roll down the window and ask, "Where do you want me to park?"

He points to the right side of the building and says, "See that driveway around the right of the clubhouse? If you follow that, you'll see some cabins behind there. You can park in one of the marked spots back there. We try to keep this front lot clear for bikes. The guys sometimes pull in and out pretty fast, not paying attention where they're going. Whiskey will meet you out back."

"Thanks, Hammer. Listen, I'm sorry about being so rude the last time I was here." I feel bad for the guy. It seems like he might have some feelings for Tempy. I wonder if she knows.

"It's okay, hun. Already forgotten." He taps on the door and walks back toward the clubhouse.

I drive around the building and park in the first empty spot I see. I jump out of the truck just as Whiskey comes out from one the clubhouse's back doors.

"You've got one heck of a set-up here, Whiskey. You even have a playground? Are there kids living here too?" I'm blown away by the amount of open space back here. There's not only the playground, but also a bunch of picnic tables, Adirondack chairs, and a giant firepit set up a bit further out. String lights are strung from the porch overhang out into the largest trees.

"We have a few kids here off and on, but none live here full-time currently. I just like for there to be something fun for them to do while they're visiting. We also have some big family cookouts, and when the families are here, the kiddos like playing together." He's really proud of this place. "You should really see it when some of the guys have a few too many drinks. They like to start daring each other to do crazy shit. One time, we had to take the tunnel apart because Steel got himself stuck in it. I think a few guys pissed themselves from laughing so hard." He chuckles at the memory. I'm liking this happy side of Whiskey.

"That does sound funny. Hey, before I forget, did the guy following us get back before you closed the gate? I didn't see anyone pull in behind me."

CHAPTER FOURTEEN

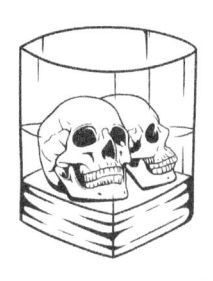

WHISKEY

The guy following us? That doesn't sound good. I didn't call anybody until just before we left her house. No one would've had time to get behind us without us passing them first, and I haven't seen any other vehicles since we crossed the town line.

I grab Kiana's hand and pull her inside and down the office hallway. We end up in the main room, where a bunch of the Brothers are hanging out and eating breakfast. I bring my fingers to my lips and whistle to get everyone's attention. Everything goes silent and heads whip around in our direction.

"Everyone, this is Kiana. Kiana, these are my Brothers. We'll make better introductions later, but right now, we've got a problem. We were followed on our way back this morning and Kiana was the only one to see them." I look down at her scared eyes and ask as gently as I can, "What did you see following you? What kind of vehicle?"

"It was a dark colored van. It was back too far, so I couldn't make out a specific color. Maybe black or a dark blue?" She's starting to shake again. I don't need her going into shock like she did earlier.

"Cypher, check the cameras. I want a make, color, and hopefully plates ASAP. Wrench, Brick, Brewer, and Saddle, I want you to double up and ride in both directions. See if you can find a dark colored van. Look for anything suspicious. Go!" And they take off.

I look down at this woman and realize that she's quickly crawling inside my heart. I may have said it as a joke to her earlier, but I'm starting to think I won't be able to let her go back home when this is all over. We've only been at the clubhouse for ten minutes, but I can already tell I like having her here with me. We're in the middle of a shitty situation, but I can feel the calmness that she brings me.

I'm the President of the Rebel Vipers MC and I think it's time for me to start a new path for our club family. Maybe when the Brothers see what it's like to have a strong woman around, they'll do whatever it takes to find one for themselves. I've always believed that depending on someone else made you look weak, but now, I think that having a partner may just make me stronger.

"I want this club on partial lockdown. Women are not allowed outside of the clubhouse without a Brother. If you want to go outside, make sure someone with a patch is with you. That also means no leaving the compound for any reason whatsoever. Not even to The Lodge or any other club businesses. Guys, if you go beyond the fence, you must have a buddy. No riding anywhere alone." I look around the room and meet everyone's eyes. "No bullshitting this time. Don't make me regret this and put us on full lockdown. Anyone with questions, just ask."

I look down at Kiana and see that she's not handling all of this very well. I pull her into my chest and try to give her some of my strength. "Why don't we go grab your bags and I'll take you up to my room. I've got some calls to make and you can lay down to rest for a bit."

"That sounds like a good idea. This is a lot to take in at once and I feel exhausted," she says.

I grab her hand and head back down the hall toward the back door. I pause and point to the double doors, letting her know that it's where we meet for Church. "If those doors are closed and we're in there for Church, you do not come in without permission. Do you understand? There are things that happen behind those doors that you don't need to know about. Okay?" I stop and meet her eyes, trying to get her to understand that I'm deadly serious about this.

"I don't get it yet, but I trust you. The whole caveman thing is weird, but this is your club." She keeps my eyes and I couldn't be prouder.

"Good girl. There are a few different rules around here, but I have no doubt in my mind that you'll be fitting in here in no time." I start us walking again and point out my office door on the right and my Pops' room on the left. When we get back outside, we both let out a heavy sigh and just pause to take in the quiet. "This may be one of the last bits of quiet we get for a while. Cooping everyone up in the clubhouse can get a bit loud. If you ever need a reprieve, this is usually the place to find it."

"Good to know. Let's grab my bags and I'll let you go do your thing. My brain needs a break," Kiana says.

When she opens the truck and pulls out just one suitcase, I'm surprised. "One suitcase? Is that all you brought? Where's the rest of your stuff?"

She laughs and pulls out two more duffel bags. "I also have two duffels and a backpack. Don't worry, I'm just a good packer. There's more in here than you think."

"Good. Let me grab those for you. You've got me for all the heavy lifting. I'm a caveman, remember?" I chuckle, trying to bring a smile to her face. After she locks her truck doors, we go back inside and I lead her through the main room, past the bar that faces the middle of the room, and up the stairs just past the main hallway.

When we're upstairs and down the hall, I stop outside the last door on the left. "This is my room. Well, our room now, so make yourself at home." I unlock the door and push it open. I flip on the light and cringe. "Sorry for the mess. I obviously didn't know that I'd be moving you in today. Feel free to move or toss anything you want." I didn't know that I could be embarrassed about my personal space, but I can definitely say I'm glad I'll have a woman's touch around here.

"It's okay, Whiskey. I know I'm just a guest here. I won't make you throw anything away. Your bed looks super comfy and that's all I really care about right now. Just set down my bags and get to doing whatever you need to do." Kiana looks up at me and I can't help but feel the need to kiss her. I put her bags off to the side and wrap her in my arms again. I lower my head and press my lips against hers. She closes her eyes and I can see the stress start to melt from her face.

"Alright, ma'am, it's time for you to get some shuteye. I'll just be downstairs, and I'll come back to get you in a few hours. If you need something to drink, I have a mini-fridge under my desk. Food is all down in the kitchen, so we can eat dinner together later. That okay?" I ask as I pull back my crumpled blankets and watch her climb in. Seeing her in my bed, laying her head on my pillow, seals the deal for me—I'm never going to let this woman go. Telling her that right now is probably not a good idea, but the wheels are spinning. I have plans to make and things to get, but when the time is right, she will be mine. Whiskey with an Old Lady? I never could've seen this coming.

I look down at Kiana one more time and see that she's already fast asleep. I kiss her on the forehead and back away quietly. I close and lock the door, and head back downstairs. As I hit the bottom step, the front doors swing open and the guys who went out looking for the van come walking in. "Any luck?"

"We didn't find anything. Wrench and I rode back toward town and only passed a few civilians." This comes from Brick.

"And we went west toward the highway but didn't see any vans or big SUVs. We can go back out, but whoever it was is probably long gone or hidden by now," Saddle, our Road Captain, says as he goes behind the bar to grab us a bunch of beers.

"That's alright, let's wait and see what Cypher digs up. If they drove past here, we'll have them on camera and know which direction they went." I plop my ass down on a bar stool and take a long sip of the cold hops. I wish I could be upstairs taking a nap with Kiana, but we need some information before I can relax.

What sounds like a herd of elephants comes running down the stairs, forcing all of us to swivel around. We see Cypher jump and skip the last two steps, hitting the concrete floor with a loud *THUD*. Somehow, he manages to land on both feet. "I got the van driving past just as the gate closed. It was a '94 Chevy Astro Cargo Van. The plates were reported stolen a week ago from Washington County, so that's a dead end, but I've got the system running a scan for any other times it might have driven by. I also looked at Wings' phone signal and there still isn't anything new."

"Now that we've got one base covered, I need all of you to reach out to whoever you need to, find out anything you can about this so-called Chaos Squad. We need to figure out who they are, where they came from, and what they're up to. And we need to get Wings back safe." An idea pops into my head. "Cypher, can you do some dark web searching for these guys? If they're selling women, shouldn't there be some sort of trace?"

"I'll look, but the dark web is a big place. But if anyone can find something, it'll be me." He laughs, and it's kind of dark and creepy, but that's exactly why we like him.

"I'm gonna go make some calls. Let me know what you find." I finish the rest of my beer and grab a fresh one before heading for my office.

CHAPTER FIFTEEN

KIANA

I begin to open my eyes and groan at the sunlight. Why is the sun shining through my bedroom window? My curtains should be closed. I roll over and realize I'm not in my bedroom. I'm in Whiskey's bed at the clubhouse.

Looking around the room, I don't see Whiskey, so I assume he hasn't come back upstairs yet. That is until I grab my phone from the nightstand and see what time it is—ten a.m. . . . on Tuesday! As in I slept for almost twenty-three hours! I don't think I've ever slept that long in my life. I must've been really out of it.

Feeling like I'm about to pee my pants, I kick back the covers and run to the bathroom, not even bothering to turn on the light. After I finish my business, I flip the switch so I can see while washing my hands. Holy crap. Now that I get a good look around the bathroom, I realize why Whiskey was a bit ashamed of his messy room. This place looks like what I imagine a frat house would after rush week. It's not dirty per se, but nothing is put away and dirty clothes are piled in the far corner. I know he said I can move whatever I want, but I feel weird touching his stuff. I don't want to be too nosy, but investigating a little won't hurt.

I pull open the top drawer of the vanity and am shocked by what I find. Why does any person need four toothpaste tubes open at one time? And razors! I stop counting at six disposable razor packages. Whiskey's beard is scruffy, so I'm not really sure why he needs razors. Closing that drawer, I reach down to the second but slam it shut just as fast. Why does he need so many boxes of condoms? I guess I should be happy that he's protecting himself, but at the same time, it doesn't make me happy that he has them at all. He's a very attractive man, so I know he can't be a monk, but I'm still jealous nonetheless.

I decide that I need a shower, so I go back in the bedroom and drag my big suitcase up on the bed. I open it up and search for some comfy clothes, settling on a pair of maroon leggings and an extra-large black t-shirt I take off a hanger in Whiskey's closet. After I grab my toiletry bag, I head for the shower. Surprised at how nice the fixtures are in this bathroom, my earlier assumption of a frat house is slowly fading away.

After showering under the best water pressure I've ever experienced, I almost don't want to get out. Finally caving, I turn off the water and grab the towel I hung on the hook just outside the curtain. I squeeze as much water as I can from my hair and tie it up in a still-wet messy bun. My curls will be a matted mess later, but even with a full day's sleep, I just don't have the energy to deal with them properly. While drying off, my stomach rumbles loudly, and I remember that I haven't eaten anything since my failed popcorn movie night. I finish getting dressed, grab my phone, and decide it's time to venture downstairs.

The hall is quiet, so I assume everyone has started their day and are at work. Speaking of work, I should really call Lynn and Angie to let them know I'll be away for a while. I get to the bottom of the stairs and take my first real look around the main room. It's one big open room, but there are different spaces with their own purposes. There's an alcove off to the right that has a pool table and a few dart boards. In the middle are a bunch of couches and recliners facing a ginormous flat screen TV. And on the far side, next to the Church room doors, is a dining area with two long cafeteria-like tables and chairs all around them. In the middle of the building, situated between the two hallways, sits the bar. There are so many stools and bottles on display, it looks like a bar you'd go to on a night out. But then again, this is where the club hangs out, so it makes sense.

"Who are you?" I spin around and see two women standing next to the pool table. I start to wonder where they came from but then notice a hallway tucked away at the bottom of the stairs. That must be the hallway of club girls' bedrooms that Whiskey mentioned yesterday. It's Tuesday before noon and their clothes, or lack thereof, make them look like they're about to go out for a wild Saturday night.

The taller girl is younger, maybe about twenty or so. She has shoulder length, bright white-blonde hair, and the prettiest green eyes. She's wearing a blue spaghetti strap tank top, high-waisted Daisy Duke shorts, and fishnet stockings. The jet-black combat boots complement her outfit perfectly. Her makeup is a bit bright, but not super heavy. She looks like your average girl next door, cheerleader type.

The second woman, on the other hand, looks like she was ridden hard and hung out to dry. She's shorter than me, and that's saying a lot because I'm only five-foot-four. She looks like could be fifty years old, but I'm guessing she might be a bit younger. And her get-up screams trashy. Unlike the tall one's pretty blonde locks, this woman's hair has been bleached so many times, it looks brassy and yellow. It's permed and kind of ratty. Her makeup is caked on, and her mascara and eyeliner make her look like a raccoon lost in the dark. She's wearing a hot pink t-shirt with holes cut all over, tiny jean shorts, and heels so high, a stripper would fall on her ass.

In an effort to not judge them, I try to go the polite route. Like Grandma Hannah used to say, you catch more flies with honey than you do with vinegar. "Hi, I'm Kiana. I'm Tempy's sister. Do you happen to know where I can find Whiskey?"

"You're Wings' sister?" the tall one asks. "Do you know where she is? Have you seen her?" She rushes at me with the saddest look on her face. I hope that means they really care about her here.

"Oh, who cares where she is? Less competition for time with the Brothers with her being gone." This comes from the older woman still leaning against the pool table. I can tell she thinks this is her territory. I only want one man here, so more power to her.

"Shut up, Jewel. You don't have to be such a bitch all the time." Looks like I might have one ally here. "Ignore her. She's just crabby that the guys have more important things to do than her. I'm Stiletto. I don't know how much you know about the club, but we're club girls, like Wings. Do you know that she's missing?"

"Yea, I do. I came here a week ago trying to find her and Whiskey said she wasn't here. Then he came to my house yesterday and said someone was attacked and I needed to come here. I just woke up and came down to find everyone missing." I look around again to see if anyone else has popped out of hiding.

"That was me. Someone tried to take me on Sunday night and things have been a bit tense around here ever since," Stiletto says.

"Oh my gosh! Are you okay?" I ask.

She gets a bit quiet and pulls me over to sit on one of the couches. "I'm fine. Got a bump to the head and some bruises from when I fell, but otherwise, I'm good. I'm honestly more worried about Wings. If the guy who tried to take me got her too, I kinda wish he would've taken me. Maybe I could've been taken to wherever she is, and then she wouldn't be alone and think no one was looking for her."

"Oh, hun, no. I would never want that to happen to you and I doubt Tempy would either. Whoever these bad guys are, I have no doubt the club will find them. I haven't been around long, but they all seem scary enough to get stuff done." I laugh and try to lighten the mood. Stiletto looks like she needs a break. I just hope she stays as nice as she is to me right now. "I just don't know how well I'm going to fit in around here. I'm so out of my element and have no idea what to do with my time."

"I'm sure you'll be fine. Whiskey brought you here, right?"

"Yea. He just showed up at my house and told me I had to come here," I reply.

"If he wants you here, then you should be here. He doesn't say things and not mean them. That's part of what makes him a good President. He sticks by his words." That's good to hear.

"And he has a huge dick and is killer in the sack," Jewel spits out as she stands behind the couch we're on.

Stiletto turns and snaps, "Good grief, Jewel, he's never gonna claim you. No one is. Why don't you go hide in your skank cave?"

"You're a club girl here too, bitch. No one is gonna claim you either," Jewel sneers and disappears back down the side hallway.

"I'm sorry about her. She's here for all the wrong reasons," Stiletto says with a sigh.

"It's okay," I say, trying to forget what Jewel said. I need to grow a thick skin if I'm going to be around the women he's slept with. "Can I ask why you're here? What's the right reason to be a club girl and sleep with any guy?" I'm not sure what would make this situation okay for anyone.

"That's fine. Girls like Jewel are here because they want one of the Brothers to claim them and make her their Old Lady. What they seem to forget is that never happens. I've only heard of it happening once and the Brother never slept with another club girl again. But the girls like Jewel wish they were that lucky. The club girls are here for the guys to use to let off steam. They have hard days and are often in rough situations, so they need someone to be there for them to get off and then go away." I can understand that, a little. "Now, I can't say that I'm not here for the variety of hot men, because I definitely am, but I also get something more out of it. The club pays for my college tuition. I don't have any family and barely graduated high school. I'm studying to be an accountant and do all my classes online. As long as I live here as a club girl, I have no rent, don't have to pay for groceries, and they give me time to do my studies. I work at the club's bar and restaurant, so I get paid, and don't have any bills other than my cell phone and car payment. It's a win-win for me."

"I guess I never thought of it like that. When Tempy decided to live here, I just couldn't understand why she would want to do this. I guess in a way, I still don't get it, because she won't talk to me about it." Just talking about her and being where she lives without her here makes me miss her that much more.

"I've asked her a few times why she came here, but she just said it felt right. I've never really understood what that meant. When she comes back, maybe she'll tell you," Stiletto says.

"I sure hope so. I wish being here didn't take me away from my work. I don't know what to do with myself. I don't handle being bored easily." I miss my kitchen already.

"What do you do?" she asks.

"I make cupcakes and cakes and own The Cake Butcher downtown."

"You own that place? Oh my God, I love all your specialty flavors. I've bought some a few times but have to hide them in my room. I made the mistake once of leaving a box in the kitchen and when I went to eat one the next day, they were all gone. Some of the guys discovered them and ate them all." That makes us both laugh out loud.

"Whiskey did tell me I had free rein of the kitchen. Maybe I can dig around and see if I can make something that everyone will like. Do you think they would eat something that isn't a boring chocolate?" I have a new flavor in mind but haven't made it yet.

"These guys will eat almost anything. If it's edible and not colored pink, they'll try it." She stands and grabs my hand to pull me up. "Let me show you the kitchen and I can try to help you. I'll warn you right now though, I'm a disaster in the kitchen. I've even burned mac 'n' cheese."

We walk past the bar on our way to the kitchen tucked behind it, and I stop to grab a bottle of Woodford Reserve bourbon. "Think they'll like booze in their cupcakes?"

That really makes her laugh. "Woman, if you put booze in their food, they'll never let you leave."

CHAPTER SIXTEEN

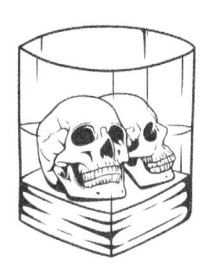

WHISKEY

"How's the weather up there?" I ask Monty. He's the one who supplies us with guns from above the border in Canada. He flies them down to us in his private plane, and we deliver them by semi-truck to our buyers down in Chicago.

"It's getting colder every day, man. We've got snow in the forecast for next week. Do you need another shipment already? The weather will determine when I can fly down."

"No, man, we're still good. But I do have a question to ask. It's gotta do with something a little more on the bad side of the not-so-legal world. Do you have any information on anyone in the human trafficking business?" I ask Monty. I don't like mixing different parts of our club businesses, but I'm desperate right now. If I don't get Wings back, Kiana will never agree to stay here with me.

"Did you say human trafficking? You mean like kidnapping and selling women? You should know me better than that by now, Whiskey. I don't like where this conversation is going, man. I don't fly around stolen women, if that's what you're asking me." Great, now I've pissed him off.

"No, Monty. I didn't mean to say that you were involved. I wouldn't ask you this if it wasn't something important. We've got a girl who was taken by a club I never heard of until this weekend. I need to find out anything I can about them. I'm just asking if you know anyone who might work in that business, and if you can point me in the right direction. I don't want you to get involved in something you want nothing to do with. I'd never mess with what we've got going on. It makes both of us too much money." I try and back myself out of the corner I unwittingly got myself in.

"I don't know anyone directly involved in the trade, but I can put out some feelers with my other contacts. I can't guarantee I'll get anything, but for the sake of our friendship, I'll try. I hate to hear that you have someone missing. That's not good for anyone." Monty sounds a bit less tense now. Thank God.

"That's fine. If you learn something, let me know. Otherwise, no harm, no foul. I've gotta go and check in with the guys. Talk soon?" I do need to find the guys and get an update, but what I really want to do is find Kiana and see what she's been up to today.

"Sounds good. Later." With that, Monty hangs up.

I walk into the clubhouse and am blown away by what I see. All my Brothers are sitting in the main room eating cupcakes. A bunch of burly, tattooed, hardass bikers stuffing their faces with desserts. "Where the hell did you get those from?" I ask Hammer as I walk up to the bar. He'd just taken a huge bite.

"Keyaannuhh made 'em," he says with half a chocolate cupcake in his mouth.

Kiana made cupcakes? I guess she's made herself comfortable in our kitchen. Good. I want her to think of this as her territory too. If she's going to be my Old Lady, I need her to feel at home here. "She made you cupcakes? Where's mine?" I ask as I look around, finding only an empty tray sitting on the bar.

I start to feel left out when the kitchen doors swing open and she comes out with another tray of chocolate frosted goodies. She looks back into the kitchen and lets out a full laugh. What I didn't expect her to be laughing at was Stiletto, who follows her out with another tray. They look like they've made friendly with each other. Kiana doesn't notice me as they walk behind the bar and slide the trays onto the bar top. Anyone within arm's distance reaches out and grabs a cupcake. Time for me to get what I want.

I walk around the bar, wrap my arm around her waist, and pull her back against my chest. She lets out a mix of a squeak and a yelp. If I wasn't so interested in trying her baking, I would've found it distracting.

"Where's mine?" I growl and take a nip at her earlobe. Okay, maybe it did distract me a bit.

"There's plenty to go around." She chuckles and wiggles her ass back into my quickly hardening dick.

"You better not be offering your sweetness to my Brothers. I want all that sugar for myself," I say as I start nibbling and kissing down her neck. I drag my nose along her shoulder and push her baggy collar out of my way. That's when I look down and get a glimpse at what she's wearing. "Are you wearing my shirt?" Damn, she looks good in my clothes.

She spins around in my arms and lifts a cupcake to my lips. "Here, try this. Tell me what you think." I take a bite and grunt around a mouthful of the greatest thing I've ever tasted. I taste the chocolate but also get a hint of something citrusy and smokey. The frosting is sweet but not enough to overpower the flavors. She plucks a piece of hard chocolate out of the frosting and says, "Taste this too. It's the best part."

"What's that?" I ask. It tastes like bacon.

"They're called Smokey Bourbon Chocolate Cupcakes. I've been wanting to make them for a while, but never had any bourbon at the bakery. When I saw the bar, I figured it'd be the perfect place to try them out. The guys seem to love them. They weren't so sure at first, but when Stiletto said they had alcohol in them, they dove right in." She laughs and I couldn't be happier to see her smile. "What do you think? Do you like them?"

"They're really good. I'm glad you made something for the Brothers. They don't eat much more than meat and potatoes." Men are not usually the ones to bake cookies and shit. "Now, back to the important stuff. Is that my shirt you have on?"

"Yes, I'm wearing your shirt. Is that okay?" I meet her eyes and see a little bit of uncertainty behind her smile.

I don't want to have this conversation in front of the crowd, even though they're trying not to make it obvious that they're listening to us. I grab her hand and pull her into the kitchen. Barely acknowledging the mess she's made, I tug her into the pantry and push the door closed. With two doors between us and everyone else, maybe she'll open up to me more.

"What's wrong, gorgeous?" I ask and pick her up, setting her butt down on the countertop. "I see the uncertainty behind your eyes."

"When I put it on, I didn't even think about it. I'm sorry," she says, scooting forward and trying to push me out of her way so she can get down.

I grab her hands and place them down on the counter next to her thighs. "Do not move them." I apply a little pressure, trying to make her understand that I'm serious. "Do you understand me?" Her eyes widen and she takes a deep breath. When she nods her head, I give her a quick peck on the lips. "Good girl."

I straighten up and reach forward, wrapping one hand loosely around the front of her throat. I don't squeeze or apply any pressure, but I do it just to see what her reaction will be. I need her to know that I'm in charge and I hope that's something she can handle. I don't like to be a domineering asshole all the time, but when something happens, I need her to listen without talking back. She needs to learn to do what I say, when I say it. She keeps her eyes locked on mine and I can feel her throat pulse under my fingertips.

"I like to see you in my shirt. I think it's fucking hot as hell. Don't ever second guess what feels right to you." I spread her thighs and step as close to her as the counter will allow. I grab the bottom hem of the t-shirt and lift it up enough to find the waistband of her leggings. I start tugging on them and she pushes her backside up so I can pull them down, and when they get caught on her shoes, I remove one of them and leave the leggings hanging off the other. I drop to my knees and get up close and personal with her black lacy panties.

She tries to close her thighs, but I place my hands on the inside of her knees and push them as far apart as I can. "Do NOT close yourself to me ever again," I bark in between placing kisses up the inside of her left thigh. I like a little harshness mixed with my tender. When I get close to her center, my mouth waters and I lick my lips. I'm close enough that she can feel my breath against her skin, and her hips start to wiggle and rock forward. God, I love a greedy pussy. Sliding one hand up, I hook my finger in the soaked crotch of her panties and rip them apart. I can't wait anymore.

I lean forward and drag my tongue through her slit. "Mmmm. So hot." I catch a little bit of wetness on the tip of my tongue, bury my face in her lap, and go to town. I swipe my tongue from her hole up into the lips of her clit. I shake my head back and forth, causing her to cry out. Lapping up her sweet saltiness, I continue to feast until she starts to shake. Hearing her moan my name out loud makes my cock harder as it presses against my zipper. The noises coming from her make me flick my tongue faster against her hard bud. I can feel her start to tense, so I know she's close to exploding.

I don't want to miss out on feeling the squeeze of her pussy, so I slide two fingers into her channel. I pump them in and out a few times, feeling her juices start to run down my palm. Curling them forward in a come-hither motion, I find that spongy patch and tap on it a few times, making her go crazy.

I devour her pussy, tugging on her needy lips, and her thighs squeeze around my ears as she comes with a scream. She shakes and grabs onto my hair, pulling it hard and humping her hips against my face. "Fuck!" she yells, gasping and trying to catch air into her lungs. I keep licking until she stops twitching and settles back on the counter.

I lift my hands up behind my head and untangle her fingers from my hair so I can scoot back far enough to stand up. I keep hold of her hands and lace our fingers together down on the countertop. Kiana looks up at me with a lazy smile and a twinkle in her eyes.

"You sure know how to show a girl a good time," she says in a slow drawl.

"If you'd like, I can show you more of what I can do," I say back and grind my hardness into her naked pussy.

"Or maybe I can show you my appreciation?" she replies with a smile.

"You don't have to . . ." I start to say as she leans forward and slides down to her knees, right between my legs. Holy fuck, this is about to get good.

CHAPTER SEVENTEEN

KIANA

I slide down to my knees, resting my butt on my heels, and look up at Whiskey. I meet his eyes as I run my hands up his jean-clad thighs and push him back a step. Being squeezed between him and the cabinet isn't the most comfortable position to be in.

He moves back and I sit up so my face is directly in front of his straining bulge. I raise my hands, hook my fingers in his belt loops, and nuzzle my nose along the denim. I let go of the belt loops and grab hold of the button, tugging it open. I pull down his zipper and his rock-hard cock bobs up against his abdomen.

Three things immediately catch my attention. First, I notice he isn't wearing any underwear. Poor guy has been dealing with the zipper rubbing raw against his dick. That sounds like a bad dick pinch waiting to happen. Ouch. Secondly, holy hell is he huge. I don't have a ruler on hand, but I'd definitely say he's quite larger than the average man. It's bigger than any I've seen before. There are light blue veins running up the length of his dick and the head is turning a darker purple color. It looks super angry and ready to pounce. Lastly, I see two shiny balls on the end of his hardness. This man has his dick pierced!

I must have a dumbfounded look on my face because Whiskey asks, "Like what you see, darlin'?"

"Pierced? You have your dick pierced? What's it called?" I ask as I run the tip of my index finger over the bottom steel ball. He has one sticking right out of the tip and a second under the crown of the head.

"It's called a Prince Albert and it's a bar that curves through the tip," he says and his dick twitches, almost like it's moving on command.

"Are you doing that?" I ask him.

"Yes, ma'am, I am. Wanna see what else it can do?" He's trying to distract me from what I knelt down here to do.

"No, that's okay. I have my own plans for him." I reach one hand up and wrap it around his cock. The skin is very soft, but underneath it is all hard. I reach my other hand around his hips and grab a handful of his hard ass. I lean forward just a bit and flick my tongue against the tip, licking up a drop of precum. Whiskey has a creamy, salty taste. Not bad at all.

He groans and rests his hands on the countertop, using it to hold himself up straight. I start to stroke him up and down, swiping my palm around his tip, catching some of his precum to help lubricate my strokes. Needing to get a full taste of him, I lean all the way in and suck the whole tip into my mouth. I lick around the head and flick my tongue into the slit.

Liking the way he tastes, I decide to go all in, opening my mouth more to take him as deep as I can. I feel myself start to choke, so I back off some and try to relax my throat a little. I start again, bobbing up and down his penis like I can't get enough. The piercing feels a little weird rubbing against my tongue, but I realize that I kind of like it.

I pull my mouth off but keep stroking and ask, "Can you feel it? Does it hurt?"

"Yea. Doesn't hurt. More of a tug," he says through clenched teeth. Poor guy can't even form full sentences.

I suck him back in my mouth and continue the job at hand. I never really liked giving a blowjob in the past. It always felt more like a job, like giving one was required to receive anything in return. But something about doing this to Whiskey feels right. I think he agrees because he grabs hold of my messy bun and starts thrusting his hips forward.

"You keep going like that, I won't last long," Whiskey whispers and tugs on my ponytail holder, snapping it and causing my wild hair to fall over my shoulders. He stands up straight and grabs two handfuls of my still damp curls, then starts fucking my face at his speed. Spit starts running down my lips and chin, but I can't do anything except grab his legs and hold on. In fact, I find it really hot.

Based on the animal-like noises coming from him, I don't think he's going to last much longer. "I'm gonna come. Can you take it?" I nod as best as I can. He starts to swell, and I can feel him explode. He holds my face tight against his pelvis as he pumps rope after rope of warm cum down my throat. "That's right. Swallow it all. Every last damn drop," he grunts, then instantly relaxes.

I pull myself back and start to lick the drops that continue to bead on his tip. I let go of his now softening cock, lick my lips, and rest my head back on the cabinet. "Was that good for you?" I ask. Yes, he came, but I need to know if it was me or just a natural manly reaction to any warm hole.

"Goddamn it, woman. I think you made my brain explode out through my dick. And I need a minute to reboot." He lets out a soft huff as he pulls up his jeans, leaving them unbuttoned. Reaching out a hand, I grasp his and we pull against each other until I'm standing up. He kneels and untangles my leggings, helping me step back into them, and slides the one shoe back onto my foot. This would be a very romantic Cinderella-like moment had I not just had his dick halfway down my throat.

Once we're both covered and standing, he takes me in his arms and kisses me deep, wrapping his tongue around mine. He must not mind his own taste because he holds nothing back. After a few minutes of playing a very adult version of tonsil hockey, we come up for air.

Whiskey picks me up again and sets me back up on the counter. "And we're back to where we started," I giggle.

"I guess we are. But I like you like this. You're so tiny, and with you up here, I don't have to bend over so far to kiss you." He leans forward and tries to come in for round two, but I raise my hand and place my fingers over his lips.

"Hold on there, cowboy. This rodeo needs to take an intermission. As much as I'd like to keep going with you, I don't think the pantry is the right place for our first time." Not that the second or third time couldn't be in here—sneaking around and having fun in random places sounds like a great time to me.

He licks my fingers and tries to bite them. I pull my hands back and tuck them under my thighs, sitting on them so I don't grab him by his beard and let him continue doing whatever he wants. His beard scraping against my thighs and scratching my sensitive nerves is a feeling I'd like to experience again very soon.

"That's fine. We can for sure continue this in our bed," he says and my mouth drops in surprise. Our bed? Where did that come from?

Before I can ask, there's a knock on the pantry door. "Whiskey, I need a word." I'm not sure who it is, but by the look that drops over Whiskey's face, it can't be good news.

"Meet me in my office," he hollers back as he reaches down to button and zip himself back up. Meeting my eyes, the corner of his mouth lifts in a half-smile. "I gotta go. Business calls."

"That's fine. I've got quite the mess to clean up, so that'll keep me busy." I try to be understanding. If I stay here for any longer, I'll need to learn that the club always comes first for him. He explained that to me the other day, but this is the first time we've been interrupted.

He gives me a simple kiss and walks out. I head back into the kitchen and start collecting all my dirty dishes. It takes me awhile to rinse everything off and run it through the dishwasher, so when I come out from the kitchen, I'm surprised to see it's now dark outside. I find Stiletto behind the bar, so I hop up on a stool.

"Hey there, lady. Did you get lost back there?" She laughs as she continues stacking glasses.

"Ha-ha, very funny. Where is everyone?" I look over my shoulder and notice the Church room doors are closed.

"They all went in there a few minutes ago. There was some yelling, but it quieted down pretty quick," she says.

I look back at her and nod. "Do we need to worry about feeding them? I didn't realize how late it was." I'm not sure how things work around here or if they eat together every night.

"It might not be a bad idea to throw in a bunch of frozen pizzas. That way they can grab and eat when they have time. They don't really care if it's hot or cold when they're busy." We head back into the kitchen and start making dinner.

CHAPTER EIGHTEEN

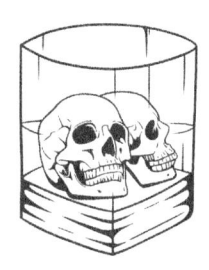

WHISKEY

"What the fuck do you mean it was torched?" I yell as I throw the gavel down and pound my fist on the table. The gavel goes sliding down the table and several hands reach out to stop it from going off the edge. I stare at Cypher and narrow my eyes. If I could shoot fire, he would be burnt to a crisp. "This is not what I fucking wanted to hear. I wanted a whole van that we could use to find clues and get us closer to finding Wings, not one we could use to roast fucking marshmallows. If we don't find her, Kiana will never stay here with me." The room goes dead quiet and I immediately know I said too much.

Ever the smart ass, Ring pipes up and says, "Kiana, huh? So that dragging her into the kitchen wasn't for cooking lessons?" The whole room erupts in laughter.

I might find it funny if we didn't now have a gutted van and a missing club girl. "Very funny, asshole, but this shit is serious. Yes, I like Kiana, but you all need to remember that Wings is her little sister. I don't need any of you joking around and messing this up for me. I like her and want her to have a reason to stay here for more than a few weeks." I fall back into my chair and run my hands through my hair. I didn't realize it wasn't tied back until now. Kiana must have pulled out my hair tie while I was eating her out. If I ever want her to do that again, I need to find her sister.

"Enough is enough. Cypher, where's the van?" I ask, needing to get out and do something.

"It's about five miles down the road in a county park trail parking lot. I lost it on the cameras I have out further, so I went riding to find it."

"Good work. Hammer, Cypher, Wrecker, Trooper, and I will ride out to look around. Wrecker, bring the rig and we'll load it up if we can. We'll bring Jacob along and make the Prospect do the dirty work. Everyone else, this is notice of a full lockdown. Any unnecessary outside business is shut down until further notice. Once we're back from getting the van, the gate gets locked. If anyone needs to call people in, now's your chance. We head out in five." Bear slides the gavel down the table, and I grab it and slam it down. "Meeting adjourned. Everyone out."

I leave the room and find Kiana in the kitchen, putting a bunch of pizzas out on the passthrough counter. "Hey there, lady." She turns and meets me with a big smile. Just what I needed to see. "Thank you for doing this. There's gonna be a bunch of people who need to eat on the run. We have to go on full lockdown." This makes her smile drop and she runs into my arms, clutching my waist as she starts shaking. I hug her back and ask, "What's wrong, baby? Why are you crying?"

She pulls her face out of my chest and looks up at me. "It's because of Tempy, isn't it? You said we wouldn't go in full lockdown unless something happened. What happened?"

"You know I can't go into details, but I can say that we haven't found her yet. I don't know what this has to do with her, but I need to go and find out. Some of the guys and I are going out to look into it, but hopefully when we get back, I'll have more answers." She doesn't like this at all.

"You're leaving? You can't go out there. If we need to be on lockdown, it's obviously for a good reason, and it's not safe out there. I don't want you to get hurt." She starts crying again and backs away from me.

"Kiana, I'm not going out alone. I need to go see this for myself. I'm the club President and the guys look to me for what to do next. I can't be the one to hide away like a little baby. Only six of us are leaving and we'll be back as soon as we can. The rest of the Brothers will be here and on watch for outside trouble." I don't like that she pulled away from me, so I reach out and wrap her in my arms again. "I need you to be here for me when I get back. Can you do that for me?" I ask.

I hate to see her sad, but I need to go. "I'll find you when we get back and maybe we can continue what we started earlier. You know that thing you said we need to do in our bed? That sound okay with you?" I lean down, reaching behind her and grabbing her ass cheeks, then I start to kiss away her tears.

She sniffles and nods. "Okay." I kiss her one more time and head out to meet the guys.

Everyone who's going out is already on their bikes, so I jump on my Harley and fire her up. We roll out the gate and follow Cypher until we reach the field. We pull over and I see the shell of a van in the middle of the gravel lot. Wrecker drives around it to back up and load it on the flatbed. Trooper shines his Maglite around, trying to see if anything is inside the cargo area. He looks back at me and shakes his head. Nothing. I don't even waste my time getting off my bike and just stay on my seat.

After the van is loaded up, we head back to the compound. I'm not a happy camper and am not in the mood for any more bad news. I need good news. I grab another handful of throttle and fly past everyone in the opposite lane. There's no one else out on the road, so I risk it and ride a bit recklessly. The few miles fly by in no time, so the next thing I know, I'm rolling back into the lot. I back my bike into its spot, kick down my stand, grab my keys, and stomp into the clubhouse.

I head toward my office, only to be met by a smiling Kiana in the middle of the main room. She walks my way and tries to come in for a hug. While I'd normally grab her and kiss her senseless, right now my mind is not in a good place. "No," I bark, and her smile drops. She turns and jogs up the stairs, but I keep walking and head down the hall, ignoring everyone's shocked stares and slamming my office door behind me. I know it was wrong, but I can't find it in me to make it better right now.

My door flies open and Hammer comes in hot. "What the hell was that? Are you trying to make sure both of us are single for the rest of our lives?"

"What are you talking about? How can we be any more single than we already are?" I'm confused as to where he's going with this.

He grabs one of the chairs in front of my desk, spins it around, and straddles it before dropping down. "You can't be mean like that to the woman you want to be your Old Lady. And since it's her sister who happens to be missing, you gotta be extra nice to her. Aaaand . . ." He drags out for way too long. "I might be finally pulling my head out of the sand and realizing I want said sister to be more than just the woman who warms my bed at night. So, we both need to kick our asses into gear and find Wings before your woman kicks your ass to the curb. And before mine disappears off the face of the planet and we never find her."

"You want to be with Wings?" I ask. I'm confused. When we were throwing away the recycling and complaining about our shitty mothers, he said he'd never settle down with an Old Lady.

"That's all you got out of that? Yes, I want to be with her. Okay? Are you happy now? I take back what I said the other day. When we get her back, if she'll have me, I'll claim her so fast, her head will spin. Then I'll never let her out of my sight again." Hammer is turning a new leaf and I think I need to take a page from his playbook. "But you can't be stomping around and being mean to your girl. Yelling at a club girl is second nature, but that poor woman is way more than that. Keeping her here is important. You need her happy."

Shit. He's right. I need to do some major groveling when I go up to bed tonight. I wonder if she likes flowers. Shit times two. We don't have any of those. This is why we need a woman's touch around here, someone to lend us a hand when we need to dig our stupid asses out of the hole our big mouths have dug for us.

But first, I need to drink this shitty night away. I spin my desk chair around and open the bottom drawer of the file cabinet behind me. I grab the bottle of Jack Daniels and two glasses, setting them down on my desk.

"Dude, where have you been hiding that? You know you can't handle that shit. You're only allowed to drink beer and clear liquors. There's a reason you got the road name

'Whiskey'. Don't you remember what happened the night you got your Prospect patch?"

He's definitely not wrong about that. I don't do well when I drink whiskey, but too bad, because right now, I don't give a flying fuck.

"I'll just have a few sips. I'll be fine." Famous last words.

Fuck.

I'm going to have a lot of ass kissing to do later.

Double fuck.

CHAPTER NINETEEN

KIANA

I hear the motorcycles come roaring into the lot a lot sooner than I expected. They must not have gone very far because they've only been gone for a little over an hour. Looking forward to seeing Whiskey, I walk out of the kitchen. Stiletto, Raquel, and I just put a second round of pizzas in the ovens, so there will be more food for the guys.

Just as I get to the middle of the room, Whiskey comes walking through the door. I make a beeline for him, just wanting to feel his arms around me and make some of the troubles evaporate.

"No," he growls, and my good mood is gone in an instant. The look on his face is one I've never seen, and quite honestly, is very scary. I spin around and run up the stairs. If he's going to act like that when I haven't even said one word, I don't want to be anywhere near him right now. Thank God he gave me a key to his room before he left or I'd have nowhere to go.

I unlock the door and shut myself in before I turn on any lights. It's a good thing I did, because if anyone saw me right now, they'd think I was crazy. I may not have had a problem with this messy room before, but now that I'm upset, I decide I can't live like this for one more minute. If he thinks it's okay to live like a damn college boy, he can find a new room to sleep in.

I grab a laundry basket from the closet and head into the bathroom, picking up all the dirty clothes and towels and tossing them in. I'll find a washing machine and deal with those tomorrow. Looking at the bathroom vanity, I decide that I don't like his lack of organizational skills. I open the top drawer and throw away all but the fullest toothpaste. The extra three were almost empty anyway. Then I go to the stupid condom drawer and pull out box after box, chucking them into the garbage can. All but two of the boxes are expired anyway. I hope he paid attention to the dates before he used them, otherwise he might have twenty mystery kids running around out in the world.

I know my attitude is a little extreme, but I don't know how else to let out my aggression. Being mad at Whiskey's stuff is just going to have to work for now.

I straighten up a few of his dresser drawers, deciding to consolidate his things so I can get some of mine out of the bags. After sorting out most of my things, I decide I'm done dealing with this for the night. My anger has mostly dissolved and the adrenaline I had when I started is gone. Before I fall asleep on my feet, I ditch my leggings, leaving on the too large t-shirt and panties, and brush my teeth.

Whiskey still hasn't made an appearance, and since my anger isn't fully gone yet, I'm going to sleep without him. Not wanting to sleep in his bed, I decide to curl up on the couch in the corner. If he decides to show up later, he can sleep alone in the bed. I plug in my phone, shut off the lights, grab the comforter, and lay down on the couch. Before I know it, I'm out.

I jerk awake and look around, wondering what woke me up. I hear another soft knock on the door and realize the noise is coming from the hall. Worried that something is wrong, I throw back the comforter and rush to the door, whipping it open and finding Hammer about to knock again.

"What time is it? Whiskey isn't here," I say with a yawn.

"I know he's not, 'cause he's right here." Hammer points down to his left.

I look down and see Whiskey sitting on the floor, leaning against the wall, softly snoring away. "For crying out loud. Why's he sleeping in the hall?"

"Not really sure," Hammer says. "We were down in his office and he left to go to bed about a half-hour ago. I just came upstairs myself and I found him out here. I thought I'd help you get him into bed." Hammer reaches down and picks up Whiskey, holding him with an arm wrapped around his back. I move back into the room and turn on the nightstand lamp. Hammer half carries, half drags Whiskey's tall frame into the room and drops him onto the bed. Whiskey groans and mumbles something I can't understand.

I look at Hammer and we both shrug.

"I'm sorry about this. I shouldn't have let him drink so much whiskey." The ashamed look on Hammer's face would be funny if it weren't for the drunk, passed-out man lying sideways on the bed. His light snores are kind of adorable though. Ugh!

"What do you mean about drinking whiskey? Why can't he drink it?" I'm confused. Why would he have that name but not be able to drink it?

"That's the thing about road names—there's always a reason the Brothers get the names they do. Our buddy here earned his name the night he got his Prospect patch. We had a huge party and he had too many shots of whiskey. The more he had, the funnier he got. But the next morning, he was seriously regretting it. When he finally woke up at noon, Mountain saw him roll off the couch and run for the bathroom, so the name was decided," Hammer explains. Another thing I don't really understand, but then again, I haven't been here long enough to get it.

I look down at Whiskey and wonder if the name bothers him.

"What about you? How'd you get the name Hammer?" Now I'm curious to hear everyone's stories.

"That's a story for another day." He starts backing up and doesn't look like he wants to answer. "If you need anything, just holler. Someone will hear you. Goodnight." And he's gone.

I shut and lock the door, then lean my forehead against the wood.

I hear rustling behind me, and turn around to see Whiskey leaning up on an elbow, trying to sit up. It's not really working out so well for him, so he lets out a huff and falls back down on the bed. I sit next to him and look down at his slowly blinking eyes.

"Hi," I say.

"Hey. You look beautiful. You're still wearing my shirt," he drawls. He doesn't sound drunk, but everyone handles their liquor differently.

"How are you feeling? Do you need some water?" I ask as I start to stand up.

Whiskey grabs my hand and pulls me down to lay next to him. "I don't need anything but you." He tries to roll onto his side, but I'm so close to him that he can't move much.

I think it's time I get him out of his jeans and tucked into bed. I stand up in front of him and pull on his hands, trying to get him in a sitting position. He's such a dead weight that it feels like he weighs four hundred pounds.

"You're gonna have to help me out here a little. You need to sit up so I can get you ready for bed," I grunt as I yank his hands.

He finally manages to get up and looks at me with surprisingly clear eyes. "Why are you being so good to me? I was an asshole to you earlier. That wasn't very nice of me."

"You were a jerk. Maybe we should have this conversation in the morning." I push his leather vest down over his shoulders and wrestle it off one arm at a time.

"Hang it on that hook." Whiskey points behind me and I turn to see a double silver hook screwed into the wall, just to the right of the door. I hang up the vest and take my first good look at the patches on the back. The arch on the top, which I learned is called a rocker, says 'Rebel Vipers' in black capital letters. The bottom rocker says 'Tellison', I guess because of where we live. And in the middle is a large patch of a bright green snake wrapped around a smiling skull. The snake's mouth is wide open, ready to strike.

I spin back around just in time to catch Whiskey from taking a nosedive onto the floor. "Whoa there, big guy. We don't need any broken noses." I catch him by the shoulders and push him back up. "I'll help you with your boots."

Kneeling, I untie the laces and pull off one boot at a time, setting them off to the side.

"I don't deserve you being nice to me. I lost your sister and can't find her. You deserve more than a dumbass like me." I freeze because I can't believe he's saying this about himself. I didn't think such a tough guy would think bad things about himself. His hands are folded together and he's looking down at his lap. "I'm not good enough for people to stay."

What is this? Enough is enough. "Hey, you listen to me." Still kneeling, I grab both sides of his face and make him meet my eyes. "I don't believe a single word you're saying. You didn't know Tempy was taken. Now that you do, I know you've been working every day to find her."

He shakes his head and tries to dislodge my hands. "Sorry for being mean before. I really wanted to hug you, but I was too angry and didn't want to be mad around you." He really is having a hard time with this.

"I understand. You're doing what you can with very little to go on."

"I just don't wanna lose you."

"Not happening. I'm not going anywhere." He opens his mouth to interrupt me, but I move one hand to use my fingers to cover his mouth. "Let's get you tucked into bed and we'll talk more when the sun comes up. Okay?" He nods. When I drop my hands onto his knees, about to stand up, he leans forward and places a quick kiss on my lips.

"Are you gonna sleep with me?" Whiskey asks as I get back up on my feet.

"I suppose I can do that. Just have to put the comforter back on the bed first. Now, are you sleeping in your jeans or can you get them off yourself?" I ask as I remember he's not wearing anything under the denim. "Do you have shorts or boxers that you sleep in?"

That makes him laugh. "No shorts. I sleep in the buff." He lays on his back, works down the zipper, and pushes his jeans down and off. I try not to stare at his hardness, but even relaxed, he's quite large. He shimmies himself backward and spins around, getting his head half on the pillow.

I pick up his discarded jeans and pull his socks off by the toes. "Hey. My feet are cold," he complains as he yanks the sheet up over his legs. Of course, he manages to twist the sheets because he grabbed the side instead of the top. I drop his clothes into the laundry basket and go back to his side to move his hands and pull the sheet the way it should be.

"Too bad, so sad. I hate socks in bed. You won't be touching me with your scratchy socked feet." I pick the comforter up off the floor, flip it around, and throw it on the bed. Whiskey put himself on the side closest to the door, so after turning off the lamp, I use the bed's edge to navigate myself to the far side. I crawl under the sheet and stare at the ceiling. I fell asleep so fast before, but after all this craziness, I'm wide awake.

The bed shifts as Whiskey rolls onto his left side, facing me. "Come here. I need to hold you," he whispers as he finds my hand and pulls me toward him. I roll onto my left side and scoot backward until I feel his warmth against my back. He pushes his left arm under my head and reaches his right arm around my waist, splaying his hand over my stomach. I think if he pulled me any closer to him, he'd be lying on top of me. I link my left hand with his and close my eyes.

"Good night, Kiana. I hope you forgive me," he says and is immediately out cold.

"Good night, Whiskey."

CHAPTER TWENTY

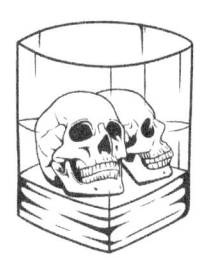

WHISKEY

Waking up with Kiana in my arms has got to be the best way to start my day. I take back what I said about being on the porch or riding my Harley—if this happens every morning for the rest of my life, I will die a happy man. She's nestled into my front and we fit together like our bodies were built for each other.

I haven't been awake for long, but I'm glad I woke up before her. I remember everything that happened after I woke up lying sideways on my bed, and Kiana had to deal with my drunk ass. She accepted my apologies, but I feel ashamed. She had to help me get ready for bed like I was a toddler. I can't believe I let Kiana see me like that. I'm not weak or vulnerable around anyone. She probably would be better off away from me, but I have no intention of ever letting her go.

Trying to push all that to the back of my mind, I concentrate on the beauty in front of me. Our left hands are linked, and we're both lying on our left sides, so I start exploring by lightly running the fingers of my right hand down her arm, then move my hand onto her hip and gently squeeze the roundness. She has a narrow waist and flat stomach, but she definitely has some junk in her trunk. I can't wait until the day she lets me bend her over so I can slam into her from behind. Thinking like this is starting to make me hard, so I push my hips forward and nestle my dick into the lace-covered seam of her ass.

She must be waking up, because her backside starts to wiggle against me. I move my hand off her hip and up onto her stomach, just underneath her shirt. I tickle her bellybutton, then continue my journey upward. Just as I reach her ribcage and am about to get a handful of her breast, she flips over and my hand slides to her back.

I look down to see she's bright eyed and wide awake. "You've been awake for a while, haven't you? You sneaky little girl."

"Maybe," she says with a laugh. "I wanted to see how far you would go with those magic fingers of yours."

"Magic fingers? You make me sound like a magician."

"What you did yesterday was magic, for sure. I don't think I've ever come that hard so fast." That makes her blush, and she ducks her head, hiding her face in my chest.

Wanting to make up for the fact that I denied her a kiss yesterday, I grab a handful of her hair, yank her head back, and dive in. I kiss her hard and deep. Our tongues battle for dominance, but I show her who's boss. I twist my hand in her fiery tresses and angle her head exactly where I want it to be, to control the kiss. Feeling her body try to get closer to me, I decide it's time to switch positions and take full control of what's happening.

I let go of her hair and push her backward using my weight, rolling her underneath me. I end up kneeling over top of her, with my hands next to her head and my knees bracketing her hips. Needing to get closer to her, I sit back on my haunches, spread her legs, and resettle myself in between her thighs.

Kiana reaches up and wraps her arms around my neck, trying to pull me close for another kiss. I let her pull me down, but only halfway. I hold myself in a push-up position and meet her eyes.

"Why'd you stop kissing me?" She pouts, and it's almost distracting, but I need to talk to her before my brain gets too far off-track.

"We'll get back to that, but I need you to listen very carefully. I need you to understand that what happened in the pantry is only a fraction of what I need from you." I thrust my hips forward and rub my dick against her wet panties. "I don't want you to think I need to be in charge all the time in bed, but I do like to be a bit bossy. I like your feisty attitude, but if I'm being bossy and tell you what to do, I want you to do it without talking back."

"So, what you're saying is that you like a little spunk but not to fight back?" She might understand me more than I thought she did.

"Pretty much," I say with a half shrug.

"Okay. Sounds good to me. Can we get back to the kissing now?" she asks and tries to pull me closer again.

"Wait, what? No arguments?" I ask.

"Nope. I like the sound of that. Now, yesterday, I said we needed a bed to have more fun. And look . . . we're in a bed. So, can we get to that fun now?"

"You'll let me do whatever I want to you?" I need to make sure she and I are on the same page.

"You said you need to be in charge, I agree to it, and you're still questioning me? Do I need to draw you a picture?" she answers with a lift of her hips.

"Girl, you are talking too big for your tiny britches. I'm the man here and whatever I say, goes. Got it?" I narrow my eyes and lower my head so our foreheads are touching.

She nuzzles her nose with mine and talks back. "Yes, sir, Mr. President, sir."

"That's it," I growl and attack.

I slam my mouth back down on hers and use my tongue to pry her lips open. I wrap my tongue around hers, and just as she starts to reciprocate, I pull back and bury my face in her neck. I lick and bite and kiss, starting behind her ear and slowly moving down to her throat. She tilts her head back, giving me easier access to her skin.

Leaning on my left arm, I shift my weight and grab a handful of her breast over her t-shirt. She must be very sensitive because she moans my name almost immediately. What I find when I run my palm over the hard nub of her nipple isn't anything like I was expecting—there's a little something extra.

In between my continued neck kisses, I ask her, "Is that what I think it is?"

"What do you think it is?" she asks back. Oh, she is for sure a feisty one in the sheets. I like it a lot.

"Is your nipple pierced?" I ask, as I shift my hand down a bit and use my thumb to brush over the peak.

"Not just that one," Kiana answers with a sigh.

I pull back and meet her eyes. "Both? You have both your nipples pierced?" She bites her lower lip and nods. "Alright, lady, enough with the secrets. This I have to see."

I sit back again and pull her up in front of me. "Secrets? It's not a secret. You just never asked."

"You saw mine yesterday and didn't say anything about yours," I playfully whine. "That's keeping a very important secret."

"I was so distracted by yours that I forgot about mine. I forget that they're there most of the time. I've had them since I was nineteen."

"Time for me to do my own investigating." I grab the bottom hem of my t-shirt that she's still wearing and pull it up over her head. Kiana lifts her arms and when they fall back down, she's surrounded by a halo of curly hair. She looks like she has a crown of fire atop her head. I really like this look on her. As I start my visual journey, I notice her lips are bruised, her neck is red from my kisses, she has scruff burn from my beard, and her eyes are a little glazed. I finally get down to her tits and lose my breath. She's incredible all over.

"Like what you see?" she asks with some sass, throwing my words from yesterday back at me.

"Hell yea, I do. Your tits are killer," I say and decide it's time to get down to the good stuff. I push her onto her back and dive in for a closer look. Leaning on my arm again, I use my right hand to flick the curved barbell dangling from her left nipple. The bar itself is silver but the balls on each end are black. "These sure are pretty. Why'd you get them done?"

"I had just bought the bakery and went out with some friends to celebrate. Long story short, I ended up at the tattoo shop in town the next morning. I lost a dare and didn't want a tattoo, so a piercing was my only other choice. These were easy to hide." When my brain wakes up again, it catches what she just said.

"Did you say the tattoo shop here in Tellison?" I ask.

"Yup. Not many choices around here. Why?"

"The club owns BIT. Who did the piercing? If it was Buzz, I'm gonna have to gouge his eyes out," I growl and nuzzle my face in between her twin beauties.

"Who's Buzz? It was an older guy, but he was super attractive, and I would've gone home with him . . ." She laughs as I start to tickle her side. "But he had a ring on his finger."

"Sounds like Skynyrd. Good. Then I won't have to explain to the club why I had to kill a Brother. From now on, no one in the club gets to see your tits except me."

I stop the tickling and lower my hand to get her panties out of the way of my dick. He's hard and ready to get acquainted with her hot, wet pussy. I tug down on the side, intending on pulling them off one leg at a time, but I pull a little too hard and hear a rip. Looking down, I notice the string dangling from my fingers. "Oops. Looks like I owe you another pair."

"If you keep ripping my underwear, you're gonna have to buy some stock in Victoria's Secret." She laughs and helps me pull down the other side.

Once those are out of the way, I scoot down and push her legs up so they're bent at the knees. Propping myself on my forearms, I get as close to her glistening pussy as I can. I use one finger to trace down her slit and find the hard nub hiding in her folds. With it right there, I flick her clit with my tongue and Kiana tenses. She shifts one leg to lay over my shoulder, resting her foot against my back. This opens her hips a bit more, so I lean forward to take full advantage, burying my tongue deeper between her folds and chasing her nub as it tries to hide.

Her clit is rock hard beneath my lips, and I take fast, quick flicks, trying to draw out as much of her sweet nectar as I can. She's drowning me in all her juices, and I'm in heaven. I feel her start to tense, so I pull back and blow a cool breath, trying to make her hold off.

"Noooo. Don't stop," Kiana yells out, grabbing a handful of my hair, trying to push my head back down.

"Let go of my hair right now. Grab hold of the sheets and do not let go. If you touch me again, I won't let you come," I thunder and turn my head to bite her left thigh, sucking hard with every intention of leaving my mark where only I can see it. She slowly lets my hair go and sprawls her arms out, spread-eagled. "You'll take whatever I give you, when I give it to you, and you'll like it."

"Please? More," she begs. I feel the sheets shift below us, so I know she's holding them tight. I can't help but smile as I dive back in for more.

"Just keep hold of those sheets and you'll get what I give you." I grab hold of her ass cheeks and lift her up closer to my mouth. While I love the sounds of her begging me for more, I'm running this damn show.

I squeeze her harder, trying to indent my fingerprints into her skin, and hope I'm adding more marks for me to trace with my tongue later. I open my mouth and latch onto her swollen folds, then stick out my tongue and shove it as deep as I can into her still weeping pussy. I swipe up and down as fast as her tight muscles allow me to and swallow the juices that are running down my tongue.

Kiana starts to tense again, and this time, I let her climb high and fall over the edge. She explodes and lets out a scream so loud, I wonder if it can be heard through the wall. I think I like the idea of my Brothers hearing what they're missing out on. If they'd hurry up and find a decent woman, they could have what I've got right now.

Lying down on my cock, and smothering him into the sheets, is getting to be a bit more than I can take. He needs to be suffocated by her pussy. I back away from her center and let her legs slide back down onto the sheets. She slowly blinks and it looks like she can barely focus. "You alright?" I ask.

"I'm good. Can we do that again?" she asks with a drunk-like smile.

"Absolutely. Time for me to get in on this." I lift her legs up from the bed, scoot my knees closer to her backside, and loop one knee over each crook of my elbow. With her spread open to me, I thrust my hips forward and back, letting my piercing rub against her swollen lips. She starts to wiggle her ass side to side, so I know she's ready for more.

"Is this what you want, little girl? Do you want my dick deep in your greedy pussy?" I ask her, knowing she does.

"Yes. I need it," she begs with a whine. Her eyes are closed, but I need to see her baby blues.

"Open your eyes and keep them on me." She does, so I let her have a little more. "You can let go of the sheets with one hand. Reach down and put him in. Line him up and he'll do the rest." She wraps her hand around my throbbing dick and pushes down on it, burying the head between her lips. I rock forward into Kiana and her pussy opens to me like a flower blooming. I give a few short pumps, and when I know she's ready, I thrust home. She yells out and comes again immediately. I use all my strength to hold back, because her inner muscles are squeezing me so damn hard, but I'm not ready to come yet.

Once I have myself back under control, I start rocking, thrusting my dick in and out of her pulsating hole, reaching every single inch of her.

I lift her legs higher, setting her ankles next to my head, and lean down against the back of her thighs. Folding her basically in half, I'm able to bury my cock deeper in her pussy, and on the first thrust down, I bump into her cervix. She lets out a squeak, so I know she's liking it. I need to be so deep inside her that she can feel me inside her later today. That way, she can remember who fucked her and want me to be the only man to fuck her for the rest of her life. I need to be her everything.

"I need . . . I need . . . I need . . ." Kiana starts chanting and I bring my lips down to hers, keeping up my rhythm. I'm now in an Army crawl position, digging my knees and elbows deep into the mattress, trying to get deeper inside her. My hips are in piston drive mode.

"What do you need?" I ask between kisses.

"I need to touch you. Please? I need to touch you." Well, since she asked so nicely.

"Grab on, darlin'. Take what you need," I say and she immediately raises her arms and drapes them over my shoulders. She can't reach all the way around, so her nails dig into my shoulder blades. The tiny bits of pain cause me to lose it.

I kick myself into high gear and plow into her even faster. That's when my balls start to rise up and the tingling feeling starts to build from my toes. It creeps up my legs and quickly reaches my back, then my spine starts to tingle and I know I'm about to explode. There's no way to stop it.

Wanting her to come with me, I tilt my hips up and angle my tip for her magic spot. One. Two. Three. And she detonates again.

Her insides tighten around me so hard, I wouldn't be surprised if my dick didn't come out molded to the shape of her pussy. I keep going through her flutters, then let myself go. If the stars behind my eyelids are any sign of what just happened, I think I died and went to fucking heaven.

"Holy fucking shit. Whoa," Kiana says with a sharp exhale.

"Right back at ya, beautiful." I lean back onto my knees and help lower her legs off my shoulders. We're still connected, and the twitching coming from her insides feels so good. Almost too good. "As much as I'd like to go another round, I think you killed my dick."

"Aww, you poor thing. Did we break you?" I'm glad she thinks my dead manhood is funny.

"Stay there and I'll get us cleaned up." I drop one more kiss on her lips and slide out of her. I roll over and sit up on the side of the bed, wincing when I set my feet on the floor. "Holy jeeze Louise, that floor is damn cold. You stole my socks and now my poor toes are going to freeze off."

She starts laughing and lets out the loudest snort I've ever heard. I whip around to see she has her hand over her mouth and is trying hard to stop laughing. I never knew I could be naked and laughed at and be perfectly okay with it.

I head into the bathroom, flip on the light, and am stunned by what I see. There are no dirty clothes or towels on the floor, and the countertop is clean. I turn on the faucet, waiting for the water to warm up, and grab a washcloth off the cubby shelf. After wetting and wringing out the washcloth, I walk back in the bedroom. Kiana is sitting up, squeezing her legs together, trying to scoot to the end of the bed. She looks like a wiggling mermaid.

"Where do you think you're going, wiggle worm? I said I was coming right back." I kiss her and use my forehead to force her to lay back down.

"I have to use the facilities." Oh, now she's trying to act like a lady, like she just wasn't begging for me and my dick.

"And you can, just as soon as I clean you up." I pry her legs apart and wipe her down with the warm cloth.

"You don't have—" she starts to say.

"Yes, I do. I made the mess, I clean it up." I pull her up to her feet and lean down to get another kiss. I'm thinking I may be as addicted to her kisses as I am to her. She goes into the bathroom and pushes the door almost closed. I wipe myself off and toss the washcloth into the laundry basket that I guess now lives in the corner.

I open the top dresser drawer to grab some clean clothes but find it full of her panties and bras. I guess she's made herself at home. I like it. I open the next drawer and find a pair of socks, then go to the closet for a t-shirt and a pair of clean jeans.

Just as I finish getting dressed, the bathroom door slowly creeps open. Kiana has a towel wrapped around her body and she's staring at the floor. Uh oh.

CHAPTER TWENTY-ONE

KIANA

I know that I have to go back out there and face Whiskey, but I'm scared shitless. I can't believe I was that careless. I stand up from the tub's edge, wrap a towel around my chest, and take a deep breath. No matter how this conversation goes, I need to be strong. I open the bathroom door and walk out into the bedroom.

Whiskey turns from the bed, and he must sense my panic because he jumps up and rushes over to me. He sets his hands on my shoulders and bends a bit, trying to meet my eyes. "What's wrong? Are you okay?"

"Yea, I'm fine. But we need to talk about something." I look up and meet his sparkling blue eyes. I'm worried about how he's going to react to what I have to say.

He grabs my hand and pulls me over to the couch, tugging me down on his right side. He sits on the center cushion and lifts my bare legs over his jean-clad thighs. "What's wrong? I didn't hurt you, did I?"

"No, you didn't hurt me. I think we know how much we both enjoyed that. And that's part of my problem. We need to talk about how we didn't use any protection. We didn't even talk about it before we got carried away, and I forgot." I pull on a loose thread from the towel and twist it around my finger.

"Shit. I wasn't even thinking about that." He pauses, and I hope he's not mad at me. I feel bad enough on my own. "I'm sorry, Kiana. I never forget to wrap it up. I'm clean, I promise. I got tested like four months ago and I haven't had sex with anyone since."

"Thank you for that, but I'm worried about something else, Whiskey." I close my eyes and try to hold back tears. I don't need him to see me sad. I can cry after he leaves and I'm all alone again.

"Connor."

"What?" I look up when he grabs my hands and untangles my fingers from the frayed towel edge. "Who's that?"

"Connor. My real name is Connor. When it's just you and me, I don't want you to call me by my road name." His real name? I like it.

"I like your name." I lift my left hand and scratch my nails down the side of his beard. "I'm worried that we didn't use anything because I'm not on any birth control. I never had a major need to be. What if I get pregnant? We haven't been together long enough for that."

"Hey, it's okay. If that happens, I'll be there for you." He turns his head toward me, nuzzling into my hand. "And even though it hasn't been long, I know I want us to be a more serious thing. I want us to be more."

"More? You want us to be together? Isn't this all happening a little fast?" I look down and realize I'm still in my towel. "Can I get dressed? I think I need to have myself a tad more put together for this conversation."

"That sounds like a good idea. As much as I like you in a towel, I think it'll be a distraction for me." He lifts my legs and spins me to sit forward. "Go get dressed and I'll be right here." I get one more kiss and hop up.

I go to the dresser and grab a change of clothes. I try to slide my underwear on under my towel, but it starts slipping. "Forget this," I say and let it fall.

"Woman, you have one fine lookin' backside. I can't wait until you let me take you from behind." I look over my shoulder and see that Whiskey is resting his head on the back of the couch, face looking up, his eyes closed. His hands are balled into fists and resting on his lap. He's trying really hard to give me space to get dressed.

I wrestle into a sports bra, leggings, and a black t-shirt, and borrow a giant red and black checkered flannel from his closet. I sit back down next to him and slide on some black fuzzy socks. I just might have a sock addiction too.

"Okay, you can look. I'm decent." I turn to face him, bending my left leg and tucking it under my right thigh. I need to look at him to really understand what he's saying. I've noticed that sometimes his face says more than his words.

He opens his eyes and turns his head to look at me. "I know it seems quick, but I knew from the moment I saw you that I wanted you. You came rolling in here all hot and angry and ready to fight, but I didn't care. Your feistiness is a huge turn-on," he says and wiggles his eyebrows. "And those pink shoes you were wearing were cute. They were the first thing I saw when you jumped out of your firetruck."

"Ha-ha, very funny. Don't be making fun of my Dragon," I say and try to make a stern face but fail and laugh.

"Dragon? You named your truck Dragon?" He chuckles.

"Yes, I did. Now enough of the gibberish. What about us?" I need to know his thoughts.

"What do you need to know?"

"What are we gonna do about Tempy? And I don't know that I'd be a very good biker girl. And there's so much going on around here that I have no idea about. I don't really like that."

"There's a lot in that, so let's start with the first part, okay?" I nod. "First concern is your sister. Even though she's still missing, she's very much still a part of this club.

She may be a club girl, but I have a feeling that may not be for much longer." He knows something that I don't.

"Do you mean Hammer? Did he say something to you?" I ask and get a little excited. If she has something to come home to, maybe everything will be okay.

"I can't say anything more. What I say with my Brothers is said in confidence. If they can't trust me, then this club will fall apart." Whiskey squeezes my hands.

"See, that's what I mean. There's a lot going on here that I'm out of the loop of. You said I need to trust you and listen to you, but I haven't had anyone to answer to since our grandparents died almost three years ago." Actually, it's been longer than that, but since they died and Tempy ran off to the clubhouse, I've really been on my own.

"Yes, I do need you to listen to me, but honestly, that's more about showing respect around the others. If you get smart and mouth off to me in front of the Brothers, that doesn't look good and reflects back on me. If I can't get you to respect me, how can I expect them to do what I say? I know it sounds a bit caveman-ish, but it's just how it works around here." I can see he's trying hard to help me understand. It's just a lot to take in.

"So, what would I be to you? Will you ask me to be your girlfriend? Doesn't that sound like we're in high school?" I wouldn't mind being his girlfriend, but I'm not sure how bikers feel about that kind of thing.

"We don't exactly call our women girlfriends. Once we claim someone, they become our Old Lady and that's a huge commitment to us. You'd be my Old Lady and I'd be your Old Man, and we'd have a whole new standing within the club. We see it as basically like being married. You wear my property patch on your cut, and you have to wear it all the time."

"What's a property patch? That sounds serious." And property? That's quite archaic.

Whiskey turns and points at his vest hanging on the wall. "We call our vests a cut. Just a biker term, but a cut, nonetheless. See the back of mine? How I have the club name on the top and the city on the bottom?"

I nod. "Yes." I learned about the rockers the other day from Stiletto. She gave me a rundown of titles and such, but I let Whiskey keep explaining things how he wants.

"Those are called top and bottom rockers. Every patch we wear on our cuts means something specific. Those three patches on the back are the most important. They represent who we are and where we come from. My name and title are on the front, and that shows everyone who I am. We have to earn every patch we get, and we protect our cuts with our lives." I can tell all of this means a lot to him. "When you become my Old Lady, you'll get your own cut. You'll have the same club logo patch as the rest of us, and the top rocker will say 'Rebel Vipers', but the bottom rocker will say 'Property of Whiskey'. That not only tells the club that you're mine, but it also shows strangers and other clubs that you belong to me. Everyone will know that you're mine and not to mess with you."

"The more you say about it, the more I worry. Why would anyone mess with me? I'm a nobody." There's so much to learn.

This causes him to fully turn and face me. When we lock eyes, he lets me have it. "You are not a nobody. You're mine, Kiana. Strangers and our enemies will see you as my weakness, and in a way, they'd be right. As soon as you put on that cut and acknowledge that you're mine, you become a somewhat honorary member of this club. Any of the Brothers would protect you just like any other member."

Everyone protects and helps each other—I like the sound of that. Whiskey continues, "It's also why we're trying so hard to find your sister. She has a place in this club and it's our job to find her. We don't go around fighting and protecting just anybody. If someone isn't in our club, they're usually not our problem. We don't just get involved in every bad thing out there. We need a reason for everything we do."

"So, you're saying that if I'm not your Old Lady, you wouldn't protect me? You couldn't save me? How is that supposed to make me feel better about all this?" I really hope he says I'm more important to him than that. I need him to prove to me that I mean something to him. I want to be his Old Lady, but this is all happening so fast. Why is this all so damn crazy? How can I not want something, but on the flip side, want it so bad?

"I know it's really soon and that you may not be ready to formally be my Old Lady. We still have a lot to learn about each other, but I do want you to be my woman. I need you to be mine. You'll learn everything that you need to know, and when the time is right, hopefully very soon, I'll give you your cut and we'll be a forever thing. I promise that I'll start to share more with you. I can't promise that it'll be everything, but I'll tell you whatever I think you need to know. Being my Old Lady will get you the inside scoop and right to know certain things that other women in the club don't get to know. The Old Lady title gives you more power."

Still mirroring my position, Whiskey puts his hands on the sides of my neck. He pulls me to him and gives me the sweetest kiss I've ever gotten. Every one is better than the last. "But make no mistake, Kiana, everyone in this clubhouse will know that you're mine. I'll protect you with everything I have. God help anyone who tries to hurt you, because we all will strike anyone who tries to hurt something that's ours. Getting bit by the Vipers is not fun."

"What about the no condom thing? Either I need to get on the pill, or we need to get you some not expired condoms. I saw all those out-of-date things you had in that drawer." I know that I want kids one day, but he hasn't said anything about whether he does too.

"We're not getting you on anything, because now that I've felt you bare, I can't imagine ever not feeling you hot and wet all around me." Leave it to him to say something dirty during a serious conversation.

He continues, "And, baby, if I make a baby with you, I'll be the happiest man on this damn planet. Whether we made one today, or we have twins five years from now, I'll be right by your side from day one. I had the best Pops growing up, and from what you've told me about your parents, we both had awesome role models. Any babies that we have will be loved by both of us and this entire club. We're one huge, crazy, dysfunctional, loud family."

That makes my heart start to race, and the tears I was trying to keep in start to roll down my cheeks. Whiskey uses his thumbs to brush them away almost as fast as they fall.

"Don't cry, beautiful. I need you happy," he whispers and starts up again with the soft kisses to my cheeks, forehead, down my nose, and finally back to my lips "What do you say we head downstairs and hang out with everyone? I have to check in with the guys, but I need you close by. Is that okay?"

"Sounds good to me. Maybe I can make us something for lunch? We've had a calorie burning morning, after all." I smile and kiss him back. His kisses are as sweet as sugar and as addicting as caffeine. "And I need some coffee. I'm surprised I made it this far into the day without it."

Whiskey stands up and walks over to the wall to grab his cut—that word will take a little time to get used to—then slides it over his shoulders and turns to look at me. "Maybe you can make some more cupcakes. I only got half of one before you dragged me away and distracted me with your womanly wiles."

Oh, now he's being funny Whiskey. "What kind would you like me to make?"

"What's that red cake stuff called? Blue used to make a red cake for me for my birthday. I guess you could say it's my favorite. The frosting was made with something sweet." I get up, walk over to him, and push him back against the door. As I slide my arms around his waist, running my hands up under his cut, I rest my chin on his chest and he hugs me back.

"That would be red velvet cake, probably with cream cheese frosting. Wait . . . who's Blue?" That's a name I haven't heard yet.

"Blue is my Pops' Old Lady, and crazy story, she's also my aunt."

"Your Pops married your aunt?" Sounds like a soap opera happening around here. "Where's your mom? Is she still here too?"

"Hell fucking no," he barks out. The look on his face is like he bit into something sour. "That bitch left and died when I was a toddler. When I was ten, her sister showed up and my Pops claimed her ass so fast, the world started to spin faster. She helped raise me ever since."

"Wow. That's crazy. I can't wait to meet her. I'll ask her if she has a recipe and I'll make sure to save some for just you.

But speaking of birthdays, when's yours?" I really hope he likes birthdays, because I love mine.

"February fourteenth," Whiskey whispers.

I pull back a bit and look up at his face. "Your birthday is Valentine's Day?" Aww . . . I love that. No pun intended.

"Yea, but I haven't had a birthday per se since I was a kid. It kinda gets lost in the mushy holiday and I've never had someone to celebrate with. It's no big deal." I let it drop because I can tell he doesn't want to talk about it, but I'll definitely be doing something special for him next year. "You'll meet Blue when we get downstairs. She should be around here somewhere."

"Okay, let's go see your Brothers," I say, sliding one hand down to smack him on the ass.

"Wait, when's your birthday? I really should know these things about my woman."

"April first," I say and turn to grab our phones off the nightstand. I shove mine in the front pocket of the flannel and Whiskey tucks his into a pocket on the inside of his cut. See? I'm going to ace this biker vocab quiz.

He spanks me back and we laugh. "That explains a lot. I'm a fool for you, woman," he jokes as we head downstairs.

CHAPTER TWENTY-TWO

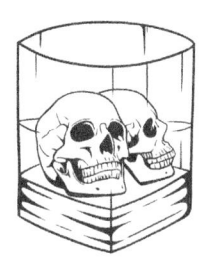

WHISKEY

The past few weeks have gone by with no news, neither good nor bad. We seem to have hit a brick fucking wall. None of our contacts have come back with any credible information about the Chaos Squad idiots. I hate even calling them an MC because if they're responsible for taking Wings, and are part of a human trafficking ring, they don't deserve to be a club. Assholes like that give us legitimate clubs a bad name.

Kiana is trying to act strong, but I can tell there are times she remembers why she had to come here. Her strength and tenacity are so amazing though, and she's been a beacon of light in this clubhouse. Every day that passes, she earns the trust of more and more Brothers.

The first Friday we came out of Church and Kiana was having a cookie decorating class with a few of the younger kids. She was being pulled in five different directions, and there were sprinkles all over the floor, but she was cool as a cucumber. When I saw her wiping tears from the eyes of one of my Brothers' sons after a frosting argument, I knew I needed her to be the mother of my children. She dealt with it like a boss and had everyone back to their own spots in no time.

A few days later, she had a few of the older kids baking with her in the kitchen. She's even taken over organizing the bigger meals that we eat as a group. She's the only woman, other than Blue and the club girls, who lives here full-time. Unfortunately for us, Blue is a horrible cook. I love Blue, but that woman somehow manages to burn something when she's boiling water, so having Kiana's help is definitely a plus.

I know Kiana has occasional issues with certain club girls, but I've seen her deal with them. I tried to interfere once, but she didn't appreciate my efforts.

Kiana pulls me out of the kitchen and pushes me out the back door.

"You can't butt into situations like that. I need them to see that I can handle my own shit," Kiana snaps and I can tell

that she's serious. "I need to be able to be taken seriously. You don't want me to talk back in front of the Brothers, so you need to give me the same with those girls."

She has her arms crossed and is tapping her pink Converse on the concrete patio. I guess she's right, and I'm going to have to do some groveling. I approach her and reach down to grab handfuls of her backside. When I lift her up, she instantly wraps her legs around my waist.

"Whiskey! You put me down right now," she says with a laugh.

"Not happenin', little lady. I got you right where I need you." I spin around and back myself up to a picnic table, propping myself up against the end. She's light enough to hold up on my own, but I've got better things that I'd like to do with my hands.

Once we're settled, I run one hand up her back and wrap her ponytail around my fist. I pull her head back and dive into her neck. She moans when I lick up under her chin and latch onto her earlobe. Her hands come up to my shoulders and she tries to push herself back, but I don't let her get too far away.

"You're distracting me on purpose. And I need you to listen to me. Please?" Kiana attempts to give me a serious face, even though I can see she's torn about letting me continue. "Please, Whiskey?"

"I don't like seeing them talk to you like that. If you'd let me put my patch on you, we wouldn't be having these issues." I'm trying every day to get her to agree to be my Old Lady,

but she keeps saying she's not ready. I just can't figure out what she's waiting for. I know it partly has to do with Wings still being gone, but considering I don't plan on ever letting her go, I don't know what else to do to show her I'm all in.

"The things they say don't bother me. I know who sleeps in your bed every night, so their words mean nothing to me. You just need to let me handle it on my own. If I needed help, you would be the first person I'd look for. If I agree to that, will you please stand back until I need you?" she asks as she runs her hands up my neck and tangles her fingers in the loose pieces of my hair. "If you let me handle my own shit, I'll handle you the way you like me to."

I rock her on my lap and let her rub against my hardness. "You'll handle me, huh? And how do you plan on doing that?"

"You know that thing I like to do to your cock? When I flick your piercing around with my tongue? I could do that again if you ask me nicely." What a temptress she's turning into. She's definitely becoming more confident in our bedroom activities.

I think I got her addicted to my dick. Or maybe he's addicted to her.

Knock knock. Fuck me. I'm pulled out of my daydream and have to press down on my growing bulge to relieve a little pressure. I'd rather not have my zipper tattooed on my dick.

"Come in," I holler through my office door.

It swings open and I'm met by two friendly faces followed by one I never anticipated them being cordial with.

Kiana, Blue, and Jewel.

My woman, my aunt, and a club girl. Sounds like the start to a bad joke—three women walk into a bar . . .

"What's up, ladies?" I ask as they come in and shut the door behind them.

Blue and Kiana sit in front of my desk, leaving Jewel standing by the door. They exchange a look and have a silent conversation with their eyes. They look a little worried and it drives my curiosity even more.

"Since these ladies won't come out and say it, I guess I have to." This comes from Jewel, the awkward third wheel of this dysfunctional trio. "We were all talking and wondering if you'd let us have a Halloween party. We've been locked up for a while now and want something fun to do." Based on her crossed arms and dramatic eyerolling, I'd say she's not happy that she's stuck inside these walls.

I look at Kiana and I can tell she's not happy to have Jewel in here with us, but she's holding her tongue.

"Do you all want to have this party?" I ask Kiana.

She nods. "Yea. We were just out at the bar and Blue mentioned it was something you normally do. Hammer overheard us and the conversation spread through the room pretty quickly. General consensus was that we needed to come talk to you."

"We normally do a big blowout for Halloween, but with the kids and families here, and the club still being on lockdown, I don't know if it's the best idea."

"What if we make it a full family thing? Make it an earlier time and let the kids dress up too?" Blue inquires.

"We'll plan the whole thing, so you don't have to do anything. Everyone will stay on the compound and it'll be as family-friendly as this crazy group can get," Kiana quickly adds.

"But what about those of us who actually want to have some real fun at this party? It's already not fair that we can't leave, but now you're making this sound like a fucking snooze fest," Jewel sneers. If she keeps making that face, it just might get stuck. If she thinks she's not getting laid enough now, that look won't help her any.

"You want to have a party just so you can fuck a Brother in a costume?" I ask.

"Well, yea. What else is there to do around here? When did this club become all about what's best for the little brats?" Jewel spits out.

Boom. I slam my closed fist down on my desk and jump up from my seat, sending the chair rolling back into the wall. "You will not call my Brothers' children brats. They're more to this club than you are. You're a club girl and nothing more."

Jewel takes a step forward. "I've been here longer than they have."

Next thing I know, Kiana is out of her chair and about to swing at her.

"Whoa there, Tyson. Nobody needs to be swinging punches today." Blue grabs Kiana around the waist and holds her back as best she can. They're just about the same height and build, so Blue's using all her strength.

"Enough!" I yell and the room goes silent. Jewel resumes her arms-crossed, stanky face pose, and Blue lets Kiana go. My woman stands tall and adjusts her rumpled clothes. Seeing a flash of her toned stomach makes me forget where we are for a split second.

When I snap out of it, I continue, "I'll allow a party, but only under the condition that everyone is included—kids, Old Ladies, and families." I look at Jewel and point a finger in her direction. "That means that any costume you decide to wear must be appropriate for children to see. No nipples, no ass, and no dirty cooters hanging out. Do I make myself clear?"

"Fine" is all I get in response.

"Oh, and anything you do with any Brother must be done behind closed doors. No private business is allowed out in the open," I add.

"That will be fine with everyone. I think everyone just wants a night to have some fun," Blue says, trying to keep the peace.

"I agree," Kiana adds.

"Who cares what you fucking think, bitch? You ain't anyone's Old Lady either, so your opinion is irrelevant," Jewel taunts.

"Oh no, you didn't." My woman has officially flipped her bitch switch.

CHAPTER TWENTY-THREE

KIANA

"You ain't anyone's Old Lady either, so your opinion is irrelevant," Jewel snaps at me.

"Oh no, you didn't." And I have officially lost my shit. Without even thinking, I reach out my right hand and slap Jewel across the face. I attempt to take another step forward but Blue pulls me back again. This makes the second time she's had to stop me from beating this bitch's ass. Clearly, she didn't take a hint the first time.

"Whoa whoa whoa." This comes from Whiskey.

I look over at him and follow his movements as he comes out from behind his desk. I know he doesn't want me to speak out of place, so I'm dreading what he's going to say to me. But then I notice his attention isn't on me—it's locked completely on Jewel. I'm not sure I like that any better.

"Are you good?" Blue asks. I nod and she lets me go again. I rub my hands together, trying to stop the tingling in my fingers.

Whiskey bypasses the chair I was sitting in and backs Jewel against the door. He wraps his hand around her throat and forces her head back. "Listen here, bitch. Nobody calls my woman a bitch except for me. And the only time I'm allowed to do so is when I'm balls deep inside of her. Now, you better clean out your ears and listen to me real good." I've never seen Whiskey like this, and I for sure don't like that he's touching her. "She might not be my Old Lady yet, but she will be, so that makes her and whatever she wants one hundred percent more important than you. Get the fuck out of my office before I throw your ass in the ditch outside the compound fence." He pulls Jewel's face forward and crouches down to be eye-to-eye with her. "I better not see your ass out of your room for the rest of the fucking week. You're also not allowed out for the party. Do I make myself clear?"

Jewel nods as much as the hand around her throat will allow. Whiskey uses his grip to move her a bit to the side, opens the door with his other hand, and pushes her out into the hallway. She falls on her ass as he slams the door shut.

"I'm gonna go find Mountain. See y'all later," Blue mumbles and scoots from behind me. "I'll just lock this behind me." She flips the lock and shuts us inside.

I turn to face Whiskey and see that he's super pissed. He's just glaring at me. "What?" I snap. "You're looking at me like that was my fault."

"Well, it kinda was." This he says with no emotion.

"How was that my fault? She called me a bitch!" I yell, confused.

"If you fucking would just fucking agree to be my fucking Old Lady, she wouldn't be saying things like that. Why can't you just give in to the inevitable and put us fucking both out of our fucking misery?" he growls.

I wish I had an answer for him. I want to be his Old Lady, but every time I open my mouth to say so, I freeze and nothing comes out. I don't know what's stopping me from agreeing, but I don't think I'm going to be able to hold back for much longer.

In an attempt to stay angry at him, I throw back, "Well, I don't like it that you touched her. You wouldn't like it if I touched another guy. And you don't need to say 'fucking' after every word."

That snaps him out of his stupor. "I will do whatever I fucking need to do. I'm the club President and she was out of line, so I dealt with her how I saw fit."

Whiskey stomps forward and grabs me around the neck the same way he did to her. I gasp to catch a breath and he uses it to his advantage, slamming his mouth down to kiss me and stroking his tongue against mine. He manhandles me until my back is against his desk, the edge digging into my ass.

Whiskey squeezes my neck a tad harder and rips our mouths apart. He turns my head and grunts in my ear. "I am your fucking man, and you will fucking do whatever I fucking say, whenever I fucking say it. Do you understand?"

"Yes," I try to say, but it comes out more like a puff of air.

"Now that I have you alone, I can remind you who you fucking belong to." He lets go of my neck and spins me around to face the desk. I slam my hands down on the top to stop my face from hitting the wood. "Good girl. Keep your hands there and do not move them."

Whiskey slaps my ass twice and I yelp both times. Even though it stings, I rise up on my toes both times. He slides his hands around my waist and makes quick work of my button and zipper. Grabbing hold of the open flaps, he yanks my jeans down and kneels behind me to pull them and my shoes off.

"Since when do you not wear pretty panties? Did I say you could walk around without a barrier for my pussy? Nope, I don't think I ever did." He smacks my ass again, and this time, I reach behind me to cover my butt cheek. "Oh, now you've done it. Put your fucking hand back on that desk."

I try to rub my skin before lifting my hand and he doesn't like that. He swats my hand away and I almost lose my balance, forcing me to return my hand quickly before I faceplant into the desk.

He grabs a handful of my other ass cheek and I moan. The combination of sting from the slap and his fingertips digging into my muscles, surprisingly, feels good. I wiggle my hips and he takes it as an invitation to bite me right on the butt. Whiskey chuckles around a mouthful of my backside. Sliding his teeth against my skin, he stops biting and licks his tongue around the sore area. As he slides his tongue up, he lifts his hands and raises them to my hips. Squeezing my waist, he raises himself to standing and pulls my ass against his denim-covered hardness. I can feel his giant bulge rubbing against my crack and I want more.

"Please, Whiskey," I plead.

"Please what, baby?"

"Please take off your pants."

"Because you asked so nicely." He laughs and I couldn't be happier.

Letting go of my hips, Whiskey reaches between us, unzips his jeans, and pushes them down. I hear a *thunk* when they hit the floor, and I look down to see him standing on one foot, kicking off his boots one at a time. He kicks both our pants to the side and uses one foot to nudge my legs farther apart.

Once I'm spread enough for him, Whiskey takes a half-step forward and resumes rubbing his dick in the crease of my ass. Grabbing hold of himself, he pushes his dick down, and since my skin is so warm, I feel the cold metal of his piercing against my folds. He rocks his hips a few times, coating himself in my wetness, then with no warning whatsoever, he pushes forward and slams into me.

"Holy fuck," I yell as he grunts and thrusts deep inside me, bottoming out. He's so deep inside me that I feel his dick hitting my cervix on every forward motion. His grip on my hips is tight, almost like he's digging into my skin. I feel one hand release my hip and start to slide up my spine, lifting my shirt as it gets higher. When my shirt is bunched around my neck, I lower my shoulders and let Whiskey slide it over my head. I lift one hand at a time, then throw it somewhere off to the side. All the while he hasn't stopped pounding his dick into my sopping wet pussy, his rhythm strong and steady.

My arms start to wobble, and I try to hold myself up, but I can't do it anymore. I give in, letting myself fold and fall forward onto his desk. Whiskey grabs the end of my ponytail and twists his wrist to wrap my hair around his fist. He yanks my head back and my spine arches backward, almost in an S-shape. One hand is in my hair and the other on my hip, giving him full control of my body. I'm basically a puppet in his hands. A marionette.

Pulling a bit harder on my hair, he tugs me up so my back is flush against his chest. He still has his cut on, so I can feel the cool leather against my skin. My head is yanked to the left and his mouth starts raining kisses and light bites down my neck. When his tongue runs behind my ear, I let out a sound I've never heard from myself before, like a mix of a cat purr and a groan.

This must make Whiskey very happy because he continues to do it over and over. His thrusts become harder and I start to yelp with every forward push of his hips. The licks turn into sucking and biting down my neck, then onto my shoulder.

"Connor," I whine.

"Do you wanna come, Kiana?" he asks with another tug of my hair.

"Yes, please. P-please?" I plead.

"Not until I say you can," he orders, and I groan with disappointment. I can feel my orgasm starting to build and don't know how much longer I can hold it in.

He releases my hair and reaches around to pull down one side of my bra. Whiskey cups the bottom of my breast and squeezes. The pressure is almost too much. Then he moves his fingers, twisting and pulling on my piercing. It's like there's a nerve that runs directly from my nipple to my throbbing center. I'm about to explode.

"I can't . . . hold it . . . much longer," I pant in between his thrusts. I'm on the edge of the cliff and ready to fall over.

"Do . . . not . . . come," he grunts each word with a plunge forward. His dick is massaging my insides so damn good. I don't know why we waited so long to do it this way. Whiskey has been threatening to bend me over and fuck me like this for a while.

"No!" I cry out and my pussy starts having mini spasms on its own. I'm not sure how he does it, but somehow my bra is unclasped and falling down my arms. I wrestle it down and off and that gives Whiskey the green light to grab ahold of my tits with both hands. Using them like handles, he presses us even closer together. I try to grab his hips behind me, but he's moving too fast and I can't get a good grip, so I just let my hands fall to my sides.

One of Whiskey's hands is still playing with my nipple, tugging and twisting my bar, while the other slides down my stomach and settles over my pussy. He uses his fingertips and starts rubbing my swollen lips, fast and rough, exposing my hard clit. I tense and he must feel my body begin to shake.

"Now," he commands, and not even a second later, I explode.

Once my pussy starts pulsating, there's no stopping the noise that comes out of my mouth. "FUUUCCCKKKK!" I scream.

Unable to fight his own orgasm, I feel Whiskey explode inside of me. He continues pumping into me as we mutually ride out our explosions. My whole body feels like it's been electrocuted, and if he wasn't holding me up so tight, I'd be thrashing around. When I stop shaking, I try and catch my breath, but no matter how many times I inhale, nothing helps. I feel like I'm sucking through a straw with no open end. I start to get dizzy and let my head fall back against Whiskey's shoulder.

His thrusts start to slow down, and I can finally get a full breath. My hearing must have taken a break too, because I can now hear his pants in my ear. Whiskey wraps his arms around my waist and tugs me backward. I feel us falling, so I grab ahold of his forearms, prepared to go down. Only I'm surprised to be met by one more thrust as he sits down in a chair and I fall into his lap. I realize then that we're sitting in the chair I was in earlier.

He moves my ponytail to one side and nuzzles his face into my neck. I turn my head and meet his mouth for a kiss. It's not a crazy, messy one, but one that's soft and gentle and more just a meeting of our lips.

"Why did we wait so long to do that?" Whiskey asks with a breathy chuckle.

"I'm not sure, but I vote that we do it more often."

"Woman, you're speaking my language."

"I think I forgot how to breathe there at the end." I laugh.

"You and me both. My legs were shaking so hard, I had to sit down. We both almost ended up on the floor."

"I guess it's a good thing you have so many chairs in your office."

"I would never let you fall." God, he's so damn sweet sometimes.

I start to turn in his lap and his softening dick slides out of my opening. I feel his cum start to run down my thigh. "Ugh, I hate that feeling." I turn sideways and squeeze my thighs together, draping my knees over the chair's arm. I try to hide my embarrassment by burying my face in his neck.

"Don't hide your pretty face from me," Whiskey scolds as he uses his right hand to lift my chin up. I meet his eyes and he softly kisses me again. "Let's get you cleaned up, huh?"

"Yes, please," I reply.

"Don't get me started again. You saying that will get us right back where we started," he says as he lifts me up and sets me back on my feet. Once he's up, he walks over to his bookshelf and grabs a roll of paper towels, twists a few pieces around his hand, then walks back toward me.

"I got this." I grab them from his hand and kiss his knuckles.

"You know it's my job to clean up my mess, but I won't argue with you."

"What happened to my tough and grumpy biker? Look at you being all nice and sweet," I joke as I turn my back to him and try to hide what I'm doing. I ball up the paper towel and toss it in the garbage can next to his desk.

"I haven't gone anywhere, little lady. I just don't see a need to fight with you about that. I'll save my battles for more important things." I watch as he picks our clothes up off the floor and makes two messy piles on his desk.

We each start grabbing items and get dressed in silence. When we're both fully clothed and he still hasn't said anything, I start to worry.

I debate dropping back in the chair but decide to take the bull by the horns. Walking around his desk, I'm met by a blank faced Whiskey. I raise my hands and push against his chest, wanting him to sit down into his chair. I turn him to face the desk and I jump up onto the top. I hook my feet around the chair's armrests and pull him towards me. His legs slide under the desk and I put my feet on each side of his hips.

I grab ahold of his face and make him meet my eyes. "What's wrong, Whiskey?"

"I don't wanna fight with you."

I'm confused. "Why would we need to fight?"

"Why won't you be my Old Lady? Am I not enough for you?" His eyes look so tormented. Oh man. I didn't realize it was bothering him so much.

"No. Never. You're everything. This has nothing to do with you not being enough. This is all on me. I want to say yes so badly, but I can't get the words out. I don't think I'm good enough for you. You should have someone who knows more about this lifestyle than me." I shake my head. I can't believe we're having this conversation less than five minutes after he fucked my brains out. Why do we always seem to have important talks after being intimate?

Whiskey snaps up in his chair and my hands settle on his shoulders. He slides his hands up my jean-clad thighs and settles on my ass cheeks. "You're more than enough for me. You're everything for me. I'm trying not to pressure you to give me an answer, but I need you to be mine." He leans forward and gives me another one of his soft kisses. How a man with such a tough and rough exterior can be so soft and kind, I don't think I'll ever quite understand.

I pull him as close to me as I can without actually sitting in his lap and gently pull out his ponytail holder, looping it around my right wrist. I run my fingers through his loose hair and scratch his scalp with my nails. This causes Whiskey to growl like a damn bear. He nuzzles his face into my chest and squeezes my backside.

"I just need a little more time. I'm really starting to feel more at home here, and I think this party will be a good test, because I think I need to prove to myself that I can do this. Let me help plan this Halloween party, and if everything goes off without a hitch, I'll be yours. We'll wake up the next morning and you can tell me whatever I need to do to officially be your Old Lady." I tug his hair and pull him up to look at me.

"You've got one week, woman." He dives in for a greedy kiss. "Actually, make that six days. Today's Sunday and the party will be on Saturday. The clock starts now." He lets out a full belly laugh. It's not a sound I hear often, but I love it.

"Challenge accepted, Mr. President." I sit back and give him a salute. "But don't forget that this is a Halloween party. That means you have to dress up as something."

"Dress up? Like in a costume?" His eyes widen and the panic on his face makes me bust out laughing.

I nod. "The kids will expect it. If you want any candy, you'll have to dress up just like everyone else." I use my feet and push his chair, causing it to roll backward, then I hop down and drop a kiss on his forehead.

"But, but, but . . ." he stutters and stands up to follow me.

I bend down to slide my shoes on and head for the door, flipping the lock and swinging it open.

I feel Whiskey right behind me, so I wiggle my hips a little. "If you dress up and I like what I see, maybe I'll sneak you some candy."

"Don't tempt me, woman. This is supposed to be a family-friendly party."

I spin around and back out into the hall. "Then leave your assless chaps in the closet, cowboy. We'll pull them out after the party's over." I continue backing down the hall toward the main room.

He slams the door behind him and starts prowling after me. "You and your ass are gonna regret that later."

I spin around and sprint into the main room, finding the first tall person I can hide behind. "Mountain, hide me. Your son's being mean to me."

Mountain straightens to his full six-foot-five height and stretches his arms out to the sides. "I got you, girly. I taught my son better than to go through a disabled man."

"Ha! Disabled, my ass!" This comes from my left, so I look and see Blue standing next to Whiskey, her arms crossed. "If you're disabled, then I'm blind. And I guess that means I can't see to do that thing you like."

That leads to a lot of *nooos* and *yucks* coming from around the room.

"Pops, we don't need to hear those kinda things," Whiskey whines and trudges over to the bar. "I heard enough of that shit when I was growing up. Prospect, gimme a beer."

I slide under Mountain's outstretched arm and he lowers it around my shoulders. He looks down at me and whispers, "Don't let his grumpiness fool you. You have my boy wrapped around your little finger."

"I know. I just need to figure out how to tell him," I say back.

He pulls me around to face him. "You'll figure it out when the time is right." He nods and walks away.

I look around the room and realize he's right, and an idea pops in my head. Now to figure out how to do it.

CHAPTER TWENTY-FOUR

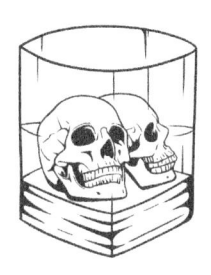

WHISKEY

It felt like this day wasn't ever going to get here. It's finally Saturday and I cannot wait to see what costume Kiana has decided to wear.

Once word got around that the Halloween party was a go, everyone got super excited. Next came the scramble to figure out what to do for costumes. Good thing there's such a thing as two-day shipping. No one was sharing what they're going to be, so it should be interesting to see what this crazy bunch of characters come out of their rooms as. One bonus has come from all these online purchases—based on the pile of smiley face boxes we have stacked on the back porch, there's plenty of cardboard to burn tonight for a bonfire.

Even though I was told I had to dress up, I had no idea what I was going to be until this morning. After I put on my usual jeans and t-shirt, I stood in front of my closet and stared at my clothes. I probably was there for a good ten minutes before a light bulb went off. I had everything I needed right there in front of me.

Black jeans, black t-shirt, black pearl snap, a Stetson Shasta 10X cowboy hat, and my Ariat Circuit Patriot cowboy boots.

I brought everything down to my office so Kiana could use our room to get ready. I get dressed and take one last look in the mirror hanging on the back of my office door. I'm not normally one to toot my own horn, but damn, I look good as a cowboy.

I lock up my office and head out into the main room. I'm shocked by what I find. Since I was cooped up in my office all day doing paperwork, I couldn't help set up. They were definitely busy out here. There are decorations everywhere. There are plastic pumpkins on the tables, skull decorations on the walls, and even a few life-sized skeletons sitting in the recliners. And the best part—bowls of candy on every surface. I have a feeling it's going to be a long night because we'll all be hyped-up on sugar.

Footsteps coming down the stairs cause me to turn around and I can't hold in my laughter. Ring comes down strutting, wrapped in a fucking bed sheet. It looks like he just took it out of the linen closet and tied it around himself. It's still got the fucking creases.

"Dude, what the hell are you? You're supposed to be wearing a costume, not your dirty laundry." I seriously can't stop laughing.

"I am wearing a costume. This is a toga. You know, like from that frat house movie?" And then he starts jumping and pumping his arms, chanting, "TOGA! TOGA! TOGA!"

And that's met by more chanting coming down the stairs. Hammer and Brewer jump in on the chanting. "TOGA! TOGA! TOGA!"

"Kick ass movie, bro." Hammer throws out a fist bump. "But be careful with all that jumping around. No one wants to see what you're hiding underneath that sheet. We don't need you having a wardrobe malfunction."

Once Hammer gets closer, I get a good look at him and realize what he's wearing can barely even be called a costume. "Are you wearing a glow-in-the-dark skeleton shirt?" I ask. "That's fucking cheating."

"It's all I had, and I wasn't about to dress up in a dumb costume. This is as far as I'm willing to go. Now, let's talk about our pal Brewer here. He looks like the guy on the roll of paper towels."

"What the fuck, man? I'm a lumberjack, you asshole!" Brewer huffs.

"Your flannel shirt and clean shaved face make you look like you should be sitting on the storage room shelf," Hammer retorts.

If this is how everyone is going to react to each other's costumes, it's going to be an interesting evening.

"Hey, you idiots, let's get this show on the road." We all turn around to see my Pops sitting in his wheelchair, but that's not even the craziest part. He's wearing a Hawaiian shirt, has a bandana tied around his forehead, and one of his pantlegs is knotted up just under his stump.

"Pops, why are you dressed like Lieutenant Dan?" I'm shocked. Mountain hates drawing attention to his amputated leg.

"Don't be giving me no damn sass, boy. I may be old and crippled, but I can still kick your ass." That makes everyone else wake from their dumbfounded stupors and laugh at my expense. "I'm dressed like this because my Old Lady made me. She said, and I quote, 'Your leg ain't growing back any time soon, so you might as well embrace the opportunity.' And since I'm not gonna sleep on the couch, I do what she says."

"Well, I for one am glad you found your sea legs," Brewer pipes in.

"Wrong part of the movie, but good one," Mountain chuckles and rolls himself toward the bar. "Now, since I'm so damn short in this chair, someone go grab me a beer. If I have to be down here all night, you all are gonna be my gophers."

Over the next half hour, more Brothers and their families make their way into the main room. We're surrounded by little spooky ghosts, cute bunnies, and a few younger boys in mini versions of their dads' biker gear. If this is a sign of the years to come, I'm happy to say we have a whole bunch of future club Brothers in our midst.

Seeing all these kids makes me think again about possibly knocking up Kiana. She would look so fucking hot with a rounded belly. She's not pregnant yet, but that sure doesn't stop me from trying to make it happen every chance I get. Maybe next year she can dress up like a pumpkin, with our baby growing inside.

I'm standing at the bar, shooting the shit with Hammer, Kraken, Doc, and my Pops, when I feel two hands grab onto my back pockets. This better not be some handsy club girl thinking she can get some while my woman isn't in the room.

"Damn, cowboy, your backside looks delicious in these jeans." Kiana. Sneaky minx.

"Why, thank you, darlin'," I say in an exaggerated southern accent. I reach my hands back and slide her fingers from my pockets, then turn around so I can see what my woman is dressed up as.

When I'm facing her, I go speechless. I honestly don't think I'm even breathing right now. She looks fucking sexy as hell. She's wearing a black lacy dress with no straps, the top shimmering with tiny jewels, and it goes down to her knees. Her hair is twisted up and there's a sparkly crown thing pushed back into her curls.

When my brain decides to start sending words to my mouth, I say, "Damn. You look beautiful."

"Why, thank you," she says with a cute curtsy.

"What are you supposed to be in that pretty, frilly dress and crown? A duchess?"

Kiana crosses her arms and pretends to pout. It might work on me if it weren't for the fact that her arms are pushing her tits up and giving me one hell of a peek down her cleavage. "No, you Neanderthal. I'm a princess." She then points up at her head. "And this is a tiara, not a crown! It even has a skull on it."

I look again and sure as shit, there's a tiny skull and cross bones. She's quickly embracing our badass lifestyle. "Well, miss tiara-not-a-crown, I like duchess better. In fact, I'm going to call you Duchess from now on." I cross my arms to mimic her snarky attitude.

"Duchess? Like how your dad calls Blue?" she whispers. The look in her eyes is one I've never seen before. The ocean blue I always thought they were before is now more like a clear, cloudless sky. The closer I look, the more colors I notice. Her pupils are rimmed with an almost silver sheen, and the surrounding swirls have a brightness that reminds me of a summer day. One where you know it'll be great weather for riding. I could get lost in her eyes if she would let me.

Sheesh. Look at me, thinking with all these poetic words and shit. But this woman here is so worth it all.

"Exactly. Just like all the Brothers have a road name, our Old Ladies get a special one too." If only she would agree.

"But I haven't—" she starts, but I cut her off with a kiss.

I grab my cowboy hat with one hand and wrap the other around her waist. "I know. We agreed to talk in the morning. We still on for that?" I need to know that what she promised me is still a go.

She wraps her arms around my waist and looks up to meet my eyes. "Yes, Whiskey, I promise."

This time, she pushes up and kisses me. I swipe my tongue over her plump lower lip and wait for her to need to breathe. As soon as she opens her lips to catch a breath, I strike. My tongue demands entrance, and she gives it to me. I dive in deep and take control, swirling our tongues around each other. All she can do is gasp for air any time I back off just enough to catch my own breath. I'm determined to show her this is exactly where she belongs.

In this family.

In my arms.

My Duchess.

"All right, that's enough kissing for you two lovebirds," Hammer jokes to bust my chops.

I reluctantly pull back from our kiss and put my hat back on before pulling Duchess around in front of me. She leans back into my chest and uses me like a back rest. "That's enough out of you, Mister Skeleton. People wearing not real costumes don't get to pick on those of us who dressed up." Damn, my woman is sassy.

"Ha! Whiskey didn't really dress up. He just put on stuff that he had in his closet," Hammer teases as he throws back a shot of Jack.

"He is too dressed up. Whiskey looks like a young Johnny Cash. The man in black." I hadn't even thought of that. "And we match. We're both wearing all black," she says as she lifts a foot, showing off a black heel with a red bottom. Close enough to all-black, if you ask me.

I wonder how those would look next to my ears as I fold her in half and devour her wet pussy? Definitely not the time or place to be having that thought.

"Okay. Whatever you say, lady," Hammer replies.

I lean my head to the right and whisper in her ear, "Do you need a drink?"

"I could go for Jack and Coke."

"What? I've never seen you drink that before."

"I figured since you can't drink Jack, I could be drinking buddies with Hammer."

That causes everyone within ear range to laugh out loud.

"She got you good, Prez," Kraken snickers.

"I can too drink Jack. I just have a very rough next morning when I do." I try to defend myself. "How do you know I can't drink Jack?" I ask her.

"Hammer told me all about your Prospect patching night. You were too busy snoring to hear us talking."

"Since I had to wake her up to drag your drunk ass into your room, I figured she deserved to know your fun secret." Hammer laughs and pours himself another shot. "Do you think you can keep up with me, Miss Duchess?" Hammer pats the bar stool next to him and Duchess climbs up. I like that my Brother has already started calling my lady by her name. It'll be official in no time.

"Probably not, but I can keep pouring for you after I've had enough."

"Sounds like a great set-up to me. I get my own private bartender. Prospect, bring us another bottle. Oh, and a shot glass and Jack and Coke for the lady."

I move to stand behind her and lean my forearms on the stool's backrest. "Are you sure this is a good idea, Duchess?"

"Don't listen to him, Hammer. He's just a worrywart." She peeks over her shoulder at me and sticks her tongue out. "I'll be fine. I don't have any plans to fall asleep in the hallway."

Hammer snorts and has to plug his nose to avoid spraying the bar top with the shot he just took.

We both laugh at that. "You'll be paying for that later," I growl at her.

"Promises, promises" is all she says before she grabs the shot glass and throws it back.

CHAPTER TWENTY-FIVE

DUCHESS

Last night was so much fun. All the Brothers and their families were able to relax and just have fun for a little while. Things have been so tense around here lately.

After we finished eating dinner, the party moved outside to the backyard area. Whiskey and Brewer lit one heck of a bonfire and the rest of us just chilled in the lawn chairs and on the picnic tables. No one left the compound, but that doesn't mean the guys didn't have any fun—the patched Brothers had some fun at the Prospects' expense.

Someone came up with the crazy idea of getting the Prospects to have a race around the warehouse. But this wasn't just any race. They had to pretend they were riding their motorcycles and run around two times. They were making vrooming noises like they were revving their engines, and they even had their arms up like they were holding onto the handlebars. Poor Jacob and Sam. When they started making laps, they didn't look very happy. But by the time they came around for the final time, both guys were laughing and could barely stand. A few Brothers had their phones out to take videos and pictures, so I'm sure there is going to be a lot of razzing done in the future.

I look down and see that Whiskey is still out cold. I wiggle sideways and slowly detangle myself from the arm and leg still hooked over me. I slide out of bed and finally get both my feet on the floor. On the way to the bathroom, I snag some clean clothes off the couch and quietly shut the door behind me. I flip on the lights and gasp when I see myself in the mirror. My hair is half falling out of its bun and my makeup is smudged under my eyes. But that's not the craziest part. My chest looks like I was attacked by leeches.

I begin to blush when the memory of last night flashes to the forefront.

The final straw is when Whiskey picks me up off my chair and throws me over his shoulder. He has a handful of my ass and I have his backside all up in my face. It may be upside

down, but damn does it look fine in those tight black jeans. I need to make him wear these things more often.

I slide my hands down his back pockets and grab two handfuls of his muscular tushie.

"What are you doing back there, Duchess?" Whiskey asks as he jogs up the stairs.

"Testing out my merchandise," I sass back.

"Best be careful. If you don't watch out, I'm gonna get you back."

"Like I said before, cowboy, promises, promises."

"That's it, little lady. You asked for it," he says as he throws me down backward on the bed. "I've about had enough of your mouth. I think I need to put mine to use to make you think twice about talking back to me."

Whiskey pulls me back up to stand in front of him and looks down at me. "How the fuck do I get this thing off of you? I need it in one piece so I can see you wearing it again."

"Just unzip the back," I say as I turn around.

I feel his fingers grasp for the tiny zipper pull and I breathe a sigh of relief as he pulls it down. When he sees I'm wearing nothing underneath, it's his turn to lose his mind.

"What did I tell you about not wearing panties to cover my pussy?" he snaps and pushes me forward, and I'm now face down, ass up on the bed. He lifts one knee at a time to get my dress down and off all the way.

I hear material rustling, so I assume he's putting my dress down somewhere. I figure out very quickly that it was not my dress making those noises—it was Whiskey's clothes. I hear his boots hit the floor, and not two seconds later, he has his hands full of my ass cheeks.

One hand comes down in a SLAP and I let out a tiny squeak.

"You're gonna take what I give you and you'll do nothing to stop me." I feel him slide one hand between my legs and he shoves a finger into my pussy. "Damn, Duchess. You're soaking wet. This is gonna make my job so much easier." He pulls his finger out and the next thing I know, I'm stuffed full of his rock-hard cock.

"Shit!" I croak out.

"That's it . . . you can take it. Take every inch of me," Whiskey growls as he starts pounding away.

"Fuck. Me. Harder," I yell back at him. I don't think I've ever been this damn horny. I don't know if it was all the Jack I was drinking, or if it was the flirty glances my man was throwing my way, but holy shit.

"Don't tell me what to do. I say what happens," he taunts me and pulls all the way out. When he doesn't slide back in, I turn my head to try and see his face.

"Where'd you go?"

"I'm right here." I finally see what he's doing—the bastard is jerking himself off. What in the actual fuck?

"Oh, I don't think so, mister." This is definitely not going to work for me. I flip over onto my back and get an eyeful of his hand sliding up and down his shiny dick. The fucker is using my juices to get himself off. Not fair!

"Where do you think you're going?"

"Right here," I say as I slide toward him.

I grab the arm he's not using to play with himself and pull him forward. He falls on top of me, which forces him to let go of his hardness. His hands are next to my head on the mattress and I'm given free rein to the rest of his hot body. My legs are spread apart and hooked up over his hips. I slide my hands under his arms and wrap them around his solid back.

When I have him just where I want him, I pull his hips forward and slide his cock back inside my greedy pussy. "Holy shit. Fuck me, woman," Whiskey hollers and finally gets back to doing what he should be—fucking my brains out.

"Yes. Yes. Don't. Stop," I grunt.

"You . . . are . . . not . . . in . . . charge," he replies in between thrusts.

Putting his incredible arm muscles to work, I watch as his biceps flex and he pushes his chest up off mine, but our lower halves never separate. When he finally has the leverage he wants, he ducks his head down and latches his mouth onto the side of my tit.

"Ouch. That fucking hurts," I say and try to wiggle my chest to detach him.

"Too fucking bad," he answers through his teeth. He finally releases, only to switch sides and bite down on the other one. "These beauties are all mine tonight. You won't be wearing anything that shows these puppies for a very long time."

Whiskey releases me again, only to scatter his love bites all around my tits. He uses his teeth to tug on my left nipple piercing and my orgasm totally sneaks up out of nowhere. I open my mouth to scream though nothing comes out but air. I'm thrashing back and forth so damn hard, I lose my grip on his forearms and throw my arms up around the top of my head. It would probably pop off if I wasn't holding it down.

"Jesus fucking Christ." I feel his body start to shake and his thrusts begin to fall out of rhythm. "Holy shit, you feel so tight. I can . . . feel you . . . squeeze me." And I can feel him detonate. "Fuck. Fuck. Fuck" is all I hear as he lets his arms go and falls down on top of me.

I can barely breathe, but feeling his body settle on top of mine is almost like heaven. "Don't go falling asleep on me now." I laugh and try to roll him off me.

"But I'm comfy right here." Whiskey wiggles his hips, sending another shock through my pussy. "If you do that again, I for sure won't be moving."

"Get off me, you brute!" I yelp. "I can't get a full breath."

"Oh, sorry, Duchess." I'm finally able to take a full breath when he rolls off me and falls to my side. He lifts my right hand and bring it to his lips, then he kisses my palm and intertwines our fingers. I've noticed that he likes to give me those gentle sweet kisses anywhere he can reach me.

I roll onto my side and look up to find his sparkling blue eyes are already watching me. "Thank you for letting us have the party today. Everyone seemed to have a lot of fun."

"Anything for you, Duchess. You know that, right? I'd do anything for you." He rolls onto his side to mirror me.

"I'm beginning to get a good sense of that, yes."

"Good. Now, let's get you cleaned up and tucked under these sheets. We've got an important day tomorrow." Whiskey sits up and uses our connected hands to pull me up after him.

"Yes, we do," I say as he leads me into the bathroom.

Neither one of us has energy for a full shower, so we just hop in long enough to rinse off. Five minutes later, we're drying off and crawling into bed. But instead of spooning me from behind like he normally does, Whiskey pushes me flat on my back and lays his head on my shoulder. He wraps his arm around my waist and hooks his right leg over mine. Once he's enveloped me like a dang octopus, I lay my arm over his shoulders and squeeze him tight.

"Good night, Connor."

"Night, my Duchess."

I grab a towel to dry my face and attempt to wrangle my hair. My hair tie snaps when I'm pulling it out, so I just use one of Whiskey's spares on the counter. I try to keep this bathroom neat and organized, but he whips through here sometimes like a damn tornado, making a mess while I follow behind to clean it up.

I slide on clean panties—that should make him happy—but forgo a bra for a camisole with one built in. Next is a pair of gray leggings and a green and gold hooded sweatshirt. It is football season after all, and I have to support my fellow cheeseheads. I pull on some socks and sneak back out into the bedroom to grab my pink shoes.

Taking my phone off the charger, I slowly open the door to let myself out into the hallway. I don't hear any noises and look down at my screen to see what time it is—6:47 a.m. Damn, I guess those early bakery hours are engraved in my brain. I head downstairs and sit at the bottom to slip on and tie my shoes.

One look around and I see we have quite the mess to clean up today. The floor is littered with random candy wrappers and a few of the decorations aren't where they started. Someone moved two of the life-sized skeletons into a very compromising position, so I walk over to the couch and pull the top one off, setting it back down next to the other. There . . . the kids don't need to be seeing those shenanigans. I mean the little kids—not the grown ass men who act like kids.

I head into the kitchen and start a pot of coffee. Maybe the aroma will start waking up some of the party animals. Once the pot is full, I pour myself a mug and add just a dash of pumpkin creamer. I guess I'm going to be a little adventurous today.

Today's a very important day. I'm hoping a lot of his Brothers will be around when Whiskey comes down. I want there to be witnesses when I tell him I'm ready to officially be his Old Lady. I want everyone to know that I'm one hundred percent committed to this club. Whiskey is it for me and this club is everything to him. I hope he really meant it when he said he wants me to be his.

I back out of the kitchen and pull one of the back doors open to let in the early morning breeze. I catch the screen door behind me, so it doesn't slam shut as I step out onto the back patio. It's so beautiful out here. Now that it's November, the leaves are about half fallen and there's a shiny layer of dew coating the ground.

I lean against one of the overhang's wooden posts and bring my coffee to my lips. I take a drink but almost choke on it when I look to the right and see my truck. Setting my coffee mug down on the nearest picnic table, I rush over to my truck, not able to believe what I'm seeing. Walking all the way around it, I notice it's the same on the other side too. Someone slashed all four of my tires. What in the actual fuck?

Reaching into my hoodie pocket, I pull out my phone but continue to look around the yard. I glance to the right, behind the cabins, and notice the fence looks kind of funny, like it was cut. I don't want to walk too far from the clubhouse, so I decide to call Whiskey and see what he wants me to do.

I swipe my screen to wake it up and hit the phone icon, then swipe on his name and bring the phone to my ear. It rings a couple times before he picks up.

"Hey, Duchess. Where are you?" I hear the morning gravel in his voice.

But before I get a chance to answer him, I'm grabbed from behind. I try to scream, but a rag is forced over my mouth and a sticky sweet smell fills my senses. I drop the phone as the lights go out.

CHAPTER TWENTY-SIX

DUCHESS

I try to roll over and snuggle closer to Whiskey, but when I go to lift my arm, it feels kind of heavy. I slowly open my eyes and realize I'm not in his bedroom at the clubhouse. I have no idea where I am or how I got here, but I know that this isn't good.

I start to panic and my head starts to spin, so I close my eyes and try to settle myself back down. My heart is beating really fast and I'm suddenly very thirsty. I breathe in and out a few times, trying to calm down. I'm freaked the heck out, but panicking is going to get me nowhere. I need to be strong for when Whiskey comes to get me . . . from wherever I am.

I squint one eye to check that the room isn't spinning anymore, and once it's not, I open the other. Still lying down, I turn my head to look around the room, and the first thing I notice is that it's extremely dark. There's only a sliver of light coming from underneath the door that allows me to see the floor, but I can't tell if there's anything else in this room other than the bed I'm lying on.

Remembering my heavy left arm, I lift it a little and realize there's a cuff around my wrist, and when I shake my arm, I hear a chain rattling. I sit up and swing my legs over the side of the bed. It turns out it's only a small twin-sized mattress, so my feet just hit the wood floor.

My socked feet feel cold against the floor. "Where the hell are my shoes?" Whoever these people are, they took my damn shoes. Whiskey is not going to be happy—he likes those pink Converse.

I push myself up to my feet and walk straight ahead until I find the wall. I have no clue how long the chain I'm attached to is, but hopefully it's long enough for me to find something that will give me a clue as to where I am. I slide my hand along the wall until I find a corner. Turning right, the wall ends at an opening, so I feel around and notice it's another door. Running my hand along the wall, my finger catches a switch and I flip it on. Holy shit is that bright! This door is for a bathroom.

Squinting, I get a glimpse of the absolute most disgusting bathroom I have ever seen. And that's saying a lot. Port-a-potties at the county fairs are really gross. This bathroom is covered in avocado green tile and linoleum. And it doesn't look like it's been cleaned since the day it was installed. There's mold growing in every corner and the toilet looks ready to fall through the floor.

I try the faucet and am very surprised to see there's clean water running. Cupping my hands together, I get a few gulps before I hear a noise coming from the other side of the wall.

In my search of the room, I forget there are probably people somewhere else in this house. Apartment? Cabin? Whatever the hell this place is.

Leaving the bathroom light on, I go back into the bedroom and notice that everything is some sort of wood. The walls are that seventies-style cheap wood paneling. The floor is bare wood planks, and it looks like they put the same on the ceiling. There are no windows, so I'm starting to think this must be a hunting cabin or something converted into a spare room. There's no furniture other than the mattress and the room is quite small.

Shit. Someone's coming. I stay standing, hoping to look intimidating, but inside I'm scared shitless. This isn't how I wanted to spend my day. I'm supposed to be at home with Whiskey. Wait . . . when did I start thinking of the clubhouse as my home? I haven't been at my house in a few weeks, and the longer I'm away from it, the more being with Whiskey feels right. Hopefully, I can get out of here and back to him.

There's a rattling on the other side of the door, and I hear a *clunk* hit the floor before it opens out into the hall.

"Well, hello there, gorgeous." This guy is slimy.

"Who the hell are you? Where am I?" I snap at him.

"Whoa there, filly. One question at a time," he says and raises his hands up like he's surrendering. "I'll tell you my name soon, but I needed to come in and check on the merchandise." He steps into the room but not all the way. "I've been having a few problems with my brothers disappearing lately. You wouldn't happen to know about that, would you?"

"Your who? What do your brothers have to do with me?" I'm so confused.

"Yes, bitch, MY fucking brothers." He charges forward, causing me to jump back. My foot catches on the chain and I fall backward. Thankfully, I land on my butt on the mattress. He squats down in front of me. "My club brothers. How do you not know about fucking bikers? You've been living in a club for months."

"I know this has to do with the club, since I was taken from there, but what do you want from me?"

"That, my dear," he says and stands up, "is the million-dollar question. You're here to be sold like your pretty little sister."

"Tempy? Where is she? Is she here?" I sit up and start to panic, looking around, almost like she'll pop out of thin air. "Where is she?"

"Don't be worrying about her. She's gone." He laughs, like an evil monster. Actually, that's exactly what he is—pure evil.

He looks like a mix between a homeless man and a movie villain. He looks to be in his mid-forties and has long, stringy black hair. His once white t-shirt is stained brown around the neck, and the jacket he's wearing looks about two sizes too big. His jeans are full of stains and tears. It honestly looks like he got in a fight but hasn't bothered to clean up in a month. How gross.

The longer I look at this idiot, the angrier I get. How dare he take me and my sister? What the hell did we ever do to him?

I push myself back up to my feet and get as close to his greasy face that his smell will allow me. "Who the hell are you? Take me back home. Right fucking now!"

The dead look in his eyes starts to glow. "My name is Bullet. And I'm your worst fucking nightmare. You're never going home, and I hope your buyer puts you in your fucking place. You're a disobedient spoiled brat."

"My buyer?" That does not sound good. "Am I going with my sister?" Maybe I can find her, then we can get out of this crazy situation together.

"Shit, I wish you were going to her buyer. That guy doesn't care what we do to her. We sure have had lots of fun with her," Bullet snickers and leans back against the door jam. "Sadly, you're going to someone with a more discerning taste. He wants you untouched."

Whatever that means doesn't sound good. "Was Tempy hurt? If you hurt her, I'm gonna get the guys to kick your ass."

That sets him into a fit of hysterics. "Your stupid club is a bunch of fucking pussies. They have no idea what the hell is going on around here. They're fucking clueless. My Chaos Squad could run circles around your fucking club."

"I don't really give two shits about your fucking club. My man and his club will find me. And when they do, they'll kill you and all your fucking cronies. I hope they spend extra time on your smelly ass." Oops... wrong thing to say.

"Listen here, bitch." He lunges at me, pushing me back against the wall. My head hits the wood and I try to hold in my cry, but a small squeak sneaks out. Holy fucking hell, that hurts.

His hands are gripping my shoulders and he's holding me a few inches off the floor. I try kicking him, but I don't have enough room to swing my leg. His whole body is pushing me against the paneling. "I'm not gonna listen to you run your mouth anymore. Women need to learn their fucking place." He stands back on his own weight but continues to hold me up. "I hope your new owner beats the shit outta you."

He lets my arms go and I crumple down onto the floor. "That's where you belong, bitch. On the fucking floor with the dogs." He swings his leg back and kicks me.

His boot connects with my right ankle and I let out a small scream. "Eekkk!"

"Oh, quit being such a pussy," Bullet mutters as he turns and walks out of the room. He slams the door behind him and I hear another *thunk* against the wood.

Now that he's gone, I can finally let my pain out. "Holy frickin' freak flag jeeze Louise hell balls asshole, that hurts!" I know that doesn't make any sense, but my brain isn't really firing on all cylinders right now. Between what I'm assuming was chloroform, my head smashing into the wall, and now the pain starting to throb in my ankle, I'm not doing so hot right now.

I slide myself over to the mattress and lay down on my side, pulling my knees up to my chest and wrapping my arms around my legs. Maybe if I curl myself into a tiny ball, I'll disappear. I just want to go back to last night. I want to be in bed with Whiskey and have him wrapped around me like a cuddly octopus.

I pull the chain attached to my wrist around to the side of the mattress. Maybe I can use it if Bullet comes back in here again. I'd like to wrap it around his neck and drag his body behind my truck.

Fuck! I just remembered that I have four flat tires. I hope whoever did it, didn't do anything else to my Dragon.

Since there are no windows in this room, I have no idea what time of day it is. I know Whiskey answered my phone call, I heard his voice, but I hope someone found the hole in the fence. Maybe they saw my truck and found my phone. I wish I could've kept ahold of it so they could track me here.

Wherever here is.

CLANK. I'm jolted out of my daydream by that noise outside the door again. I really hope Bullet isn't coming back for more, because I don't know if I can handle anything else.

The door opens, and this time, it's a younger guy. I stay curled up on the mattress, just looking at him. I'm not going to say a single word. I don't know him, so he's automatically one of the bad guys.

He turns around and picks up a bag from out in the hall. It's one of those plastic bags from a grocery store and I recognize the pig logo on the side. We have that store in town, so I hope that means we're still somewhat close to Tellison.

"I got you some food," he says as he holds the bag out. He's standing in the doorway, making no move to come into the room, but I'm for sure not about to get up and go over to him. With my luck, it's a fucking trap. Plus, I don't even know if I can stand on my ankle.

I think he gets the hint that I'm not going to move because he finally walks into the room. This guy is a lot cleaner than Bullet, but I can see he's wearing a club cut. It has a Prospect patch on the front, so I now know why he was sent in here to feed me—he's this club's bitch boy. Dumbass man picked the wrong kind of club to join.

He drops the bag at the end of the mattress. It makes a rustle and a thud when it hits the floor. Sensing I don't have anything to say, he turns and walks out of the room. The door shuts again and I can hear the *thunk* before it happens.

Not even bothering to see what's in the bag, I close my eyes again. I don't trust that the food wasn't tampered with or drugged in some way. They did it to get me here, so I wouldn't put it past them to do it again.

I feel myself start to drift off and let sleep take over. I just hope Whiskey finds me soon. I need to tell him that I'm his Old Lady.

CHAPTER TWENTY-SEVEN

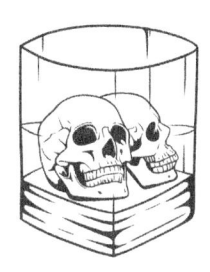

WHISKEY

Ring. Ring. What the hell is that?

Ring. Ring. Someone better be dead to interrupt my sleep. I better answer that before it wakes up Kiana. Grabbing my phone off the nightstand, I squint at the brightness of the screen.

DUCHESS CALLING. I quickly look to my left and see that she isn't in bed like she should be. What's going on?

I swipe the green icon as I swing my legs over the side of the bed. "Hey, Duchess. Where are you?"

I hear a small squeak and some grunting, but then it sounds like the phone drops to the ground. When I don't hear anything else, I start to get worried.

"Duchess? Is everything okay?" I get no answer. The line is still open, but I don't hear any more sounds. I think it's time to go look for her.

I jump out of bed and start grabbing clothes from the scattered pile on the floor, throwing on my black jeans and t-shirt from last night. I slide on my riding boots and grab my cut off the hook as I run out the door.

"WAKE THE FUCK UP, PEOPLE!" I yell as I jog down the hallway and continue down the stairs. I hear a few doors open but don't bother to look back and see who it is.

Hitting the last step, I look around the main room and don't see anyone. The room is a bit messy but nothing too crazy.

Maybe she went to get coffee and spilled some on herself. Maybe that was what the squeak was and she dropped her phone trying to clean it up. Maybe. Hopefully.

Turning left toward the kitchen, I notice that one of the back doors is open.

"What's going on down there?" I turn back to see Hammer, Brewer, and Ring coming down the stairs.

"I was woken up by Duchess calling my phone, but she never said anything." I hold out my phone and look down at it. I notice that the call has now ended, but I don't know if that was me or her. "I heard some noises, but then it sounded like she dropped it. Then she didn't reply when I kept talking. I just noticed the back door was open and was going to check it out."

"Okay. That's a good idea." Hammer kicks into gear. "Brewer, run back upstairs and wake everyone up. Ring, get the girls up and then meet us outside. Whiskey, we'll go look outside. Let's go." Thank goodness he's taking the lead, because I don't know if I have it in me right now. "Dude. Move your ass."

I snap out of it and head down the back hall. I push the screen door open and sweep my gaze across the backyard. My heart deflates when I don't see her. Where is she? "DUCHESS!" I yell at the top of my lungs. The only response is a flock of birds flying overhead.

"There's a half-full mug over here," Hammer says and I walk over to him at the nearest picnic table.

I pick it up and it's still warm. "Still warm, so she can't be far. Where the hell is she, Hammer?" Now I'm really starting to freak the fuck out. My heart is about to pound out of my chest and I'm starting to sweat. "Where did she go?"

"Hey, guys, look at this!" We look to the right and Ring is standing next to Duchess's truck. "All four tires are flat. They've been slashed."

I rush over to her truck, and sure shit, all four are flat and the truck is sitting at a funky angle. Who the hell would do this? I look around and notice the whole clubhouse has emptied onto the back patio. Brothers, women, kids, and club girls are bundled up and looking around like they're lost.

My brain snaps awake and I holler out, "CYPHER!" He works his way through the crowd and heads toward me.

"Whatchya need, Prez?" he asks.

"I need you to trace her phone. She called me, but she never said anything. Maybe she has it with her. Trace it and we can go get her." I need him to find her. "Please."

"You got it." And he's gone running back toward the clubhouse. The group parts to let him through and it's almost like moving has woken them from their confusion. Everyone starts talking at once and it's almost too much.

A whistle trills and the talking stops. Hammer whistles one more quick tweet and we all turn toward him. "Women and kids, get inside. Brothers are to be stationed at every door. The rest of us will split up and look around the compound. Look for footprints and any disturbances to the ground. It's still early and there's still a bit of frost on the ground. Eyes open, people." He claps twice and the crowd starts to disperse.

I must be looking pretty rough because I'm soon being pushed to the porch and down on a picnic table bench. Someone sits down next to me and I look over to see that it's my Pops.

"Don't be jumping to conclusions, son. We don't know what happened yet." He's trying to be helpful, but I just can't listen.

"I don't want to hear it, Pops. I know that she's gone. Someone came in here and took her from right under our noses. This is my fault." I jump up and start pacing back and forth. "This is all my fault. Wings was taken and now my Duchess is gone. I don't deserve her."

"ENOUGH!" he yells. I freeze and look at him, because it doesn't matter that I'm the President, Mountain is still my Pops and he gave me this title. "No matter what happened, we will find both of the girls. We will find them and bring them home. And you do deserve her. You both deserve each other. That woman was made for you and she knows that too. Understand me, boy?"

"Yes." I look down at my boots, immediately feeling like I'm five years old again and in trouble for doing something stupid.

The back door slams open and Cypher comes running out. "I found it. It's still here."

"Where is it?" I ask just as I hear another whistle coming from the woods.

"OVER HERE! WHISKEY GET OVER HERE BY THE FENCE!" I don't know who's yelling, but I take off running.

I round the back of the family cabins and head toward Ring. He's a few feet into the tree line, standing next to a hole in the chain link fence.

"What the fuck?" I mumble.

"Someone cut this fence. There's no rust on the cuts, so it was done recently. And there are some drag marks through the leaves and dirt. Maybe three or four people." He points back the way we came and also on the other side of the fence. "Trooper and Sam just went through to see what they can find."

"Alright. I'm going out." I take a step toward the fence, but there's a pull on the back of my cut.

"You're not leaving this compound." I spin around and take a swing. Hammer ducks to the side and my punch goes wild. I trip over my own feet and have to do a shuffle to avoid falling to the ground.

"What the actual fuck, man? You can't fucking stop me from going to find my woman," I roar.

"Yes, I actually fucking can. I'm the Sergeant-at-Arms and it's my job to protect the members of this club. And yes, that includes you right now." He crosses his arms and taps the title badge on his cut. "My badge. My rules."

"But I'm the President. I overrule your rules." I mirror his position and stare him down.

"Not if I say you don't." This comes from Mountain, who's coming up behind Hammer. "I gave you your title. I can and will take it back just as fucking fast. Do not question him again. Hammer is now in charge until we get Duchess back. Do I make myself clear?"

"Fine." I'm put in my place for the second time and I don't like it one damn bit. "So, what do you suggest I do then, huh? Sit around and twiddle my thumbs?"

"First, we all go back inside and lock down the clubhouse. No one in or out. Then, we go in Church and catch everyone up." Hammer turns and looks at Pops. "That good with you?"

"Good plan. Call everyone back in." Mountain turns and heads back through the trees. He's not moving as fast this time and I see him watching the ground. Whoever thought it was a good idea for a man with a prosthetic leg to go traipsing in the woods was damn crazy. I should tell Blue on him. It would serve him right.

"Nothing out there," Trooper says as he and Sam come back through the fence. "But we do need to get this fence closed up. "Sam, run back up and find Wrench and Wrecker. They'll know what's needed."

"Let's get you inside." Hammer grabs my arm and pushes me to walk in front of him,

This time, I keep my hands to myself and my mouth shut. The guys are probably right. I need to put all my focus on Duchess and let my Brothers do what they need to do. We all have our jobs and titles for a reason.

I step back into the clubhouse and Cypher hands me Duchess's phone. I wake up the screen and see a picture of myself. It's my profile as I'm sitting at my desk. She must have snuck this picture when we were in my office the other day. Seeing myself on her phone makes me smile. Maybe she is ready to be my Old Lady. We never got to have that talk this morning.

"CHURCH IN TEN MINUTES!" Hammer yells and everyone heads off in different directions.

I jog up the stairs and shut myself in my room. I lean back against the door and inhale for what feels like the first time today. My head is starting to spin and my heart is beating too fast again. Making my way to the closet, I pull a box down from the top shelf. Sitting on the end of my bed, I place the box in my lap. Just holding it is helping me calm down.

I take the lid off and pull the leather out, letting the box fall to the floor. I hold up the cut and look at the new patches I had sewn on the back. I really hope I can give this to her soon. I stand up, open the closet, and hang it inside on an empty hanger.

When Duchess gets back, I'll give this to her.

She will have her cut.

She will be mine forever.

"Am I allowed to sit in my own chair, or is that for you today?" I snap at Hammer.

"Sit the fuck down and shut up," Brick snaps and slams the door behind Cypher. "Grow the fuck up and listen to what you're told for once."

"Let's get this show on the road." I slam the gavel, plop down in my chair, and wait for someone to start talking.

"I guess I'll start," Cypher pipes up from the left side of the room. He stands up and plugs his laptop into the wall. "I scanned through the footage starting from last night. It shows a van driving by, the first time about three this morning. It then came by again five minutes after your call from Duchess." He looks directly at me and I can tell there's something he isn't saying.

"What else?" I ask him.

"What do you mean?"

"There's something you aren't telling me and I wanna know what the fuck it is. Tell me right now, Cypher." I spin my chair fully around and face him.

"I switched to another camera angle and it shows them driving away."

"You have footage of them taking her? Why the hell didn't you start with that? Let's see it," I demand.

"I don't know—"

I cut him off. "Show me the goddamn footage!"

Cypher puts his laptop in front of me and Hammer and I scoot closer. He pushes play and I see the road that runs alongside the compound fence. A van drives in from the left and comes to a stop, then two men come walking out of the woods and one of them is carrying something over his shoulder.

"That's her!" I point at the screen.

The footage continues to show them opening the side door, laying her in the back, climbing in, and driving away.

He reaches forward to hit the space bar and the screen goes black. "I got a shot of the plates, so I have my programs running to see if it shows up again. Once I get an alert, I'll let you know. Until then, I don't have anything else."

"Nothing else? What the fuck do you mean, you have nothing else?" I yell.

"Whiskey, that's enough. Thank you, Cypher," Hammer says and pats him on the shoulder. "I want to set up some search parties. We'll do rotating groups and ride in different directions. But nobody goes out alone or for very long."

"I'm going out."

"No, you are not," Mountain barks. "You will stay here if I have to sit on you my damn self."

"Fine! If you all think you can run this damn club better than I can, you go for it. But let me make something perfectly clear first. From now on, Duchess is my Old Lady. That now makes her your responsibility as well, so you will find her. I'll stay here and wait and bug you all until she's back in my arms. Get fucking moving!" I slam the gavel again and get up, walking out of Church and heading straight for the bar.

I grab three beers from the cooler and get comfortable on a bar stool.

I'll be the first and last thing people see when they come in and out from their search rides, and I'm not leaving the main room until she's back home.

CHAPTER TWENTY-EIGHT

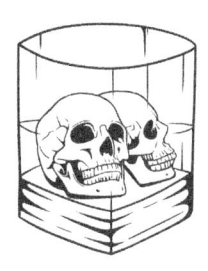

WHISKEY

"WAKE UP, EVERYONE! WAKE THE FUCK UP!"

Why the hell does it seem like everyone is yelling around here all the time? Can't a guy get a decent night's sleep?

"Whiskey, wake up. I found the van."

That makes me wake up, alright. I jump up and stumble as I almost fall off the side of the couch. Getting to my feet, I look around to see Cypher standing next to the bar. "Where is it? Do you know where Duchess is?" I get up in his face.

"I don't know if she's there for sure, but it would be the first place I'd look." Cypher doesn't even flinch with me all up in his personal space. He backs away and walks toward one of the dining tables. He puts his laptop down and drops into one of the chairs. He flips open the lid and starts typing away.

"Where's the van? And where do you think she is?" I pull out the chair at the head of the table and spin it around before straddling it.

"Remember the trail parking lot where we found the burned van? That's where I have footage of it driving past." Cypher is still typing away. Apparently, the kid is very good at multitasking. He's only twenty-one years old, and he showed up one day with Buzz and has been here ever since. Lately, I think this club would be lost without him. No one else here knows how to do any of this techy stuff.

"Show me whatchya got."

He spins the screen my way and I'm watching a van pulling into the parking lot. It parks, a guy climbs out, and then he walks off into the woods.

"Can I ask where you got this footage?" I look at Cypher with a raised eyebrow.

"You can ask, but I don't know if you really wanna know the answer." He smirks back, then pulls the laptop in front of him and starts typing again. "If you didn't like me having that, maybe you shouldn't watch how I'm getting what I'm gonna show you next."

"At this point, I don't care how you get what you get. As long as it brings my lady home, I'll turn a blind eye." I sit back and wait for whatever is next.

"What's going on, guys?" Ring asks as he walks over. Behind him are Hammer, Kraken, Brewer, and Trooper.

I look around and notice the room is filling with all my Brothers. Some of them already have Old Ladies, most of them don't, but they've all supported me from the start of this craziness. We are definitely stronger together.

"Cypher found the van that took Duchess. It's in the same parking lot where we found the other van," I explain to everyone.

"And this is where I think she's being held." Cypher spins the screen around again and this time I see a satellite image of a small cabin. It's in the middle of a small clearing surrounded by a forest of endless trees. There's one truck parked next to the cabin, but other than that, it looks deserted.

"Why do you think she's there?" Hammer asks.

"First, this cabin is only about a half-mile from where the van is parked. Second, when the guy walked away from the van, he walked in this direction." He draws an imaginary line on the screen, from the parking lot to the cabin. "And lastly, because we need to start looking somewhere. We'll never find her if we don't start fucking looking." His voice gets sharper and angrier the more he says. He's taking this very seriously and I couldn't be more thankful.

"Thank you, Cypher."

"No need to thank me, Prez. This is my job." Cypher goes back to his computer. "It's daylight now, so I wouldn't suggest we go balls out and rush in there now. But I do think a ride by couldn't hurt. Maybe you can see something I can't get from the one camera view. And I need to get off this satellite before I get caught."

"Do what you need to do on your end." I swing out of my chair and turn to face the group behind me. "Trooper, Hammer, and Cypher, I need the three of you to ride out with me. We'll ride by only one time, so keep your eyes peeled. Grab what you need and we leave in five. Oh, and wear a coat over your cuts. We don't need them seeing us and realizing who we are." We never ride without showing our patches, but today is definitely an exception.

I run up to my room to change out of yesterday's clothes. I ended up falling asleep on the couch last night because I couldn't be in my bed without Duchess. Actually, now it's our bed. She's my Old Lady and everything I have is now ours. I grab my keys off the dresser, loop my knife through my belt, and pull out my Carhartt jacket, then head back downstairs.

I head out to my bike, climb on, and fire her up. Three more motorcycles start to rumble and we roll toward the front gate. Sam is standing there and he pushes it open just wide enough for us to get out in a single file line.

The first few miles are pretty smooth sailing, but as we get closer, Hammer raises his fist and we slow our speed just a bit. The parking lot comes up on our right and I see a black van backed into a spot at the back of the lot. If you were going by at full speed, you definitely would've missed it.

We continue down the road a bit and notice a gravel driveway almost hidden in the trees. If it weren't for the mailbox and the approach, it would be invisible. I look over to Cypher and he nods back at me. He must see what I do. There's one truck, like the satellite showed, but now there are two guys standing in the yard. They don't even bother looking up when we roll past.

Another few miles down the road, we hang a left and start our ride back to the clubhouse. We can go around this block and not have to ride past the cabin again, so we won't draw any unnecessary attention to us.

The gate rolls open as we pull up and we ride back in the same way we left.

I park my Harley and shut it down. I climb off and start pacing back and forth across the parking lot, finding myself in front of the fence, and I kick it in frustration.

"AAAAAHHHHHHHH!" I scream out loud and then kick the fence again.

"You alright, man?" I spin around to see Hammer standing with his hands tucked in his coat pockets.

"Am I alright? Are you seriously asking me that?" I'm beyond fucking pissed right now. "No! I am not ALRIGHT! We just rode past some dumpy ass fucking cabin in the middle of the woods and my woman could have been inside it. But all I could do was pretend like I didn't even see it. I'm not gonna be okay until she's back home. How the fuck do you think I'm feeling?"

Hammer loses his shit right back at me. "I know exactly what it's like to lose my girl. Don't forget that Wings is still missing too," he hollers back in my face.

"Well, maybe if you would've claimed her, she wouldn't have left your ass! She left here because of you," I yell back. "But no, all you did was fuck her every night and not make her your Old Lady!"

Punch. Before I know it, I'm lying on the ground and Hammer is on top of me, throwing more punches. I swing back a few times, but before I can get in any good hits, Hammer is pulled backward.

"Knock it the fuck off." Gunner has Hammer by the hood of his coat and I quickly jump up. "We're not babies having a scuffle at the playground. You're grown ass men who need to put your dicks away and come inside."

"Whatever. Let's go." Hammer heads inside and I look over at Gunner.

"You good, Whiskey?"

"Yeah. Thanks for that." I hold out a fist and he bumps me back.

I head straight for Church when I get inside and park my ass in my chair. I don't even bother calling for a meeting, but I don't have to wait long for everyone to follow.

Brick shuts the doors, so I pick up my gavel and slam it down on the table. I look at Hammer and we settle our scuffle with just a nod at each other.

Trooper raises his hand and starts the conversation. "Based on what we saw, I agree with Cypher's earlier statement. We shouldn't go in there during the daytime. We can go back after it gets dark and kick in some doors. If we park at that lot, we can walk through the woods and surround the clearing. That way, we can see trouble from all directions and have an eye on their van."

"I like that idea. Just make sure we don't go crazy and shoot each other," Doc says and the room erupts in laughter. "I don't need to be digging slugs out of any of your asses."

When the laughter dies down, everyone turns and looks at me. I guess I have the final say here.

"Sounds good to me. If anyone needs anything, get with Hammer." I look at him and point. "You're in charge tonight. If we find Duchess in that cabin, I'll be one hundred percent focused on her."

"You got it," Hammer replies. "Cypher, can you put a copy of the satellite image up on the screen? We need everyone to see it so we can set up a perimeter."

"Let me go grab my laptop. It's just by our phones." He jumps up and is back in no time.

Cypher heads to the plug behind me and we all turn to look at the screen that's still down from the other day. Someone turns the lights off and the screen comes to life with an overhead view showing the cabin, the parking lot, and the space in between.

"This is where we'll park." He points to the right side of the screen. "And this is the area we need to surround."

"Everyone split up with your Enforcer teams. We'll go in that way. Ring, Trooper, Wrench, and Gunner will each take a direction. Four teams for the four sides of the cabin. Ring, take the front. Trooper, to the left. Wrench, take the right. Gunner, come in from the back. We only saw one door on the front, so we don't have a count on windows or any other ways in. Once we get the clearing surrounded, look for your wall and act accordingly. Any questions?" Hammer is in full leader mode.

Buzz raises his hand. "Are we shooting to kill any bad guys we find?"

"Let's try and not kill if we don't have to. We need them alive to ask questions," Hammer chuckles.

"Awww, man. I'll try my best." Buzz folds his arms and pouts like a toddler who got his toy taken away.

"Any more real questions?" Hammer asks as he throws a crumpled-up piece of paper at Buzz.

"We need to vote on this, Brothers." I lean forward and brace my elbows on the table. "All in favor of going in to kick some ass and hopefully find my Old Lady, say aye."

"AYE!" comes from around the room in a resounding boom.

"Anyone opposed?"

And everyone is deathly silent.

"That's a full pass," I say and slam the gavel down. The wood hitting wood makes a thunder-loud crack and I look down to make sure nothing really broke.

"Meeting adjourned?" Hammer asks me.

"Yup. Meeting adjourned." And I slam the gavel again.

Time to get ready to bring my woman home.

CHAPTER TWENTY-NINE

DUCHESS

I roll over and start counting the boards on the ceiling again. That's all I seem to be doing today. There are forty-seven boards. Forty-seven. That number is going to be ingrained in my mind for a long time.

I'm not exactly sure how long I've been here. Based on the amount of times the guys have come in to try and feed me, this is the second day. I still haven't eaten anything they've given me, but I have taken the soda bottles and dumped them out to fill with water from the bathroom sink. I'm hungry and my stomach is starting to gurgle, but the water is helping some. Thank goodness the bathroom has toilet paper and the chain attached to my wrist is long enough that I can reach the toilet.

I go to the bathroom, and just as I'm done, the bedroom door swings out. A man I've never seen before walks in with another plastic bag.

"Why the hell aren't you eating? Do you want to starve yourself?" he snarls. This guy is not in a good mood. The look on his face is unfriendly and hateful.

"I'm not hungry." I have to walk past him to get to the mattress and I almost make it. My ankle is still super swollen, so I'm more limping than walking.

He grabs me by the bicep and pulls me in to his chest. "You will eat tonight if I have to force it down your throat. You need to be healthy for your buyer." He lets go of my arm and I try to back up, but he slaps me across the face and I fall backward again onto the mattress. But this time, I don't hurt my ankle.

BOOM! Something crashes out in the main part of the house.

BANG! That sounded like a gunshot. The guy runs out of the room, and I try to get up and make it to the door, but it slams shut in my face at the last second. The clank happens again and I sag against the wood floor. I really wish the door opened in. Maybe I could get it open somehow. No matter how hard I try to push it open, the door doesn't budge.

BANG! That was another shot. I move away from the door and just listen.

There's some rustling and yelling, so I make my way into the bathroom. I hope the uninvited guests are friendly, but

I can't be too careful. I try to climb into the bathtub but realize there's no easy way to do it with one bad leg. I sit on the edge and slide down into the tub, pulling the curtain closed and waiting for I'm not exactly sure what.

The house instantly becomes deathly quiet.

"DUCHESS!" I hear someone yell. "ARE YOU HERE?" It's Whiskey.

I open my mouth to answer him back, but nothing comes out. I try to shove the curtain out of my way, but end up pulling the whole rod down. It makes a loud clatter and I can hear more voices talking. I can't tell what they're saying, but I'm glad they haven't left without me.

I climb out of the tub on my hands and knees and flop down onto the floor when I knock my ankle against the edge. I let out a scream and the talking stops.

Someone starts knocking on the bedroom door and I call out with a sob, "I'm in here."

"I'm coming, baby. Just hold on for me," Whiskey says through the wood.

"Back up, Whiskey. I can get it open," offers a voice I don't recognize.

I hear a bunch of different sounds as I start to crawl out of the bathroom. Just as I make it into the bedroom, the door disappears and Whiskey walks in with his gun drawn. I look up at him, my arms give out, and I immediately crumple to the floor.

"Shit. Take this." Whiskey drops down next to me and pulls me into his arms. I cry out when his hand accidently hits my ankle. The chain also gets in his way. "What is this? Get this off her. NOW!"

I'm numb. I look up at Whiskey and can feel my vision start to fade. "Connor," I whisper.

"I'm here, baby." He kisses my forehead.

"My ankle hurts" is all I get out before the darkness takes over.

CHAPTER THIRTY

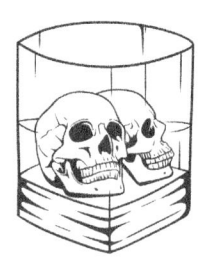

WHISKEY

The sun finally set about an hour ago, so the sky is now pitch black. The main room is a flurry of activity as my Brothers finish getting themselves ready to head out.

A few of them are saying goodbye to their women and kids, and I have to look away. They all know the risk of leaving on this mission, but thinking that this might be the last time they see their families hits me hard for the first time. Is this what Duchess is going to feel when I leave the clubhouse on a run, or when we have to go rescue someone else? I shake my head and snap out of that thought really quick. I can't be thinking like that. This is my club and we will all make it back in one piece. And the next time I do leave this compound, she'll be here to say 'see you later' and welcome me home.

"Time to ride, Brothers," Hammer shouts and everyone starts to file out the front doors.

"Son." I turn and see my Pops standing there with his arms around Blue. Her face is buried in his chest, her arms around his waist, and it looks like she has a death grip on him. "I'm gonna stay here with the ladies. Is that alright with you?"

I'm not really sure what's going on with them, but it looks like Blue needs Mountain more than I do right now. "That's fine." I tilt my head to the side, silently asking if everything is okay. He nods his head and leads her toward the couches.

I look around the room to figure out who will drive the van now in case we need it. I see two of the Prospects standing just outside the front doors.

"Sam and Jacob," I bark out.

They spin around. "Yes, Whiskey?" Jacob answers.

"You two are on van duty. Mountain is staying behind, so you're both going with Doc. I don't care who drives, but you do whatever he tells you to. Do I make myself clear?"

"We got it." Jacob turns and shoves Sam out the door.

I follow and head over to my bike. The parking lot comes to life with the rumble of all my Brothers' Harleys. I raise my fist and they all do the same. The gate rolls open and we start filing out two by two, me leading the way with Hammer to my right.

When we make the last curve before the parking lot, everyone shuts off their headlights and we coast into the lot. The van comes in last and parks right at the end by the road. I see Sam jump out of the driver's seat, gives me a nod, and stands guard to watch. Everyone else meets in the middle and waits for instructions. The other van is also in the lot, but it's tucked toward the back edge. There's no way it could get out of here even if someone tried.

"Team up and let's go. Wait for my signal and then we all go in at once," Hammer whisper-shouts and everyone heads off in the same general direction.

Walking through these woods in the dark isn't the easiest thing to do, but luckily, tonight we have a full moon. A majority of the leaves have fallen from the trees, so the bare branches are letting in just enough light for us to see where we're going. Also, the damp leaves are providing pretty good ground cover to hide the sound of our footsteps.

We finally reach the edge of the woods and the cabin comes into view. Everyone stays back a few feet as the other groups spread out to their assigned sides. I see that the cabin has a door and one window on the front, and two windows on the right side. All the windows I can see are boarded over, so I guess we'll all be going in the front door. The truck we saw when we drove by earlier is gone, so I'm wondering if anyone is even here.

The team I've included myself in is Ring, Hammer, Brewer, Wrecker, Cypher, and the Prospect, Jacob. I see a quick flash of light from the other three directions and as soon as Hammer flicks on his flashlight, everyone starts moving at once, their guns up as we jog toward the cabin.

Hammer makes it to the front door first and kicks it down at a full run. The door busts off the hinges and makes a loud *BOOM* as it hits the floor flat.

Someone runs out of a room from the left and Ring is the first to fire. *BANG!* The bullet hits the guy's chest and he goes down face first.

I look at Ring and he just shrugs it off. "It was him or one of us."

"Watch out!" someone yells and I turn to see someone coming out of the back hallway with a gun raised, pointed straight at me. My gun is still up, so I turn a few inches to the left and pull the trigger. *BANG!*

The bullet enters the middle of his chest, but he's still moving toward me. Wrecker barrels into him from the side and knocks the both of them to the floor. There's a bunch of yelling and rustling, but finally there's a crack and silence. No one moves a muscle.

"DUCHESS!" I yell out. "ARE YOU HERE?" Hopefully, she's somewhere in this cabin.

I head down the hall and start opening doors. There's a kitchen to the left, a bedroom on the right, followed by a closet and a bathroom on the right.

I hear a small squeak and freeze where I stand. I think it came from the door at the very end of the hall. Brightness fills the hall and I turn back to see Brewer and Jacob behind me. Someone must have found the light switch.

I walk forward the last few steps and start pounding my fist on the closed bedroom door. I hear a voice on the inside call out, "I'm in here."

"I'm coming, baby. Just hold on for me," I yell into the door. I go to grab the handle and realize it's locked and there's a metal bar laying across the door frame. Brackets are bolted to each side and the bar is barricading the door from swinging open.

"Back up, Whiskey. I can get it open." Jacob appears next to me with a screwdriver in his hand. I back up to let him around me and am stunned silent to see him take over. He lifts the bar and drops it to the left, then uses the flathead and pries the pins up and out of the door hinges. When he has all three removed, he grabs the door handle, pulls hard, and the wood panel falls toward us. Jacob grabs ahold of the sides and picks it up, moving it to the right.

I lift my gun back up and slowly step into the room. There's a light coming from the left side, so I turn that way first. Looking down, I see my Duchess crawling out of a bathroom on her hands and knees. She looks up at me, and as soon as we lock eyes, her arms start to buckle and she crashes to the floor.

I realize I'm still holding my gun up, but I don't even bother putting it back in my holster. "Shit. Take this." I hold my hand out and someone grabs my gun. I don't know who, and right now, I really don't fucking care. I fall to my knees next to Duchess and pull her into my lap. She cries out when I move her legs to the side. I feel something cold rubbing against my arm and that's when I realize she has a cuff and chain around her left wrist. "What is this? Get this off of her. NOW!"

I look down at her and she's blinking really slowly. "Connor," she mumbles. I love when she says my real name.

"I'm here, baby." I lean forward and drop a soft kiss on her forehead.

"My ankle hurts." She whispers before her eyes roll back and she passes out.

"Duchess." I shake her and try to get her to wake back up. "Wake up, baby." I shake her a little harder, but still no response, so I lower my ear to her face and can hear her breathing. Holy fuck, that was scary.

"Let me get this off her arm." Trooper drops to his knees beside me and uses a key to unlock the cuff from her wrist.

"DOC!" someone yells and takes off running as I stand up with her still in my arms. I take off down the hall and everyone moves out of my way. Doc and I almost collide in the living room when he comes running through the front door.

"Let's get her to the van," Doc says and leads the way outside. I walk forward and notice someone has pulled the club van into the clearing. Doc opens the back doors, climbs in, and reaches out his arms. "Give her to me."

"I got her," I snap back and try to climb in with her still in my arms, but I can't lift my leg high enough and Doc raises an eyebrow at me.

"I need to look her over, Whiskey. Hand her over so I can do my job," Doc snarls at me. He reaches forward, loops his arms under her body, and lifts her right out of my grasp. He turns and lowers her to a mat on the van floor. I try to climb in but he turns back my way. "No. You cannot be in here. There's not enough room." He immediately goes back to Duchess. I'm not really sure what he's doing to her, but he's touching her a lot more than I would normally be okay with.

"Whiskey." A hand drops onto my shoulder and I turn to see Hammer standing next to me. "You can't ride back with them. You have your bike in the parking lot and we can't leave it behind."

"But I need to be with her." I point into the van.

"I can ride it back if you need me to." Both Hammer and I turn around to see Jacob standing behind us. He has his hands crammed in his pockets, and I can tell he's trying to stand up tall and prove he can handle anything. He surprisingly has been very helpful tonight. And it takes some serious balls to offer to ride the President's bike. That's something that is never done.

I get as close to him as our boots and chests will allow. I'm all up in his business. "Do not make me regret this, Prospect. If you wreck my bike, your ass will go up in smoke."

"Yes, Whiskey," he replies.

I pull the keys from my pocket and hand them over. He grabs them and jogs off into the trees.

"You sure that was a good idea?" Hammer asks with a chuckle.

"I'm not sure I care right now. It makes it back in one piece, he'll be one step closer to earning his patch."

"Quit your yammering and shut those damn doors. We need to get moving," Doc hollers.

"I'll ride up front." I shut the doors and jog to the passenger side. I jump in, Sam puts the van in drive, and we pull out onto the road and are on our way home.

The ride is even quicker than normal and we're back at the clubhouse in no time.

I jump out as soon as we stop moving and roll the side door open. Before Doc can even speak, I pick up my lady and take off. The doors are still open, so nothing is in my way.

I notice the main room is empty and I head straight toward the room where we hold Church. Doc is hot on my tail and he gets around in front of me, pushes a few chairs out of the way, and points at the table. "Lay her down softly. She has a pretty good bump on the back of her head."

I lower her to the table top and cradle her head in my left hand. Doc tries to push me out of the way, but I hip check him back. "I'm not leaving her."

He turns and growls in my face. "If you don't get out of my way, I'll have someone come in here and force you out of the room."

"Whiskey, let the guy do his work." Pops is at my side with a folded towel. I lift her head just enough for him to slide it under my hand, then I turn her head to the side and lower her cheek onto the towel. "I'll get out of your hair."

"Thanks, Pops." I back away but only go and sit on the other side. Grabbing ahold of her left hand, I kiss her knuckles and close my eyes. I stay out of Doc's way and hope he has good news fast.

"What's the word, Doc?"

"Other than the goose egg, her right ankle is swollen. Nothing feels broken, so my guess is it's just sprained."

"You guess? What kind of answer is that?"

"Without an x-ray, I have no way of seeing her bones. Do you wanna take her to the E.R.?"

He's got a point. That's drama we don't need right now. "Not unless we need to. Why isn't she waking up yet?"

"She's probably exhausted. We don't know what went on before we got there, and she might have a small concussion. Let me check her pupils again." He uses a tiny flashlight and shines it in both of her eyes. "They're both responsive, so I'm gonna say no on the concussion."

"Uhnnnn," Duchess groans and we both freeze.

"Baby, can you hear me?" I jump up and get close to her face.

"Back up, man. Let me do my thing," Doc replies.

I back up again and go back to the chair.

"Duchess, can you hear me, honey?"

"Connor?" She finally starts to blink and move her head.

"No. It's me, Doc. Can you understand me?"

"Yea. It's too bright," she whispers.

Doc steps back, hits one of the light switches, and half the room goes dark. "Is that better?"

"Yea."

"Good. Can you open your eyes and look at me?" Doc asks.

She nods and slowly her eyes open all the way.

"There you are, Duchess. I've been waiting to see your beautiful blue eyes." I grab her hand again and lightly squeeze.

She turns and looks at me. "Whiskey, I missed you."

"Hi," I whisper and lean forward to kiss her lips.

"Hi." She kisses me back.

"I hate to ruin your moment, but I need a few minutes to talk to our patient here," Doc interjects.

I don't take my eyes off my woman. "I'll be right over in my chair. Is that okay?"

"Don't go too far, please," she says with a small tremble.

"Never too far, baby." I kiss her one more time and go sit in my chair at the head of the table. I'm far enough away to be out of earshot but not too far to be able to get to her side in a hurry.

Doc and Duchess whisper a few things back and forth for a few minutes. He takes her blood pressure and checks her pulse, looks at both of her wrists, and then starts running his fingers around her sore ankle. I see her flinch a few times, but I force myself to stay in my seat, folding my hands to avoid punching Doc in the face. He's causing my woman pain and I don't like it.

"Alright. You can come back now, Whiskey." Doc looks at me and I jump out of my chair.

"What's the news, Doc?" I stand next to the table, all of a sudden afraid to touch her until I know what's wrong.

"I'm still saying no to the concussion, but my guess is she passed out because of what we call psychogenic shock."

"Big words there, Doc. Speak for the dumb person in the room."

"Psychogenic shock is the technical term for the body's way of shutting down after a stressful situation. When your pulse increases but your blood pressure drops, the brain doesn't know what to do. That caused her to pass out. It's fancy talk for the body's way to shut off and reboot."

"What do I do now?" Duchess asks.

"You need to get rest for a few days. For at least tonight, I don't want you to use a pillow. Your body needs to restore normal blood flow. And for your ankle, I'll wrap it in a bandage and you need to keep it elevated. I'll come see you again in the morning and we'll go from there. Sound good to everyone?" He makes eye contact and speaks directly at me.

"Sounds good. I got her." I look down at her. "You ready to head up to our room, Duchess?"

"Yes, please. I need our bed."

"Let's get you upstairs." I scoop her up again, trying to be as gentle as my rough and tumble arms possibly can. I'm not usually known for being soft or delicate.

I head out into the main room, and unlike when we walked in, the room is now packed to the gills. It's super crowded and looks like everyone has just been waiting for us to come out.

"Whiskey?" Stiletto slides off a bar stool and rushes to my side. "Is she okay? Is there anything I can do? Does she need anything?"

I appreciate her asking, but I just need to get Duchess up to our room. "Thank you for offering, but I got this."

Raquel appears next to us. "If she needs something, just let us know."

Duchess turns her head toward the girls and whispers, "Thank you."

I start walking again and more people try to stop me, but I ignore everyone and keep going. Duchess is my priority. She'll be my only focus for the rest of the night.

CHAPTER THIRTY-ONE

DUCHESS

"Whiskey," I full out whine. "You need to let me out of this bed. I'm going crazy in here." It's been two days and I have to see something other than these four walls. "It's like you have me in jail up here."

"I don't think so, little lady. Doc said you still need to stay off your ankle," he yells from the bathroom.

"I can keep my leg up on a couch down in the main room," I sass back.

He comes out of the bathroom and crosses his arms. He's trying to look mean and intimidating, but all I see is sex on a stick. Yum.

"I know you wanna go downstairs, but we have some things to talk about first." He comes over to the bed and sits down next to me. He slides back against the headboard and grabs ahold of my hands. "We need to talk about what happened while you were gone."

I knew this talk was coming, but I really didn't know how long he was going to wait to bring it up.

"Can you tell me what happened? Start from the beginning?" he asks.

"I went downstairs to get coffee and went outside to get some fresh air."

"We found your mug out on the picnic table. That was our first clue that something was wrong. Then Ring saw your truck."

"Yea, I noticed it was sitting at a funny angle, so I ran over to look at it. I pulled out my phone and called you. I heard you answer, but that's all I remember." I pull my hands from his and tug the blanket up higher over my legs. "When I woke up in that room, I was so scared."

"Oh, baby." Whiskey wraps an arm around my shoulders and pulls me close.

"I had to calm myself down. I knew you would find me and I needed to be strong."

"What happened next?"

"This dirty, gross guy came into the room to tell me that someone had bought me." I tell him what the man said about taking Tempy and how I was supposed to stay untouched for my buyer.

"He didn't do anything inappropriate to you, did he?" Whiskey pulls back and grabs my hands again. "If he did,

I'll go back there and kill him again." His eyes are wide open and on fire.

"No, no, no. He didn't do anything but grab my arms and kick my ankle."

"Phew." His shoulders slump and he lets out a deep breath. "What did he look like? The guy who talked to you?"

"He had long black hair. His clothes were dirty and torn up, and he smelled like he hadn't showered in way too long. And he was a little older, maybe forty something."

"That doesn't match either of the guys who were there when we found you. They were both younger and had short hair."

"He was talking like he was the one in charge. He kept saying 'my' everything. My club. My brothers. It was kind of annoying. He said something about a squad and how his brothers were disappearing."

Something I just said makes him jump out of bed and start pacing. "Squad? Like Chaos Squad?"

"That's it! He said it was his club. I think he's their leader."

"Did he tell you his name?" He places his hands down on the bed and his face is an inch from mine.

Okay, now I'm freaked out. "Yes."

"What was it?" he asks with a growly whisper.

"Bullet."

Whiskey stands up, grabs his pillow, and throws it across the room. It flies into the bathroom and something crashes on the counter. "Son of a fucking bitch!" he shouts.

I scramble across the bed and sit right on the end. "Who is he?"

"He's no one important." The pacing starts again and he starts mumbling to himself.

"It obviously is important if this is how you react to just his name. I need to know who had me taken." This must be a very big deal.

"Fine." He sits down next to me again and leans his elbows on his knees. "We heard that name from the guy who tried to take Stiletto. He mentioned that Bullet was the one calling all the shots and he was just doing what he was told. He must have left before we got there."

"I only saw him the one time. He came in to check on his merchandise."

"Shit." He drags his hands through his hair and ties the long pieces back.

"It's okay now. I'm here. I'm back with you." I try to calm him down, but really have no idea what to do. If I thought him getting angry at a snarky club girl was scary, this is a whole other level.

Knock knock. "Go away." *Knock knock*. Someone is determined to get our attention. Whiskey gets up and swings the door open. "What do you want? Damnit, Blue, I'm sorry."

"Go downstairs, Whiskey." Blue comes in the room.

"Not happening. I'm not leaving her."

"Connor, do not make me pull my aunt card and kick your ass. Get your ass downstairs right damn now!" She barks the last few words.

"Fine. Make sure her foot stays elevated." He grabs my chin and tips my face up to him, then his mouth comes down to mine and he devours me whole. This is not a gentle kiss by any means. This is a kiss that tells me he's in charge and I'm supposed to just take it. His lips are demanding and all consuming, and we're practically sucking each other's face as he plunges his tongue into my mouth. He finally lets me come up for air and drops one last kiss on my forehead. "Do not let her get out of that bed." The door slams and he's gone.

I scoot back to my side of the bed and put my ankle back up on the pillow. "Is everything okay, Blue?"

"I should be asking you that question." She pulls out the desk chair and drags it next to my side of the bed, then she sits down and kicks her feet up on the mattress.

"Make yourself comfortable, why dontchya?" I laugh.

"Might as well get comfy. I came up here to keep you company and get Whiskey out of the room. He's been ignoring every text he's been sent, and everyone is wondering what's going to happen next."

"He probably put his phone on silent. I haven't heard it go off since we got back."

"Damn stubborn boy. He's just as headstrong now as he was back when I came to live here. You should have seen him as a ten-year-old boy. Connor was surly and angry at me for months. After what his mother pulled, he didn't trust women and thought I was taking his Pops away from him."

"He hasn't told me a lot about her, but I get the gist of it."

"Yea. Roxy sure didn't know what she gave up." Blue puts her feet back on the floor. "But enough about the past. Tell me how you're feeling now."

"I'm honestly not really sure yet. I don't think it has kicked in fully. I haven't even cried. I keep waiting to snap and freak out."

"I get that. I had no idea what I was getting into when I came here."

"How did you do it? I mean, get used to everything bad that happens here?"

"The truth?"

"Please."

"Mountain didn't give me the opportunity to leave. He told me that once he claimed me, I was his forever. I agreed to be his Old Lady after being here for only three days."

"Three days? Are you serious?" I came to the clubhouse after only three days. We met on a Friday and I was here that Monday. Three days. Wow.

"Yup. Now, do you think you have what it takes to be a President's Old Lady?"

"Don't hold back any punches, would ya?" She's going for the jugular.

"I'm being serious. Can you love Whiskey even though he does bad things? Are you strong enough to be what he needs when he's having a bad day? He may be this club's leader, but he'll have some off days here and there. And what about when he can't tell you things that happen to him? He can't share everything with you, and you'll have to learn to accept that."

"That's a lot. I don't know what question to answer first." I stare straight ahead and try to sort the multiple things buzzing in my mind.

"I didn't mean to bombard you with everything at once. I'm sorry for that. I just want you to think about what staying here means for you. And for Whiskey too. If you can love him as much as I think he does you, you'll be just fine. I see a lot of Jethro in him, and trust me, that's a very good thing." Blue winks, stands up, kisses my cheek, and leaves me to my thoughts.

CHAPTER THIRTY-TWO

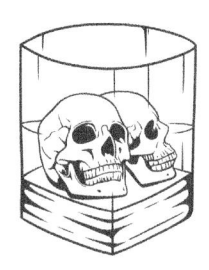

WHISKEY

I drop a kiss on her forehead and give Blue one last warning. "Do not let her get out of that bed." I grab my cut off the hook and am out the door.

If they're going to kick me out of my room, I might as well take the time to fill the guys in on what I just learned.

Bullet is the one who took Wings and Duchess.

Fuck.

Before I even reach the last step, I'm calling out for my Brothers. "Anyone here, Church, now. Call everyone else in." I drop my phone in the lockbox and don't stop my stride until I get to my chair. I lean back in my seat and close my eyes to collect my thoughts. How did this happen? What did we do to piss these assholes off?

I listen to the shuffle of boots and chairs for a few minutes, then sit up and look around the room. We're missing a few guys who are working off property, but due to us still being on lockdown, the majority are here.

"What's up, son?" Mountain asks from the far end of the table.

"I just got kicked out of my bedroom by your wife." I stare him down, trying to convey my unhappiness about it.

"She probably had a good reason for it." He leans back in his chair, crosses his arms, and looks way too happy with himself.

"She threatened to beat me up, so who fucking knows. Girl talk or some bullshit." I shake my head and that gets a chuckle from the room.

"You wanted an Old Lady, so you have to deal with the consequences," Brick comments back.

"Yea yea, mister lifelong bachelor. Enough of the chit chat. We've got a problem." I crack my knuckles and ball my fists. "It seems Bullet has made an appearance."

"Bullet?" Hammer pounds a fist on the table. "Like the name we got from that dumbass Loony? He was telling the truth?"

I nod and get down to the brass tacks. "I finally talked to Duchess about what happened when she was at that cabin. She said Bullet was the first person she saw. He told her his name after telling her she had been sold to someone. Based on her description of him, he wasn't one of the two men we encountered when we got there. He apparently has long black hair and is super dirty."

"We must not have missed him by long, because that truck was still on the satellite image just before it went dark," Cypher growls.

"He probably used the darkness as a cover to leave undetected," Ring interjects. "It's basically what we did."

"My thought exactly. Cypher, I know we haven't gotten anything yet, but can you search the name? It's not really anything, but a name is better than nothing."

He wiggles in his chair and looks ready to run to his computers. "I'll get right on it when I'm out of here."

"One last thing, then you can go. Duchess said Bullet admitted to taking Wings too, so now we know for sure she was taken. He said she had a buyer, but she didn't see her at the cabin."

That news causes Hammer to pound the table again and he stands up so fast, his chair tips over. He stomps out of the room and doesn't even bother shutting the door.

Jacob peeks his head in the doorway. "Need me to shut this, Whiskey?"

"It's fine. Meeting's over anyway." I slam the gavel and the room slowly empties. The bombs I just dropped have really put an even bigger damper on our already shitty situation. I'm not paying much attention to anything until the door shuts, and I look up and see my Pops is still in the room.

"What do you need, Pops? I don't know if I have anything to give right now." I'm lost on what to do next.

"Is Kiana who you want for your Old Lady?" he asks and props himself against the table.

"Hell yes, she is. I already made my announcement to the club. What kind of fucking stupid question is that?"

"Then you need to man the fuck up and be strong for her. You need to give her some time to figure out what her role in this club is. She's proven herself the last month she's been here, but giving her the official title will flip the switch with the Brothers. They'll expect more from her." He's got a point. Not only do Old Ladies hold a higher place in the club, but by being the President's Old Lady, she'll be held to a higher regard.

"She has it in her. I know she does. I have no question about her. It's me I question sometimes. Can I be what she needs? I never expected to be President this young."

"I never would've handed the patch over if I thought you couldn't handle it. I could've given it to one of the others until you were older, but seeing the way you stepped up after my accident, I knew it was yours."

"Thanks, Pops." I get up and meet him halfway for a handshake and back slapping hug. He may be a tough, grouchy, old biker, but my Pops has always put being my dad first.

"Just don't give up on her. I have a feeling she needs you just as much as you need her. Everything happens for a reason, whether we understand it at the time or not."

"When did you become a philosopher? Giving all sorts of thoughtful advice," I chuckle and head for the door.

"This was all Blue. She told me to talk to you."

"Son of a bitch. She set us up. I bet she's upstairs playing fairy godmother to my woman."

That sets Mountain off into a deep, loud, full belly laugh. "She for sure is. You better get up there before she unintentionally scares your lady away. Blue can be a bit harsh sometimes when she's trying to be thoughtful."

"Fuck. And that's my cue to get going." I leave the room and grab my phone. "Jacob, can you get the room back in order, please? There are a few chairs up on their ends," I say as I head for the kitchen. "And don't forget to lock it up."

I hit the kitchen door a bit hard and it swings wide, hitting the wall. Hammer comes running out of the pantry with his hand on the butt of his gun. "Slow down there, killer. It's just me."

"Sheesh. Do you need to be running around, slamming doors and shit? Gonna give a man a heart attack." He turns around and disappears for a second, and when he comes back out of the pantry again, he has a couple bags of chips and a bottle of Jack in each hand.

"You're one to talk about running around. You just up and left Church without a word. You know that isn't allowed." I think I need to kick some sense into him again. "I know you're not in a good place with this Wings situation, but you need to rein your shit in. You're an officer in this club and need to start acting like it. The Brothers look to you for leadership and you need to step the fuck up."

"I'm trying, man, but this is hard. I wish I would've gone after her when she left. I almost did but backed out last second. If I had gone, I could've saved her." He sets the bottles down and I can tell this is hitting him hard.

"Shit, man. I wish you would've told me this sooner."

"No one needs to hear my whining. By the time we realized she was missing, we had other shit to deal with. Fuck, why are we acting like little bitches? This isn't us. We're fucking Vipers, for fuck's sake. I need to man the fuck up." He grabs the chips and goes to leave the kitchen.

"Are you gonna take the Jack?" I point at the bottles he left on the island.

"Nope. I don't need them. I'm gonna go find Cypher and see if he needs anything. The sooner we find Wings, the sooner I make her my Old Lady."

"That's the spirit, Brother. Go find your woman." And he's gone.

I put the bottles back in the pantry and grab the things I need to make Duchess and I some lunch. I need one more chill and lazy night with my woman, and then tomorrow I'll bring her downstairs. The club needs to see that she's okay.

Arms loaded with a couple plates and a few beers, I head upstairs to my lady. I open the door and find her sprawled out like a starfish on our bed. "Hey there, bed hog."

"There you are. I was starting to wonder if Blue scared you away for good," Duchess chuckles and scoots back, putting her back against the headboard.

"She could never do that. I'd come for you no matter where you are." I set the plates on the nightstand and pull off my cut to hang it up. "I brought us some lunch. I thought we could do a movie day and tomorrow I'll let you out of your jail cell."

"You will?" She perks up. "Thank you, Whiskey."

I lean on the bed and go in for a kiss, stealing a small, soft one before backing off and settling in next to my woman. Once we're under the comforter, I put the plates on our laps and hand her the remote. "Here, have some lunch. It's not much, but I wasn't about to cook anything. And you pick us a movie to watch. Nothing too girly or cheesy though, please."

"*Steel Magnolias* it is." She laughs and scrolls through Prime.

"Please no," I beg her. "I don't think I can handle watching Ouiser again."

"Aww, you poor baby," Duchess mumbles with a mouthful of food.

"Can we please at least watch the *Fallen* movies? I know you like that British guy."

"He's Scottish, not British. There's a big difference."

"Whatever you say, gorgeous. As long as I don't have to watch another Easter egg hunt." Anything but that. I wanted to smother myself with the comforter the third time she made me watch that damn movie. "I'll even give you a back rub."

"I know what happens when you give me a massage. You get distracted and then you jump my bones. I know your games, mister."

She has me figured out. "I can't help it that you're hot. When I get my hands on you, I just can't stop myself."

"Fine. You win. You're one hell of a smooth talker. Bad guy movie night it is." The movie starts and we relax together for the rest of the night. I win.

CHAPTER THIRTY-THREE

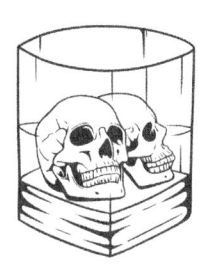

WHISKEY

"Be careful out there, Duchess. I don't know why you won't wait for me to be done. I don't want you to fall." I talk loud over the shower spray.

"I'm just fine, Whiskey. My ankle doesn't hurt as much anymore. I can walk into the bedroom by myself."

"Just please be careful. Walk slow." I don't need her falling while I'm still in the shower.

"Yes, dear." And now I know she's just appeasing me.

I finish rinsing and dry off before getting dressed. I promised I would take Duchess downstairs today, and just in case she needs help, I want to be ready before she is.

I rub my towel over my hair one more time as I walk into the bedroom, only to stop dead in my tracks when I see what my Duchess has in her hands.

She's standing in front of the closet, holding her cut. "What's this?"

I toss the towel back into the bathroom and slowly approach her. "It's your cut."

"When did you get this?" She holds it out toward me like she still doesn't understand what it is.

"I got it the day before Halloween. I planned on giving it to you the morning you went missing. We were supposed to have our big talk and I wanted it to be ready for you." I wanted so much to happen that morning. Instead, I got the biggest scare of my life.

"I wanted to talk that morning too. I shouldn't have left the room without you." Her shoulders slump and she looks down at the floor.

I take the last step toward her and lift her chin with my hand. I hold her up by supporting her neck in my palm. "You're here now. That's what's important." I drop a soft kiss on her forehead. "I still need to have your name put on the front of the cut. I ordered it before I gave you your name."

"Duchess," she whispers as she looks down at the leather still in her hands.

"It really does suit you." I can't wait to see her put it on.

"Do you really think I can do this Old Lady thing? I thought I could, but after what happened, I need you to tell me that I can." Her eyes start to water and the next thing I know, the tears are flowing down her cheeks.

"You can do anything you put your mind to. You made it through that shitty situation and bounced back like a badass." I brace her head in my hands and try to kiss the tears away, but they're falling too fast. I grab the cut from her hands and hold it out for her to slip on. She turns her back toward me, sliding one arm in at a time, then I lift it over her shoulders and can feel her tug it closer to her chest.

"Is there something in the pocket? It feels kinda heavy." She looks at me over her shoulder.

Grabbing her hands, I pull her to the couch. "Why don't you take a look? I may have slipped something in there." When we get settled with her curled up next to me, she reaches in the inner pocket and takes out a rectangle jewelry box.

"You've given me so much already. You didn't need to get me anything." She tries to hand me the box.

"I saw it and immediately thought of you. I found it before I gave you the name Duchess, but now it makes even more sense." I grab it from her hands, open it for her, and turn it around so she can see what's inside.

"Oh my gosh," she gasps. "It's a crown."

"It is. It's a crown skeleton key on a necklace. I got it for you to wear. That way, if you're ever not wearing your cut, you'll remember who you belong to." I remove the necklace and snap the box shut, setting it aside. "Let me put this on you." I fumble to open the clasp and slip it around her neck after she turns around and moves her hair aside. After I get it hooked, I run my hand down the patches on her back. Her finally wearing this cut is the best thing I have ever seen.

Duchess turns back to face me and grabs the key. "It is perfect for us."

That's when I notice that she's still crying. She tries to blink the tears away, but they keep flowing. And she starts again with the questions.

"Why do you live like this? Everything that has happened is so dangerous and you could be killed. You already shot someone to get to me. Why do you do this?" Duchess asks through her tears.

"Do you not get it yet, Duchess? I deal with all of this danger for you. I shot that man to save you. He had a gun pointed at me first, so I did what I had to do to protect myself and my Brothers." I turn all the way to face her. "Loving you isn't a choice for me. It isn't a mistake or a problem for me. I will deal with any bullshit and would walk through countless bullets to keep you safe." I can tell this is going to be a fight. She's so damn stubborn, but I need her to understand me or this will never work.

Talking about more bullets sets her on fire. She jumps up and starts pacing at the end of our bed. "I didn't ask for any of this. I just came here to find my sister. And if you weren't a damn biker, I wouldn't have been taken by those fucking thugs," she yells.

I get up and put myself in the middle of her path. "If I wasn't a damn biker, I never would've met you. And that's not an acceptable choice for me. I may have been born into this life, but I chose to be in this club as an adult." I can't hold it in anymore. "I may not have always known why my life led me here, but now that I have you, I finally understand. Every bad thing that has happened to me, and every morning I've woken up alone, they've all led me to you. It fucking sucks that things have happened the way they did, and I'm so sorry that your sister is missing, but if I knew where she was, I would bring her home to you in a heartbeat. So, until we can find her, I need you to stand at my side and fight." I let it all out because I need her to understand me.

"Making the choice to be here is one thing, but why do you want ME here? Why me? Why do you want me?" This side of her right here, this is the scared and vulnerable Kiana hiding in the shadows. She's lost everyone she's been close to, and she needs reassurance and love to remind her that she's important. My brave and strong Duchess is having a hard time dealing with the stress and I need her back in the light.

"Did you miss it the first time, baby? Maybe I just need to say it straight out. I love you. I love you, Kiana. That's why I need you here." I thread our fingers together and pull her hands up to my lips, kissing her fingers and talking through her tears. "I need you by my side because you make me a better man, a better Brother, and a better

President. I love you and I know deep down that you love me back. You say it with your touch and your smile and those damn pretty blue eyes." I kiss her forehead, trail my lips down her cheek, and whisper in her ear. "I love you, Duchess, and I need you."

"You really love me?" she gasps.

I pull back and meet her eyes. "Of course, I do. It may make me sound like a selfish asshole, but I'm never letting you go. We're stronger together and we'll fight any bad thing that comes our way. I need you to put the scared and hurt Kiana away and bring out the tough and strong, badass Duchess. I know she's in there." I bring our arms down and wrap mine around her waist.

And just like that, the switch flips.

My Duchess is back.

She stands up taller, pushes back her shoulders, and looks me straight in the eyes. "What do you need from me? What can I do to make this easier for you?"

If I didn't already love her, that would have done it for me. "That right there, Duchess. Doing exactly what you just did shows me that you were perfectly made for me. Standing tall, asking questions, and doing what needs to be done. All you need to do is be strong, stand by my side, and we'll get through anything life throws our way."

I know I finally have her when she reaches behind her back and grabs my hands, pulling them down and in between our bodies. "I love you too, Connor."

I slam my mouth down on hers and try to steal her breath with my kiss. She doesn't need air to breathe—she has me. She's meant to be mine. After a few minutes, we come back up for air. I could kiss her all day, but I can tell she has more she wants to say.

"I think I've known it for a while now, but I didn't want to let it show. I thought that being part of this life was a bad thing. I just wanted to find Tempy and get back to my normal life. But I realize now that I wasn't really living. You make me happy, and I would deal with a hundred bad guys if I could wake up every morning with you."

"You know, Duchess, you can't wake up with me if you don't go to sleep with me first. And I know just the way to fix that." I shake her hands loose and turn us so her back is to the bed, pushing her down and crawling over her. She grabs ahold of my shoulders and tugs me down so that I'm putting all of my weight on her chest, basically smooshing her into the mattress.

"Oh yeah? And what's that?" She smirks and wiggles as best she can under my bulk.

I lean up on my elbows, trying to give her some room to breathe. "Move in here with me."

"Move into the clubhouse? Like live here all the time?" Her mouth hangs open and she looks like a gaping fish out of water.

"Uh yeah. This is where I live. Pops, Blue, and I lived in one of the cabins out back, but I moved in here when I started Prospecting. When he lost his leg, we converted a storage room into a suite of rooms because it's easier for him to be inside with no steps. Maybe we can clean the cabin out and move out there. That way, you won't have to be surrounded by all these smelly guys." Now I feel like a rambling teenage girl. Why am I so damn nervous?

"Okay. But only under one condition," she says as she wiggles her arms free and wraps them around my neck.

"What's that, Duchess?" I ask, knowing I would probably give this woman any damn thing she desires.

"I get the top drawer in the bathroom. You have zero organizational skills and we do not need three open tubes of toothpaste." She busts out laughing and her eyes are now sparkling with happy tears.

That's the look I need to put on her face every day.

"If I agree, you'll be my Old Lady? You'll wear my patch and let everyone know that you're all mine?" I need her to say the words.

"Yes, Whiskey. I will be your Old Lady."

I kiss her again, only this time I do it gently and let her keep her breath. She's all mine, and I'll love and take care of her until the day I die. And every day after that from my grave.

"And don't forget, no clothes on the bathroom floor. I'll buy us a hamper and you can toss your dirty laundry in it."

That gets us both laughing and I roll over to lay next to her. "I can see it already. Lacy curtains and fancy towels and damn funny shaped soaps. The guys will never let me live this down."

"What about matching bath robes? You would look so cute in a fluffy pink robe."

Now it's my turn to look like a gasping fish. "Please tell me you're joking." I really hope she is.

CHAPTER THIRTY-FOUR

DUCHESS

It's just after ten o'clock and the New Year's Eve party is going strong. Everyone is hanging out in the main room, but Whiskey doesn't seem to care about that. He's too busy pulling me down the hall. We reach his office and he doesn't miss a step as he kicks the door shut, walking until he reaches his desk, where he picks me up and sets me down on the edge.

Whiskey's kiss starts out soft and smooth, but it quickly turns heavy and hot. He lets go of my hips and starts sliding his hands up to my waist. I can tell he's trying not to rush things, but once he tickles my ribs and I giggle into his mouth, things kick into high gear. He reaches up and grabs twin handfuls of my breasts, his fingers immediately finding my nipple piercings. He can zero in on them even through my shirt and lacy bra. Whiskey gives them a little tug and I think he does it because he still can't believe a woman like me could have such a wild side.

"This damn shirt is in my way," he rasps. Before I can even blink, he pushes off my cut, grabs ahold of the bottom hem of my shirt, and lifts the material over my head. The shirt goes flying somewhere and I couldn't care less.

Staring at his pecs, I press my hands against his rock-hard chest and drag them over the eight ridges of his abs. Even through his long sleeve t-shirt, I can feel every single bump. My fingers hit denim and I get excited. I hook my fingers into the waistband of his jeans and yank him as close to me as the desk allows, then I unfasten his belt and tug open the button and zipper. I'm about to reach my hand inside his pants when there's a loud knock at the door. *Knock knock.*

"I'm sorry, baby." I deflate and he drops his forehead to mine. He gives me a kiss and dangles my shirt in front of my face. In typical Whiskey fashion, it's halfway turned inside out, so he flips it back right and hands it to me.

Knock knock. "Hold your damn horses," Whiskey yells. "They really like to interrupt us, don't they?"

Once I have my t-shirt and cut back on, and am returned to somewhat normal, he calls out to whoever for them to come in.

The door opens and it's Buzz. He's standing with his hands behind his back and looks a bit ashamed, but I know he wouldn't interrupt unless it was important. "Hey,

Duchess, sorry to butt in, but I need to run something by the boss man really quick. Bloodlines stuff."

"It's okay, Buzz. I'll leave you two to your business." I hop down from the desk and give Whiskey a quick peck on the cheek.

I'm almost out of the office when he calls out, "Duchess, why don't you head on up to our room? I'll be there as soon as I'm done here."

"Yes, sir." I drop him a wink and head out the door. Not wanting to get stuck talking to anyone, I make a quick beeline for the stairs. As I move up the stairs, I take in the craziness going on in the room.

It's a good thing this isn't a family party. Jewel just disappeared down the club girl hallway with Saddle. Stiletto is currently butt ass naked and dancing on top of the coffee table with another club girl. And Raquel looks like she'll need to be surgically removed from Wrench's lap. He's got them in a recliner in the corner and they're one lacy thong away from full-out sex for everyone to see. Not my cup of tea, but to each their own.

Other Brothers are playing pool, crowded around the bar, and huddled on the couches, just shooting the shit. The music is loud, the booze is flowing, and it looks like a good time is being had by all.

Not even ten minutes later, Whiskey comes walking in, hangs up his cut, and drops down on the foot of the bed to kick off his boots. He looks up at me, reaches out to grab my hand, and pulls me to stand between his legs. I lay my forearms on his shoulders, thread my fingers through the back of his curly hair, and climb up to straddle his lap. The first thing he does is nuzzle his face deep into my cleavage. I think he would live in them, if he could.

Every time I get close to him, I feel like we're two puzzle pieces clicking together. I feel at home in his arms.

"Is everything okay with Buzz?" He has yet to say anything and I'm worried something is wrong.

He nods his head and mumbles into my skin. "Yea. Just an ordering snafu he caught when he was doing paperwork earlier. It could've waited 'til tomorrow, but Buzz isn't one to let shit lay around."

"It's good he caught it," I say and start to rub myself against him.

"Mmmhmmm" is all I get in response, but he definitely cannot hide the way his cock is straining against the front of his jeans.

Speaking of the front of his jeans, I can tell they're still unbuttoned. That means this asshole walked all the way through the crowded clubhouse and up the stairs, strutting like a damn peacock. My lover doesn't believe in the concept of underwear, so even though his cock was still tucked into his jeans, people definitely were able to see more of him than I'd like.

Not only that, but this idiot basically let everyone know what had started behind closed doors and what he was leaving the party early to do. Honestly, I don't really mind one bit, but I wasn't going to tell him that. It's not uncommon to hear things happening behind our closed doors, because my Old Man doesn't like when I try to be quiet. I think some of these Brothers have a secret pact to see who could make the most noise with their lady, because there are mornings when they'll razz each other for hours.

Whiskey finally stops suffocating himself in my chest and tilts his head back to lock eyes with me. The smirk on his face lets me know that he knows exactly what he was doing walking around with his pants undone. The right side of his mouth is creeping up in a sneaky smile, and before he can say something he thinks is funny, I let him have it.

"You've made it quite clear that you don't like it when I wear things that show off too much skin. That the parts of me that you like to call 'mine' are all yours. So, I would greatly appreciate if you didn't walk around the clubhouse with 'my' cock hanging out of your pants," I sass. Ever since I agreed to be his Old Lady, the word 'mine' has become a new part of his vocabulary.

"Oh really?" he smirks. Whiskey has that gleam in his eye again—the one that says I'm about to be in trouble for talking back. "I think it's time for you to show me more of what is mine then."

"I'll show you mine, if you show me yours." I scoot off his lap and stand back on my feet.

"Take off my cut," he whispers as he traces the front edge of my leather.

I may be the one wearing it, but he calls it his. I walk over to the wall, showing him my back, and slide it off my shoulders.

"Damn, Duchess. You look hot as fuck with my name on your back. Fuck, woman," he growls. He's sitting a few feet away, but his voice is so deep, it feels like it's right in my ear. My whole body breaks out in goosebumps.

I hear some rustling behind me, so I turn back around to see what he's doing. I'm gobsmacked by what I see. He's still sitting on the bed, but he has his t-shirt off and the whole top of his left arm is wrapped in what looks like black plastic wrap.

"What's that?" I ask.

"It's a tattoo."

I know it's covering a tattoo, but I don't think my brain has caught on yet. "I kinda figured that, but where did it come from? You didn't have that this morning when we took a shower." I definitely would have remembered seeing that this morning. I think I covered every inch of his body with kisses before I dropped to my knees and gave him one hell of a good morning blowjob.

"I went and got it when I told you I was going to The Lodge to do a walkthrough for the party there tonight." He tugs on a piece of tape and starts to peel it back.

"Here. Let me do that for you." I kneel on the bed to his left and gently pull the tape from around his bicep and shoulder. "Is this why Buzz came to talk to you before? Because of this?"

"Yup. I forgot to grab the cream he gave me to help keep the skin from drying out."

"Why didn't you tell me you were getting a tattoo today? I could have come with you." I have all the tape off and am suddenly hesitant to pull the bandage off.

"It wouldn't be a very good surprise if I told you ahead of time. I wanted to show you after it was all done."

"So, you snuck around with Buzz and here we are," I laugh. Typical Whiskey. He always has a reason for the things he does. "Does it go with your other ink?" I drag my fingernail up over the ghost and skull on his forearm. Other than having the Rebel Vipers skull and snake with the top and bottom rockers on his back, the ink on his forearm is the only other tattoo he has. Until today.

"In a way, but this one has more meaning. It's for you and me. Peel it off slowly and you'll see what I mean." He winks and gives me that lopsided, sneaky smile again.

I tug the upper corner off his shoulder and the first thing I see is a swirl of black. When I get the plastic down over his bicep, it falls away on its own and reveals the whole piece at once. I'm stunned speechless again.

It's all black and white, and I love it immediately. There's a skeleton wearing a jeweled crown that reminds me of my skeleton key, and it's kissing a woman by holding up her chin with its boney hand. That's what Whiskey does to me all the time—he holds up my chin and places gentle, loving kisses on my lips. It's haunting and beautiful at the same time.

"Oh, Whiskey, I love it." I can't take my eyes off it. I wish I could touch it, but I don't want to cause him any pain.

"Do you understand what this means? Why I got this design?" He lifts my chin and I have to meet his eyes.

"It's us," I choke, trying not to cry happy tears.

"It is us. You're my Duchess, but I'm also your King. Every leader needs his woman by his side, so from now on, you're by my side no matter where I go. And you'll be there forever."

"I love you, Connor." I lean into him and kiss him like he does to me, gentle and soft, almost like the touch of a ghost.

"I love you too, Duchess." He deepens the kiss and pulls me into his lap.

Minding not to bump his arm, we slowly pull the rest of our clothes off each other and I end up straddling his naked body. I drag my hands down his chest again, but this time when I reach his hardness, I don't have to stop because of a knock on the door. I wrap my hand around his hardness and he throws his head back with a groan.

"If I don't get inside of you, and fast, this show will be over before it even starts."

Still holding his hard length in my hand, I lift up onto my knees, line him up to my opening, and slide down onto his cock. I slowly lower myself all the way down until my pussy lips meet his short, wiry curls. When he's all the way inside of me, I bounce my hips just a bit, then Whiskey goes buck wild. He lays down on his back and pushes his butt up in the air. Using the leverage my knees have on the mattress, we start thrusting against each other, quickly finding our rhythm. I immediately start feeling my inner muscles start to throb around his dick.

"I'm gonna come," I pant out.

"Fuck me hard, Duchess. Fuck me hard," Whiskey growls behind clinched teeth. He's glaring at me with fire in his eyes, his pupils like pin pricks and the veins of his neck straining.

I lean forward and drop my hands next to his head, continuing to pump my hips up and down. Up and down. My thighs are starting to burn and I'm squeezing my insides as hard as I can. I try to hold on, but the explosion hits me like a wave over a breakwater. You see the tiny waves, but all of a sudden, a big one hits and crashes over everyone in its path. I'm done.

"Now. Now. Now." I scream so loud and the bed starts to rattle against the wall.

Whiskey gives a few more thrusts before wrapping me in a bear hug and shouting into the room. "That's it. Fuck. I'm coming."

He grabs a handful of my hair and pulls my head back. He's holding me tight but my necklace is flinging around, almost hitting him in the face.

Then, out of absolutely nowhere, I start to come again. I have no idea how I do it, but this one makes me float away into the ether. I gasp an attempted scream, but nothing comes out other than air.

Whiskey rocks our hips together until the spasms slow down and eventually stop. He rolls us to my left and his hardness slides from my opening. Neither of us speak a word, but we lock eyes and they say everything for us. That may have been quicker than our usual bedtime fun, but it was just as powerful.

We make no attempt to move, and he lets out a chuckle. "Let's do that again."

"Maybe later. I don't think I could even if I tried." I flop onto my back and stare at the ceiling.

"Not today, Duchess, but maybe tomorrow?"

"Are you trying to kill me?" I look his way to see that he's still laughing.

"Nope. I can't kill you. I need to knock you up first. I'm surprised I haven't done it yet. I bet I did it just now."

"It takes some people years to conceive. Three months is nothing in the time of things."

"Whatever you say, love." Whiskey gets up to turn off the light and crawls back in bed, pulling the covers up over us. He arranges us so his head is on my chest again. My arms are wrapped around him and I remember to keep away from his new ink. I look down at his face and see he's already out cold. How he falls asleep so fast, I have no clue.

I look back up at the ceiling and think about how lucky I am to be loved by this man. Every woman on this planet has loved a bad man at least once in her lifetime. He usually teaches us the lessons on what we shouldn't be looking for in a soulmate. But somehow, I got lucky, and my bad man and soulmate happen to be the same person. I may have found him under crazy circumstances, but I wouldn't have it any other way.

My phone flashes from the nightstand and I can just read the screen from here. I set an alarm for when midnight hits. I can hear a muted cheer come from downstairs and I kiss the top of Whiskey's head. Talk about starting the New Year with a bang!

CHAPTER THIRTY-FIVE

DUCHESS

Now that the holidays have passed, and we're in a new year, things around the clubhouse have calmed down a bit. The Brothers all have their motorcycles parked for the winter, and let me tell you, none of them are happy about it. I think I saw Whiskey shed a tear or two when he rolled his bike into the storage unit behind the garage. I asked him why they don't ride on the non-snowy days and he went into this longwinded tangent about salt and rust and shitty drivers. I just sat there and nodded when it seemed appropriate, until he ran out of steam. It was so dang cute.

I'm still running the bakery but only going in three or four days a week. I hired two more people to help pick up the slack and things are going smooth so far. Whiskey likes having me around more and I'm getting to know the Brothers better every day.

It's Monday afternoon, and since both the bakery and salvage yard are closed, Whiskey and I are hanging out in his office. He's going through some club paperwork and I'm researching new recipes for the bakery.

Our peace and quiet is suddenly disrupted when yelling comes from down the hallway. Someone yells "WHISKEY!" and he jumps out of his chair in a blink.

Just as he gets around his desk, Trooper comes running through the doorway. His breathing is labored and he's trying to talk, but nothing understandable is coming out.

"Breathe, Brother. What the hell's going on?" Whiskey asks.

"Wings," Trooper whispers and I join the huddle.

"What about her?" I ask, afraid to be too excited.

He's finally able to piece some words together. "She's on her way here."

Whiskey grabs him by the shoulders and gives him a shake. "What are you talking about? Where's she coming from?"

"Remember my old co-worker, Thomas?"

"Yea. You worked together at the Bureau and now he's at the county," Whiskey answers.

"He was on patrol and saw her walking down the side of the road. He pulled over and she asked to be brought here. I don't know much else, but they're on their way here."

That's all I listen to before I push them out of my way and take off running for the main room. I don't care if they follow me, but I'm going to be waiting for her outside when she gets here. I really hope this isn't a dream. I don't think I'll be okay if it's not really her.

There's a crowd of Brothers and a few club girls standing out in the parking lot and I push my way through them.

I start to lose my footing on a patch of ice and Gunner catches me before I fall. The gate is already open when a county police SUV turns into the parking lot. The passenger side door swings open and Tempy steps out wrapped in a huge blue blanket. The crowd is dead silent until I start to cry, running forward and wrapping my arms around my sister for the first time in almost five months.

"Kiana? What are you doing here?" she asks through her own tears.

I pull back, still holding her shoulders and let out a small laugh. "I came here to find you a few months back and kinda haven't left."

"What does that mean?" Before I can think of how to explain things to her, an arm wraps around my waist. Whiskey.

"She's with me," he answers for me.

"What? Since when?" Tempy gasps. "No, you can't be here. You can't be with him. Kiana, this isn't the type of place for someone like you." She's getting very angry at me.

"Don't talk like that to her. She can make her own choices," Whiskey barks at her.

"You fuck anything that walks, so why would I want my sister with you? I've fucked you myself. Does she know that?" Every sentence comes out louder than the last.

"I haven't touched you in almost two years, and it was only once, so don't even throw that in my face. And yes, she does know. We don't keep important secrets from each other," Whiskey replies with steel in his voice. It's the tone he uses to let people know he's not to be questioned again.

I lost my grip on Tempy when he got in her face, so I work my way between them and tuck my arms around Whiskey's waist. "Why don't we take this conversation inside? It's pretty frickin' cold out here. Please?"

"Fine." Whiskey looks around, and when he finds the deputy, he points at him. "You. Stay out here. I want to talk to you."

"Need me, Whiskey?" Doc appears next to us.

"Yup. Let's get Wings inside and check her out. Looks like she has some nasty bruises I want you to look at. That okay with you?" he asks Tempy.

She shrugs. "That's fine."

Whiskey drops a kiss on my lips and lets me loose. "Why don't you go with them? I've got stuff out here I need to figure out."

As much as I'd like to hear what they're going to talk about, it's club business, and my sister is my priority right now.

"Love you," I whisper.

"Love you too, Duchess."

I wrap an arm around Tempy and we walk toward the clubhouse. She gets nods and hellos from the group as we pass by, but she keeps her head down and doesn't say a word back. I lead her down the hall toward her room.

Stiletto comes out of her room when we round the corner. "Holy shit! You're here!" She throws her arms around Tempy and they both burst into tears. "Are you okay?" I hear Stiletto ask.

They pull apart, and Tempy nods in my direction. "I'm okay. We're just gonna go in my room and wait for Doc. We'll catch up soon. Okay?" She turns away, not waiting for a response.

Stiletto and I look at each other, confused. She's been gone for months and she's acting like she just saw us yesterday. What the hell?

"Alrighty then, I'll let you have your sister talk. I'm glad you're home, Wings."

"Ready to go in?" I ask Tempy as we continue down the hall. Her door is the last one on the left.

"It's probably locked," she mumbles. I pull a set of keys out of my cut pocket and unlock the door. "What the hell has been going on around here?" And with that, her sass is back.

"The door was locked, so I had Trooper pick it for me. I wanted to see if you left anything behind that would give us a clue as to why you were gone."

Knock knock. "Sorry to interrupt, ladies, but I'd like to talk to Wings alone, if that's alright?" Doc announces as he enters the room.

"She can stay. I'd like to get this part over with and not have to tell the story more than necessary." Tempy sits down on her bed and drops the blanket from her shoulders.

I shut the door and lock us in.

CHAPTER THIRTY-SIX

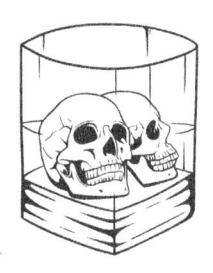

WHISKEY

I watch Doc and the girls walk into the clubhouse and I'm struck dumb. How in the hell did she find her own way back? Cypher couldn't find anything about her on the dark web. I wasn't in any hurry to tell my Old Lady that I was out of ideas on how to find her sister.

"I guess we're having Church out here tonight, boys," I shout to the Brothers. There are a few groans, so I let them have a little respite. "Run in and get some coats on. Make it quick." Most of the guys hustle inside, but a few make their way closer to me.

Pops and Brick come walking out, and Brick holds out my Carhartt to me. "I grabbed this out of your office. Thought you'd want it."

"Thanks. I don't want to let him out of my sight," I point at the deputy, "otherwise, I would've gotten it myself."

The rest of the Brothers come back out and we form a large circle. Thomas walks over with Trooper and I hold out my hand. We shake and I thank him for bringing Wings back.

"No problem. Honestly, I almost ran her off the damn road. I came around a curve over on Highway 97 and she was walking on the gravel. She was about a quarter-mile away from the abandoned motel."

"I'm just glad you found her," I reply.

"Now, I have to ask, because she wouldn't tell me anything, why was she out there all alone? Is something happening out here that I need to know about?" He grips the top of his bulletproof vest and stands in that typical police officer *'I'm the law you have to listen to me'* stance. Too bad for him, I'm very stubborn and I don't fall for that line of bullshit.

I cross my arms and mirror his attitude. "That would be club business, so I can't say. We'll take care of it."

The group starts to get antsy and I need this guy off my compound. I can't have one of my Brothers opening his mouth and starting trouble by pissing off an ex-fed. We haven't been outside long, but it's too damn cold for us to be out here—perfect excuse to get this guy on his way. "Trooper, please show your friend back to his vehicle. We have things to do." I spin away from them and walk up the porch, standing out of the winter wind while I wait for him to leave. I hear his SUV back out of the lot, and as he pulls away, a truck comes peeling in like a bat out of hell. It's Hammer.

He stops just before hitting a porch post and jumps out, truck still running. "Where is she?"

I step in front of him before he can make it to the door. "She's in her room with Doc and Duchess. I know you wanna see her, but we have more pressing business to deal with first."

"But I—" I cut him off again.

"No, Hammer. We know where she was and we need to go check the place out."

"Fine, but when we get back, she's all mine."

"That's fine. All right, gentlemen, sounds like we have a motel to go check out. Who's with me?"

I drive Hammer's truck with him and Ring, and Trooper drives his with Cypher and Wrecker. I know exactly what abandoned motel Thomas was talking about, so I lead the way. It's about an hour away on a normal drive, and I try not to push the speed limit too much because I don't need us getting pulled over, but we make it there in just under forty-five minutes.

The lot has a few inches of snow, but there are a few tire tracks going in and out to the road. We pull right up to the building and hop out, rounding the front of the trucks with guns drawn. We split up, each taking one door at a time. Kicking in the first six doors, we find nothing but empty rooms. Two of the next six give us exactly what we're looking for.

Trooper yells out, "I got a body."

Hammer follows with "This was Wings' room."

I walk into Trooper's room and the stench hits me immediately. "Holy fuck, that's ripe." The smell of a decomposing body is hard to explain—just imagine mixing together one hundred skunks, then multiply it by a thousand. I pull my sweatshirt collar above my nose and try to breathe through it. "Smells like he's been here for a while."

"I'd say probably three of four days," Trooper coughs. "I found a burner phone on the nightstand, so we'll be taking that with us. Other than that, this room is just fast-food wrappers and dirty clothes."

I step myself out of that room real damn fast. I really hope I can wash that funk out of my clothes, otherwise I'll have to burn them. We walk to the neighboring room and find Hammer in the back corner, frozen and staring into the bathroom.

"Hammer, you okay back there?" I slowly walk over, almost like approaching a spooked puppy.

He doesn't say anything and just shakes his head, pointing into the bathroom then turning away, only to kick the closet door. The glass shatters and he kicks the wood paneling that is now half hanging off the tracks. I walk into the dingy room and instantly see what has him so worked up. There's a pile of blood-stained towels tossed in the corner. It looks like someone had one hell of an injury and bled more than they should have.

"Did she . . . did she look hurt?" Hammer asks from just outside the door.

I flip the light off and push him away from the doorway. "I didn't see anything major, but she was wearing clothes and wrapped in a blanket when she got to us. Don't think the worst until we know all the facts."

"But what if she *is* hurt? What if she's hurt and I wasn't there when she needed me?" And now his panic is kicking in. His breaths are coming out faster and he starts pacing the room.

"Slow yourself down. Let's not jump to conclusions. Calm your anger because we need to search this room. Find anything that will help us figure out who these assholes are. That's the only way we can help her right now."

I'm not sure if my pep talk helped any on the inside, but his demeanor shifts. Hammer starts opening drawers and pulling out clothes, tossing them on the floor. I kneel down to look under the bed and Trooper is next to me with his Maglite. We find nothing but dust bunnies under either of the beds. The room is pretty much a bust. There are a few receipts in the garbage can, but we take those with us to look at back at the clubhouse.

The six of us head back out to the parking lot and I look to Trooper. "What's the best way to light this place up? Should we pour gas on everything?"

"We'll blow it to smithereens. We puncture a few gas lines, that way it'll look like an accident. I'll get the furnace line in the room with the body so that can be the point of ignition. The rest will go when enough gas builds in the rooms. It'll take me two minutes to bust the line and then we wait about fifteen for the rooms to fill. Then I'll jog back and toss in a lit box of matches. That should be plenty to get it going." The more he says, the more excited he gets.

"Are you sure you weren't a pyro back in your fed days?" Wrecker jokes and we all laugh in response.

"Ah, fuck you, asshole. I learned a lot about stuff like that working too many cases. But let's move our trucks. I don't need burning shit falling on my new paint job. I just got my baby a new color this summer."

We shut all the exterior doors, but open the connecting doors. Trooper does some fiddling with the furnace in the room with the dead guy, and we all hustle back to the trucks. We get out of the parking lot quickly and drive a little ways down the road.

The clock ticks by super slow until Trooper comes running back toward us. Just as he jumps in the driver's seat of his truck, the explosion goes off and we can see the flames through the trees. That's our clue to leave, so I throw the truck in gear and we take off.

"Holy shit!" Ring laughs from the back seat. "We need to do that shit more often. I could get on that bandwagon."

"I don't think we need to go around blowing shit up, Ring. That's one way to draw unwanted attention to the club. If you want to watch bodies burn, you can be in charge of the incinerator from now on."

"Deal." He meets my eyes in the rearview mirror and nods. The smile on his face is way too big. We really have some fucked up Brothers in this club. I wouldn't trade any of them for anything.

We drive the speed limit on the way back and pull in the gate an hour later.

Cypher is the first in the clubhouse and he heads straight up to his room. Trooper follows him, carrying the bags holding the burner phone and receipts.

"What'd you find, son?" Mountain asks from behind the bar. He pulls a bunch of beers from the cooler and passes them out. We each grab one and the group disperses, all except me and Hammer.

"A decomposing body and a burner. We blew the motel and got the hell out of dodge." I pop the top and drink half the bottle. "Any word from the girls?' I ask.

"Nope. Doc came out about an hour after you left and went straight out onto the back porch," Pops says.

"I gotta go see Wings." Hammer sets his beer down and heads down the side hallway that leads to the club girls' rooms.

I follow him a few steps back and wait for Duchess to come out. I have a feeling she'll need me.

CHAPTER THIRTY-SEVEN

DUCHESS

Doc comes out of the bathroom and closes the door behind him. "I told her she can shower, but you need to bandage a few of her scrapes when she gets out." He digs through his backpack and pulls out a tube of antibiotic ointment, a roll of medical tape, and a few different size bandages. "Use what you need and leave the rest for her."

"How is she?" I want the truth and I'm not sure how much Tempy will tell me.

"She's good considering how long she was in that motel. Physically, she's strong, but mentally, I'm really not sure. She wouldn't say much, and I'm not really trained for that even if she did." He closes up his bag and heads for the door.

"Thanks, Doc. For being here to help." Anything I say will never be enough, but I try anyway. He nods and is gone.

I sit back down on the edge of the bed and drop my head into my hands. What the hell do I do now? Do I leave and give her space, or should I stay and pull the big sister card to get the answers I need?

The shower turns off and I decide to stay and make her talk to me. Tempy opens the bathroom door a crack and pops her head out. "Can you come help me with those bandages?"

I jump up and grab everything Doc left behind. "Of course." She opens the door all the way and I join her in the bathroom. Her bedroom is almost the same size as mine and Whiskey's, but the bathroom is a lot smaller. There's only a single vanity, toilet, and a square shower stall.

"What do you need bandaged?" I ask and set everything on the counter.

"I'll put ointment on my arm, but I need help with the gash on my leg." She twists her hip and I see a red line on the back of her calf. It looks fairly new and still angry red in color. The wound is closed, but I still don't want it to get infected.

"Stand in front of the sink and do the ointment. I got this one." I grab a few square gauze pads and the medical tape, and I kneel down and get to work. Once she's all fixed up, we head back out to her room.

Tempy grabs some clothes from her dresser and drops her towel to get dressed. I gasp when I see a giant tattoo of angel wings on her back. They cover her from shoulder to just above her waistline. "When did you get those? They look so real." It almost looks like she could just fly away.

"I got them not long before I came here. It took a few sessions and I talked to Buzz a lot while he worked. That's how I found out about the club."

"I always wondered how you ended up here," I say and sit at her desk. "I asked, but you wouldn't tell me."

After slipping on a baggy t-shirt and flannel pajama pants, she sits crossed legged on her bed. "I'm sorry about that. I didn't think you'd understand and I had no interest in fighting with you once I decided to move here." She laughs and I join her. It feels good to have her back.

"Can you tell me what happened? How did you end up with those guys?" I ask, hoping to get some answers.

She grabs a pillow and hugs it to her chest. "I was coming to visit you. I don't know how much you know about Hammer, but he and I had an argument and I needed to get away for a few days. I packed a bag and was coming to spend the weekend with you, only I ended up with a flat tire. This van pulled up behind me and I thought they were there to help, but I was wrong. I noticed their cuts and when I didn't recognize the patches, I panicked. I screamed, but they knocked me out, then I woke up in some cabin in the woods."

Holy shit. I wonder if it was the same place I was. "Then how did you end up at a motel?'

"I got moved to a different place every few weeks. I tried to keep track of the days, but after a while, I lost count. Every new place, I was told that my buyer was coming to get me, but no one ever showed. I would ask, but that only made whoever was watching me mad, so I stopped asking. I knew something was wrong with this last place when no one came back for like four days. The room started to smell and I busted the lock to get the window open. I crawled out, and when I found one of the guys dead in the room next to me, I knew I needed to get out of there. I started walking and that deputy found me. I didn't tell him anything other than I needed to get to the Rebel Vipers clubhouse. He called Trooper and here we are."

I don't know how she can just summarize the last few months into so few sentences. It's crazy.

"Can we address the leather elephant in the room?" she asks with a giggle.

"What?" I laugh and pretend to brush off my shoulder. "This old thing? It's just something I found lying around and decided to wear."

"Nice try, Kiana, but I know you better than that. How the hell did you end up with Whiskey?"

"I told you, I came here to look for you. You hadn't answered my calls in almost two weeks and I was worried. You never ignored me for that long before and I knew something was wrong. I got here and yelled at Whiskey.

They thought you were with me and I thought you were here. Didn't take long to figure out something was wrong. Then Stiletto was attacked behind The Lodge, so Whiskey came to the house the next morning and made me come stay here for protection. Things just kinda grew from there."

"That doesn't explain the property patch. They don't just go around handing those out like candy. I know that all too well." She drops her gaze and I can feel the sadness coming off her in waves.

"I'm gonna kick Hammer's ass all the way to Timbuktu. And I thought I liked the asshole. No more cupcakes for him."

"Don't be mad at him. It's not all his fault. I shouldn't have let things go as far as they did." She takes a big breath and zones back in on me. "Quit trying to distract me. Keep telling your story."

"Fine, where was I? Oh yeah, I came here mid-September and got the cut after I was rescued a few days after Halloween. That about sums it up." I stare down at my shoes and hope she ignores the last part of my sentence.

It's quiet for too long, and I look up to see her staring at me like she sees a ghost. "Rescued? What the living fuck does that mean? Why did you have to be rescued?"

I start talking and try to get it all out fast. "The morning after Halloween, I woke up and went outside for some fresh air. I got chloroformed and woke up in a cabin. The next day, the guys found me and brought me back. A few days later, Whiskey gave me the cut and told me he loved me."

Tempy falls back on the bed and starts laughing out loud. She sounds like a damn hyena. "Oh my goodness. This would only happen to you."

"Hey! I love him too and I'm happy here. If you don't want to stay here anymore, you can have the house, but I'm moving in fully in a few weeks." I don't find my relationship funny or something to be laughed at.

She sits straight up and scoots forward to grab my hands. "No, no, no. That's not what I'm laughing at. I think it's funny because the reason I never wanted you to come visit me here was that I didn't think the biker life would be your thing. And then you go and end up shacking up with the club President."

I squeeze her hands and crack a smile. "I wanted to punch him the day we met. He was all bossy and grumpy and told me to leave. Of course, I talked back and left in a huff."

"Sounds like you."

"Yup, that's me. And now the grumpiness is hot as fuck."

"There's a lot of that floating around here."

"I've noticed. So . . . are you planning on staying in the clubhouse? Do you still plan on being a club girl? I don't think I can see that while living here." I really hope she doesn't keep sleeping with all the Brothers. The more I get to know them, the less I want to picture them fucking my sister just to get their rocks off.

"I'd like to stay here if Whiskey will let me, but I don't know how that'll go over when I tell him I don't want to be a club girl anymore. He would have every right to boot me straight back out the doors. I've seen it happen."

"If you want to stay for a while, I bet I can get him to agree. If he doesn't like it, I can always threaten to cut him off," I joke.

"You don't need to do that. To be honest, I'm hoping that by staying around for a little while, maybe Hammer will wake up and we can figure us out. I'm not counting my chickens, but I can always hope."

"Why do I have a feeling there's something you aren't telling me about him?"

"If I tell you something, do you pinky promise not to tell anyone? Not even Whiskey? I can't tell you unless you swear it won't leave this room. I really don't want to talk about it, but I'll tell you just this once, then we'll never discuss it again until I'm ready." She holds out her right hand, pinky pointed in the air.

We haven't pinky promised since we were teenagers. "I pinky promise you that I won't say anything. Not even to Whiskey. He may be my Old Man, but you're my sister first."

She leans forward and whispers her secret in my ear. I'm so shocked, I almost fall out of the chair. I can't believe she's been through all of this, and she was all alone.

"And you cannot tell Hammer. I'm not ready for him to know yet. I'll tell him when I'm ready." She tightens our pinky grip until I nod my agreement.

I don't really agree, but this is what she needs. "I understand why you don't wanna talk about everything that happened, but I just want you to be prepared for it to come out when you least expect. Because no matter how hard you try to keep them to yourself, secrets always find a way of coming out at the worst time. And if I've learned anything in these last few months, these men don't like to be kept in the dark about important things. Hammer needs to know everything."

"I know, and I will. One day. Just not today," she whispers.

Knock knock.

"What is it with this place? Does everyone around here have a radar to detect when people are having important conversations? It's getting really annoying." Tempy busts out laughing again and it pops the tension bubble. We keep laughing until my stomach starts to hurt and there's another knock on the door. "Hold your goddamn horses!"

I get up and head to the door, swinging it open. It's Hammer. I look back at Tempy to see what she wants me to do.

"It's okay. You can let him in." She stands up and walks toward us.

"I'll let you two talk. But if you need anything from me, you know where I am, okay?" I ask while giving her a hug.

"Yes, big sister. You'll be upstairs boning the boss."

"Hardy har-har. Love you, Tempy." But one last thing. I turn to face Hammer and let him have it. "If I hear one more bad thing about you from my sister, my standing in this club will be the least of my concerns and I will come for you. Do I make myself clear?"

"Crystal clear. I'll be on my best behavior. I swear on my cut," he says and taps his finger on his Sergeant-at-Arms patch.

"I'll hold you to that." I walk out of the room and the door shuts behind me.

"Duchess? Are you okay?" I turn and see Whiskey at the end of the hall. I run to him and jump up into his arms. The tears start falling as he picks me up and carries me up the stairs. He knows just what I need, and I need for us to be alone.

CHAPTER THIRTY-EIGHT

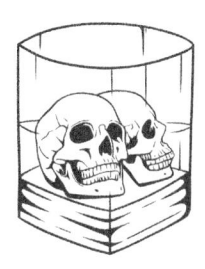

WHISKEY

Hammer knocks on the closed door and nervously looks back at me.

"Are you sure you wanna do this now?" I ask him.

"Yup. I need to know everything and then we can move forward." He nods and the door swings open. It must be my Duchess who's there because very quickly I can hear her telling him the brass tacks.

Duchess stares at the door as Hammer closes it and she looks so lost, I don't think she even realizes I'm standing here. "Duchess? Are you okay?" I call out.

She jolts and spins to see me down the hall, then she starts running and I catch her when she jumps into my arms. I pick her up and she wraps her legs around my waist.

Immediately, I start to feel her shake. The tears are falling, so I need to get her up to our room.

I head back down the hall and make the left turn up the stairs. Taking them two at a time, I make it to our room in no time. Needing to get the keys out to unlock the door, I brace her back against the door and dig them out of my pants pocket. The door swings open and I carry her in, kick it shut with my boot, and flip the lock, and we're finally alone.

I sit down on the bed and start to rock her back and forth. "What's the matter, Duchess? Are you okay?" She shakes her head and burrows further into my body. It's almost like she's trying to climb inside me. I've never seen my woman like this, and I have no idea what to do for her. "What do you need from me? What can I do for you?"

Her head lifts and she looks me square in the eye. "I need you, Whiskey," she whispers. "I just need you."

I feel her hips start to grind in my lap, and my dick definitely is getting excited and wants to join the party. Not knowing how to react, I try and give her an out. "Are you sure, love? I know you're upset. Are you sure this is what you need?" The tears and crying tell me she's upset and emotional, and I don't know if sex is the right thing. If she told me she just needed me to hold her, I would sit like this all damn night.

"Yes, I need you. I need to let it all out," she whines and continues to rub her chest against mine. We couldn't be closer if we tried.

"Stand up," I bark, and she hurries off my lap. "Take off your cut and hang it up."

"Shirt too?" she asks.

"Shirt too." The material goes flying and lands across the room on the couch. "Now, come back up here. Kneel over my lap."

Duchess crawls back up and with her hands back on me, she goes straight for my belt, unbuckling it and diving her greedy hands into the denim. Before I can blink, she has me gripped in both of her hands and starts stroking me hard and fast.

I enjoy the feeling for a bit, but when the tingling starts in my back, I know I need to get moving. I use one hand to unclasp her bra, then push her leggings down to her knees. Thank the Lord for the stretchy material—they've helped me get quick access to her pussy several times. I rub my index finger over the lace of her panties and Duchess lets out a soft moan. I can feel the tension start to lift from her body as she leans her head on my shoulder and continues to jerk me off between our bodies.

Hooking one finger in the bottom of her panties, I pull them aside and use the other hand to start rubbing her skin to skin. Her folds are already damp, and I know she's ready for me to be inside her. She just doesn't know that my plans are not what she may be expecting.

I trace two fingers down her slit and quickly push them into her opening.

"Fuck!" Duchess screams out and she immediately starts to shake. With only one push into her channel, she comes all over my fingers. "More," she chants. "I need more." And I'm going to give her exactly what she wants.

With my fingers still inside her, my wrist holds the material out of my way, and I wrap my other arm around her waist, pulling our torsos closer together. Our arms are stuck between us, but neither of us slow down our movements. Her hands keep stroking me and I don't stop slamming my fingers in and out of her pussy.

I have my hand flipped up and my middle two fingers are plowing in and out of her opening. The liquid flowing from her is collecting in my palm, and every time I slam my hand up, it makes a wet slapping sound against her skin. The noises coming from her mouth, combined with my grunting and the wet slaps of our skin, make the perfect symphony of sound.

Duchess starts swirling her hand up over the head of my dick and I feel like I'm almost ready to blow. Her sheath starts to squeeze my fingers, so I know she's right there with me. We're going to go over the edge together.

"That's it, Duchess. Let it happen. Come all over my hand like the dirty girl you are," I growl at her.

"Yes," she begins to chant, and that's it. Game over. She jolts one last time, freezes, and screams out my name. "Connor!"

I feel the tingle run down my spine and I explode in her hands. The cum rushes out in ropes and it coats her fingers. Her hands keep stroking me, using the slickness to continue her movements.

"I . . . stop." Duchess gasps for breath between each word. She finally lets go of my quickly deflating flesh and pushes down on my wrist. My fingers slide out of her and I untangle my hand from her panties. We both just sit there for a few minutes, catching our breath.

Since her head is still on my shoulder, I turn mine to whisper in her ear. "Let's get cleaned up." I wrap both arms around her waist and stand up.

Duchess lets out a laugh. "Put me down, you caveman." Her leggings are still down to her knees, so her legs just dangle in front of my body.

I hike her up tighter, carry her into the bathroom, and plop her butt down on the counter top. No words spoken, I strip off my clothes before pulling off hers as well. I run a washcloth under some warm water and use it to wipe the wet stickiness off both of us. I step away to toss it in the hamper and she hops down to wash her hands.

We go about our nightly routines and turn to leave the bathroom at the same time, but we collide in the doorway and both start laughing. She tries to push me out of her way, but I nudge her with my hip and beat her back to the bed. I crash down onto the mattress and yell, "Victory!"

"That's cheating," she huffs as she crawls in her side. "Didn't your Pops ever tell you to let the girl win? That's just the polite thing to do."

"Nope. He always told me to be the first one through a door. You never know what's on the other side, and you need to protect whoever is behind you." I yank her closer to me and she cuddles into my chest.

"I'm sure he did, but I don't think that's what he had in mind when he said it." Duchess does this little full body worm wiggle to get herself close to me and comfortable.

"You're probably right, but in this case, I still win." I lift her face up to mine and kiss her like there's no tomorrow. It's not a crazy, sloppy kiss, but one to convey to her that she's my everything.

When we come up for air, she opens her eyes and her whole face smiles. Her cheeks are flushed, her eyes are squinty, and her lips are plumped up from my kiss. My kiss. I did that to her.

I don't want to burst her happiness bubble, but I need to know what made my Old Lady so sad before. She lays her head back on my shoulder and I use a finger to start playing with one of her curls. "Are you okay, Duchess? Did Wings say something to upset you?"

She lets out a deep exhale and melts further against me. "No, she didn't make me upset. I was sad because of everything she went through. I can't believe she was gone for so long, but I'm glad she managed to get herself away."

"I can understand that. I'm sure she has more to tell us, but we'll worry about that another day." I hug her tighter and drop a kiss on top of her head. "How about we get some sleep and we'll start tomorrow like a new beginning?"

She nods. "I like the sound of that."

"I love you, Duchess."

"Love you too."

CHAPTER THIRTY-NINE

DUCHESS

"Where do you want this wood box, Duchess?" Whiskey yells from the living room.

I peek my head out the bedroom door and see him holding my grandma's hope chest in his arms. That thing weighs a ton and I have no idea how he isn't dropping it. "Put it next to the bookshelf, please." I duck back into the room and listen to the footsteps of all the Brothers helping us move into the cabin.

It's Valentine's Day, and Whiskey's birthday, but once he decided this was the day we were moving in, there was no changing his mind. Yesterday was Saturday and the guys moved in all the big furniture I wanted from my house. Today, we took the club's box truck and filled it with the boxes of my personal things.

Tempy and I had a long talk about what to do with the house and we decided to keep it for now. She made a comment about maybe moving into it come spring, but she hasn't made any final decisions. I still go into town because of the bakery, so I can stop in and check on it whenever I want.

Things have somewhat calmed down in the last month. Whiskey lifted the full lockdown, but everyone is under orders to remain vigilant and never leave the compound alone.

We do have one new full patched member of the club. The Prospect, Jacob, was given his new patches last weekend and there was a huge party here at the clubhouse. He was given the name Smoke because of how he always seems to be around when he's needed most.

Whiskey told him, *"You've proven yourself to be a great asset to this club, and we would be lucky to have you as a Brother. Your patch gives you the road name Smoke. It's because you're always around when we need you but then disappear in a flash. And I did threaten to send you up in smoke if you crashed my bike."*

It made the whole club laugh. Smoke is moving out of the Prospect bunk room and taking over the room Whiskey and I were in.

"That's the last box," I hear Ring say, and that's my cue to get my surprise ready. I push the door shut a crack and grab the bag I hid in the closet.

"Thanks for the help, Brother," Whiskey replies and I can hear all the guys saying their goodbyes before the front door closes.

"They're gone," Whiskey hollers. "Do you need help with anything?"

"Can you grab the small blue tote off the couch and bring it in here please?" This cabin has three bedrooms and I'm in the one across the hall from our master. Apparently, this was Whiskey's room growing up.

Whiskey's boots thunk as he walks down the hall and the door swings open. He freezes in the doorway when he sees me in the room.

"Where did that chair come from?" he asks. I'm sitting in a wood glider with cream colored cushions. It's new and just part one of my surprise.

"Ring went and picked it up for me. I bought it from the furniture store in Henderson."

"It looks nice." The tote falls to the floor and that's the moment I know he sees what I'm holding in my lap. "What's that? What are you holding?"

Standing up, I hold it out to him and he finally walks into the room. "Take it. It's your Valentine's-slash-birthday present."

He grabs it and holds it in his hands. His body is tight and he looks like he's holding a bomb. In a way, he is. "It's a teddy bear." He's a man of few words right now.

"Yes, it is. Did you read what the shirt says?" His present is a teddy bear wearing a white t-shirt that has something printed on the front. I ordered it custom from an online store. It says, '*HAPPY BIRTHDAY DADDY!*'.

"Are you serious? Is this for real?" Whiskey looks up from the bear and asks.

"Yup. Look in the tote. There's more in there," I tell him.

Still holding the bear, he turns around and kneels to open the tote. He pulls out the item I specifically left on top—a tiny black leather jacket. He climbs back to his feet and stands right in front of me. "What's this all for?"

For such a smart man, it's taking him a minute to really get it. "I went a little crazy online and bought a bunch of stuff. That's what else is in the tote. I bought it all for our baby."

That's when all the puzzle pieces fall into place and he gets what I'm telling him. "Baby! We're having a baby?" he yells.

"Yes!" And the tears start falling. "A baby." Whiskey drops the bear on the chair and grabs ahold of me in a giant full body hug. His body is shaking and I'm starting to get worried, so I ask him, "Are you okay?"

"Of course, I fucking am." And he lets out a giant laugh. He pulls back and gives me a quick kiss. "Is that why you wouldn't let me open any of your boxes? You were hiding this from me?"

"I couldn't let you see what was in them. It's not often you don't know what's going on around here, and I wanted to surprise you with everything at once. The bear was the last thing to arrive yesterday."

He turns us to the side and looks down at the chair. "Well, it sure was one hell of a surprise. When I walked in and saw you sitting in that chair, I almost had a heart attack. I could read the shirt, but my brain wasn't connecting the clues."

"That's okay. I know it was a shock you weren't expecting." I hug him tight.

"I really shouldn't be too shocked. I've been trying to do this for months now." He pushes me back and has a serious look on his face. "Is everything okay? I was kind of rough with you last night. Are you okay? Is the baby okay? Do you know how far along you are? Do you know what it is yet?"

Now that he started talking again, he doesn't seem to be shutting up. That makes me start laughing so hard, the tears start flowing again. I push out of his arms and have to put my hands on my knees to avoid falling over.

"Yes, I'm fine, and you were fine last night." I finally stop laughing and stand back up. "It's way too early to know the gender yet, but I think I'm about six weeks."

That makes him think. "Six weeks. That'd be around New Year's. HA!" He laughs. "I was right. I knocked you up on New Year's Eve."

He grabs ahold of my face with both hands and kisses me dumb and silly. Any argument I have about him being right goes right out the window. "Whatever you say, Whiskey," I reply when my brain can form words again.

Whiskey lets go of my face and drops his hands to my waist. He pushes my cut open and starts tracing circles on my belly. "Thank you, Duchess."

"What for?"

"For growing my baby. Our baby. For making us a family."

That gets the waterworks flowing again, but this time with extreme happiness and wonder.

"Don't cry, Duchess. I don't like it when you cry. This is the best birthday I've ever had." The words rush out.

"Even better than red velvet cake?" I meet his eyes and ask with a giggle.

"So much better than red velvet cake." He grabs my face again and starts wiping my tears away with his thumbs.

"Don't let Blue hear you say that. She made you a cake."

"She did?" He's stunned.

"Yup. When I took the pregnancy test, I had to tell someone. I knew she would keep my secret. She was the one who suggested I tell you today." Blue has been my savior these last few days. Every time I wanted to blurt it out, I would find her and she would talk me down.

"If you're so happy, why are you crying? I can't get the tears to stop." He's still holding my face.

"Hormones. There's gonna be lots of emotions and tears for the next eight months or so." I pat his hands and pull back from him.

That makes him freeze again. "More tears?"

"Yes, sir. You did this to me," I point to my still flat belly, "so you get to deal with everything that comes with it."

"Fuck. I'm gonna need a drink."

"No more whiskey for you, mister." I point and shake my finger at him.

"Not even in a mixed drink?"

"Nope."

"What about a shot? Just one?"

Now, he's just messing with me, so I sass right back at him. "Don't even think about it, it's not happening. No mixer, no shot, no nothing."

"Fine." He kisses me one more time and grabs my hand, pulling me tight into his arms. "No whiskey on the rocks."

THE END!

EPILOGUE

PENELOPE

I drive around a curve and what I see to my left makes me slam on the brakes. The height of the chain link fence, topped with barbed wire, shocks me. I'm going to go out on a limb and say this is the place I was hoping to find. The Rebel Repairs sign to the left is another indication that I'm at the right place.

Realizing I'm stopped in the middle of the road, I look around to find a place to park. I see a very tall man appear in the driveway just ahead, standing next to a small building of some sort that is set back into the fence line.

I look him up and down and notice he's completely dressed in black. His boots, jeans, t-shirt, leather vest, sunglasses, and even his hair is black. Another thing I notice right away is he's covered in tattoos from his neck down to his knuckles. I'm not close enough to see any detail, but every bit of skin I can see has something inked on it. I wonder if they continue under all his clothes.

Penelope, I scold myself, *now is not the time for those thoughts. You're here for a reason, and it's not to ogle this man.*

I lift off the brake and turn left into the driveway approach. There's enough room for my van to be off the road, but I can't pull ahead too far because of the closed gate.

When I get the van in park, the guy starts walking toward me. He walks all the way around my van before knocking on my driver's side window. I hit the button to lower it and he drops his giant paws on the window sill. Now, I can see the details of his ink a lot better.

The guy coughs, and when I look up at his face, I'm struck stupid again. Holy shit is he hot!

"Can I help ya, darlin'?" That snaps me out of it.

"What's your name?" I squeak out.

"Ring," he says, pointing to his chest. Sure enough, it's embroidered on his vest.

"I need to talk to someone in charge."

"Why's that? I can't just let anyone in here. You may be very pretty, but that's not enough sometimes." He finally breaks into a half-smile and chuckles.

Oh . . . he's trying to be flirty with me.

I pull the picture of my mother from my purse and hold it out to him. He grabs it, looks at it, and walks away. "Wait!" I open the door and get out to chase him down. "You can't take that."

He stops at the hood and pulls a phone from his pocket. "Whiskey. You need to get out here. No. I can't describe it if I tried. Okay." And he hangs up but is still staring at the picture in his hand.

I walk around him and get as close to him as I dare. "Give me that," I snap and yank it from his hand. We're now locked in a silent stare off, neither of us moving.

"What the fuck is so important that you make me leave my sick pregnant Old Lady?" This bark comes from another guy wearing a leather vest, but his is over a white t-shirt. The vest says 'Whiskey' and that he's the President. I'm not exactly sure what that means, but I'm guessing he's the one in charge.

"I'm looking for someone."

"Who's that?" he asks.

"This guy." I hand him the picture and his eyes about pop out of his head.

"Where'd you get this? Who's this woman?" He points at the photo, his demeanor not happy or friendly.

"I need to know where he is." I'm not telling him anything until he gives me the information I need. I know it's not rational, but I don't care.

"He's not here unless you tell me what the fuck is going on in this picture," the man named Whiskey roars in my face.

"Well," I take a deep breath, "I need to know where he is because I think that man is my father."

TO BE CONTINUED...

ACKNOWLEDGMENTS

Mr. J – I still wouldn't be doing this if it weren't for you. I love you to the moon and back!

Rebecca Vazquez – I don't know why you got picked to be my book fairy godmother, but thank the heavens you're here! With you, I know I can curse at the words and we'll just laugh when typos somehow sneak through three rounds of editing. Thank you for responding to me like I'm a normal person, because let's face it, I'm kinda crazy!

Kay Marie – To my long-distance other half, You Rock! We may have missed all the book signings this year, but that means we get to see each other more next year. You'll always be "My Person". You are the Meredith to my Cristina!

My KM Alpha friends – Kay, Becca, Heidi, and Olivia. We trade complaints about the weather and send each other inappropriate TikToks, but I wouldn't want to do it with anyone other than you crazy ladies! Again, I wouldn't trade our Alphaness for the world!

Charli Childs – I'm so sorry for all the hassle I caused you in making this cover! Finding the perfect Whiskey was so important and you nailed it! You are a miracle worker!

Heather M. Orgeron – Thank you for allowing me to reference my favorite book of yours in my story. . . even if it was only for two lines LOL! I've gushed to you so many times about how much I love Breakaway, and I couldn't resist a tiny Colton reference!

And last, but definitely not least, YOU! THANK YOU, READERS! Thank you for reading Whiskey and Duchess's story. I hope you had as much fun reading their journey as I did writing it. These two put me through my paces and I had to just see where they led me. What's coming next in the Rebel Vipers world is going to knock your socks off, so hold on tight, it's about to be a bumpy ride.

ABOUT THE AUTHOR

Jessa Aarons was born and raised in the frozen tundra of Wisconsin. She has had her nose buried in books for as long as she can remember. Her love of romance began when she "borrowed" her mom's paperback Harlequin novels.

After experiencing a life-changing health issue, she had to leave the working world and dove back into books to help heal her soul. She would read anything that told a love story but still had grit and drama. Then she became a beta reader and personal assistant to another author.

Jessa is the boss of her husband and their castle. He really is her prince. Thanks to his encouragement, Jessa started putting pen to paper and creating new imaginary worlds. She spends her free time reading, crafting, and cheering on her hometown football team.

SOCIAL MEDIA LINKS

Facebook Author Page

FB Reader's Group

Instagram

Twitter

Amazon

Goodreads

Bookbub

Pinterest

Spotify

TikTok

OTHER WORKS

<u>Rebel Vipers MC</u>
A Mountain to Climb
Whiskey on the Rocks
Ring of Steel
Hammer's Swing
A Smoke Filled Haze
Top of the Mountain

<u>Standalones</u>
Pure Luck – cowrite with Kay Marie

Printed in Great Britain
by Amazon